Volume Two of

The Muse of Mischief

Clyrea X9

ISBN: 978-1-7324052-4-0 (Paperback)

ISBN: 978-1-7324052-5-7 (Kindle)

First printed edition 2019

Any references to historical events, real people, or real places are used fictitiously. Names, characters, and places are products of the author's imagination.

Cover image by
Derrick Briscoe Photography, LLC
www.derrickbriscoe.com

Published by
Catrina Briscoe Photography, LLC
www.catrinabriscoe.com

Worry not that no one knows you;
seek to be worth knowing

~Confucius

G'SAAR IS BORN

"Was he born like that? Look at his hair, it's out of control! And he's... huge!" Emperor Bartala said, putting forth his best effort to look disgusted as he looks up from the image on his tablet.

"Hush Bartala, you're being rude." scolded Empress Nalau.

Emperor Bartala knows he's being rude, but he also knows he's right. The child is not attractive. He looks for a rescue from his oldest friend, the Muse of Mischief, but doesn't receive one.

"Wait, YOU'RE insulting his hair? It wasn't that long ago that you were wearing yours styled like Londo, the science fiction character from Earth. It stuck straight up, kind of like a wave was framing your face. Besides, aren't most infants ugly? Most of them seem to have smooshed faces and..." The Muse of Mischief said.

"Smooshed? What is smooshed? You know I'm right; I can see it on your face. Even Ferocity agrees." Emperor Bartala interrupted.

M refused to turn and look at Ferocity, they had a telepathic link so she was already well aware of what the Dragon was thinking. Instead she looked at Empress Nalau, hoping to steel herself. It didn't work. Instead they both started laughing, soon they were all laughing.

"Oh, I am so sorry, so sorry, that is mean." Nalau cleared her throat and attempted to regain her composure. "It is just amazing that they were able to have a child, the combining of DNA from a Rogsaar and a Xinood has never been done before - and they are ecstatic, very proud parents."

The infant they're speaking of is a marvel of modern science. Doctors on Xinood figured out a way for Rogs, an asexual, oviparous, Myaad, and G'ist, a male Xinood to combine their DNA and produce offspring. The infant was carried by surrogate, a female Xinood. All Myaads have pale skin, shockingly white, messy hair, and black eyes. Xinoods on the other hand have skin and hair as black as obsidian, but they have brilliant green eyes, except when angered. Then their eyes turn red. G'saar is a combination of the two. The infant has G'ist's skin and eye color, but Rogs' white, messy hair.

They've gathered in the great green sitting room of the Ploosnar Palace. Emperor Bartala and Empress Nalau are dressed in their usual fashion - he in a long coat with colorful trim, and she in a gown that matches the color of his trim which is purple today. Bartala leads his wife to her usual winged chair, once seated he takes a seat in his chair next to her.

"Well we should get it all out of our system now, they arrive tomorrow." M said taking a seat on the sofa. She's tempted to put her feet up on the table, but that would be just a little too relaxed for the green sitting room. Instead she crosses her long legs, covered with her favorite striped stockings. Ferocity pulls a stool over and takes a seat near M. His tail and wings do not work well with chairs. Now that he frequently visits the palace, a variety of stools have been placed in every public room. Emperor Bartala and Empress Nalau may not be able to hold their laughter when presented with shocking images of an infant, but they are more than gracious to everyone they know.

"Speaking of infants, how many days of freedom do you have left?" M asked.

2

"Five, only five, and we are too excited to think of much else." Nalau answered.

M was pleased to see her so excited about the arrival of their first child. Ploosnarian reproduction completely incapacitates the mother for several months and so Empress Nalau had invoked the ancient right of using a surrogate - much to Bartala's disappointment. Nalau is somewhat indifferent to being a mother, she has nothing against children, but doesn't want to devote her life to raising them. It took some negotiating, but they had finally come to the agreement that a surrogate would carry the child and Emperor Bartala would be the primary parent.

"And have you selected a name yet?" M asked.

"Probably, but we cannot make it known until we meet him. We have selected three possibilities and when we meet him, we will decide which name seems appropriate." Bartala answered. "When will that partner of yours get here? He said he was going to bring espidrun."

"He's here now." M answered.

Ferocity snorted with laughter.

There was a knock at the door, a butler stepped in, "Your Majesties, Agent Brzko has arrived."

Brzko steps past the butler and enters the room carrying a brightly colored titanium bottle of espidrun in each hand. He hands them to the butler to hold, the titanium bottles came together for just a second and let out a pleasant clinking sound.

"Oh that telepathy thing you two do now is just too cute, stop showing off." Bartala said waving his hand dismissively.

"You're just jealous." The Muse of Mischief said as she stands to greet the love of her life. As is his custom, Brzko sweeps her back, planting one if his best Hollywood movie star kisses. He rights her and releases her, he turns to the Emperor and bows, "Emperor, a pleasure." Then he turns to Empress Nalau, gently takes her hand and bows while kissing it, "As always it's a pleasure to see you Empress Nalau." He removes his hat and his coat and trades them to the butler for the espidrun bottles. The butler hangs them on the coat tree near the door and leaves the room. He nods to Ferocity. "Ferocity, you are looking well."

Ferocity just nods in return.

"Here, I brought one for each of you." He said as he hands one bottle to the Emperor and one to the Empress and then settles in on the sofa next to M.

"Wonderful, thank you Brzko." Bartala said. "Now I won't have to get into that stash your wife keeps in her rooms. You know, the one she thinks I don't know about." He grins at M, like a triumphant sibling.

"This reminds me of our trip to Trella." Nalau said. "Let's drink your bottle first darling. We need glasses." She retrieves them from a side table and places her bottle behind the table - effectively hiding it.

"Oh! I see how you are... stashing your bottle for later. M is really rubbing off on you." Bartala stands and pours a little espidrun in each glass. Lifting his high, he toasts "To ugly infants! May we not see another anytime soon." This makes them all laugh. Brzko catches the image of the infant via telepathy from both M and Ferocity.

They haven't even put their glasses down when a familiar voice brings M, Brzko, and Ferocity's earcom links to life.

"We have a situation. Your immediate assistance is needed on Chyke 2C95. Are you available?" It's Lelelu, their assistant.

M answers for them, "Yes Lelelu, what's wrong?"

Bartala and Nalau know something serious must be happening, they stay silent, waiting to hear what the situation is.

"A team of Jreyonian researchers is trapped. Initial reports are that about ten beings are at risk."

"Where's the Gaznzulian ship? Aren't they in orbit?" M asked. There is always a Gaznzulian ship in orbit around Chyke 2C95. Their main responsibility is to monitor the fresh lava flows. The inhabitants of Chyke 2C95 live in old lava tubes, far from the currently active volcanoes. But the Gaznzulian ship in orbit, monitors the planet's surface, ensures that the unpredictable lava flows don't take them by surprise. But Jreyonians don't live on Chyke 2C95, these researchers are only visiting the planet.

"Yes, but they are on the far side of the planet. The research team deviated from their original exploration route and got too close to an active volcano. They've taken shelter in a cave but there's lava all around them and it's already taken over their shuttle craft. There's no place for them to go. Commander ShyUst doesn't think they can get there soon enough to save them."

"Send us the images Lelelu, we're on the way."

"Surface or underground?"

"Both."

Brzko and Ferocity look over M's shoulder as she unrolls her tablet. They can see a huge lava flow heading toward a small cave from all directions. It's too close to the entrance to provide them a safe egress. If the flow changes directions slightly the cave will be filled. The images inside are just as disturbing. In a small cave there is a group of Jreyonians huddled to one side. They look uncomfortably hot -sweat pouring down their long narrow faces.

"Ferocity, we don't have time for you to travel by ship." Brzko said putting on his hat and coat. He takes Ferocity's arm and they're gone.

"Sorry, we'll be back when we can." M said to their friends as she put on her own hat and coat. She doesn't wait for a response.

~~~

They arrive near the lava flow, between it and the side of the cave. Ferocity immediately takes flight and begins attacking the flow with his frozen breath. That begins to slow it down, but he won't be able to stop it entirely. It takes more energy for the Dragon to breathe ice than it does for him to breathe fire. The Muse of Mischief leaves Agent Brzko's side and enters the cave.

Her sudden appearance startles the already frightened researchers. She sees the group move as one, like a school of fish, pushing themselves further back in the cave, forming a tighter group. "Don't be alarmed, I will not harm you, I'm here to help. We have to get you out of here."

They just stare at her completely terrified. They huddle even tighter. Jreyonia are not social beings. They rarely mingle with other species. M considers the best way to get them to trust her when she notices a disturbance at the back of the group.

"Let me out, let me out." A very small Jreyonian works his way to the front of the group. It's a child and, what M assumes is his nervous mother follows him out with her hand on his shoulder. "We have to go with her, this is the one I told you about. This is the Muse of Mischief."

They all turn and look at her, apparently they've heard of her. She reaches for Brzko, *"Are you ready Brzko? There are about ten of them."*

"Yes, Ferocity has slowed the lava, they should be OK out here until the ShyUst can get here."

M steps up and takes the child's arm, they are instantly outside with Brzko. She immediately returns to the cave to get his mother next. One at a time she moves them out of the cave. The fourth one she approaches resists; M can only move a willing being and this older female does not want to be transported by M. She ends up outside the cave alone.

"Oh no, one of them is too frightened to..." Brzko said. He knows that has to be the reason she appeared outside the cave alone.

M didn't stay around long enough to let him finish; she wasn't sure how long Ferocity could hold that lava flow away from the cave entrance. Instead she answers with her mind, *"Yes, I'll take her last."*

She was already back out with another, and another. Now it was just the frightened female in the cave. She has her back pressed against the wall of the cave, her eyes huge with fear. M finds the child she had taken out first, "Can you help us? One of your group is too frightened to come out but I don't know how much longer we can keep the lava away from the cave."

"Please save my aunt Drudrilia."

"OK. Agent Brzko here is going to take you back in with him. Then you can tell her not to be frightened and I can bring her out, got it?"

"Yes." They were gone.

As they entered the cave Brzko reached for Ferocity. *"Ferocity, keep an eye on them. We're both going to be inside the cave."*

"Affirmative."

Inside the cave the child approaches the lone female, "Drudrilia, they will help us. See I'm fine, it doesn't even hurt."

While Drudrilia's attention was on her nephew M takes her arm and moves her out of the cave before she has time to resist. It works. They've rescued all ten of the researchers but they aren't safe yet. Ferocity is exhausted, he has no more ice to breath, he lands near them. The group shrinks back, away from the Dragon. Brzko stands next to Ferocity and addresses the group.

"It's OK, this is Ferocity. He will not harm you. He's here to help us."

Once again, the bravest in the group is the child. He shrugs out of his mother's grip and runs toward Brzko, stopping at his feet and looking up at him. "Is he a real Dragon?"

Brzko turns and looks at Ferocity, making it clear that he expects him to answer for himself. Ferocity takes a knee in front of the child. "Yes, I am a real Dragon. Do not let my appearance fool you. I'm one of the good guys."

The child reached toward Ferocity. "Can I touch you? What do your horns feel like?"

Instead of answering, Ferocity bowed his head, and allows the child to touch him. It only takes a second for him to satisfy his curiosity and confirm that Ferocity is indeed real. He trots back to his mother. "It's real, it's real, a real Dragon." The adults seem to relax, but still keep a watchful eye on the Dragon.

They hear ShyUst via earcom link. "We're here. It looks like we have just enough space to land the shuttle. Would they prefer that to transports?"

"No one has presented themselves as the leader and I don't want to waste any time by trying to locate one, send the shuttle." M answers.

Within a second there's a flash as the Gaznzulian shuttle breaks through the atmosphere and descends toward them. ShyUst lands the shuttle near them, the side door slides up and the ramp descends. Two Gaznzulians jump out and head toward the group of Jreyonians, causing them to be even more frightened now. Gaznzulian soldiers on one side, a Dragon on the other, and hot lava all around them. To them the Gaznzulians looked like Jreyonians but they know that these are not Jreyonians, they begin to scatter but there's nowhere to go.

Agent Brzko closes his eyes and focuses, he projects calmness. It is one of his most amazing abilities, he can calm individuals or large groups. It works, they stand still and wait for instructions.

The child and his mother were still standing near M, she looks down at him, "Tell them to board the shuttle, these are Gaznzulians and they are here to help you, they will return you to your ship in orbit."

He doesn't waste any time, he runs to the front of the group, "Come on follow me!" Surprisingly they do. M, Brzko and Ferocity follow behind them, making sure no one gets left behind. The Jreyonia quietly board the shuttle as the child stands at the bottom of the ramp motioning for them to enter the shuttle. Once everyone in his group is boarded, he turns and runs back over to M, "Thank you for saving my Drudrilia Muse of Mischief."

"You're welcome, you better get on that ship, it's not safe here." He ignores her and turns to Brzko.

"I think you must be Agent Brzko. Thank you."

"I am and you're welcome, now get going." He also ignores him and turned to Ferocity.

"Thank you Mr. Dragon. You saved all of us. I hope I get to see you again someday." With all three of his rescuers properly thanked he finally turns and runs back to the shuttle. ShyUst immediately takes off. H knows that The Muse of Mischief and Agent Brzko can take care of themselves.

"Thanks, ShyUst, you got it from here?" Brzko asked.

"Yes, we've located their ship and we'll get them back to it. Thanks for getting here so quickly. We wouldn't have made it in time."

"No problem ShyUst, it's what we do." M said via earcom link.

Brzko turns and looks at M, "Do I look as bad as you do? You've got ash all over your face and clothes."

Before she can answer, Ferocity does, "Yes, you look just as bad, we are all covered in ash. Let's get out of here."

Agent Brzko takes his Dragon's arm and the two of them return to Ploosnar. M goes home, to Earth.

~~~

Agent Brzko and Ferocity don't return to the palace on Ploosnar, at least not the main palace. Emperor Bartala has been kind enough to provide Ferocity with quarters in the west wing of the palace. There is a hangar for his ship and a few private rooms. Ferocity doesn't technically live in hiding, but he does keep a very low profile. Most beings think that Dragons are mythical, or ancient and extinct. His rooms are three stories tall - not quite large enough for Ferocity to fly but he can at least fully spread his wings. There is a private garden patio on the backside, behind a very high wall. Ferocity has even been assigned his own Ploosnarian butler, Whotov, who is too old to keep up with the day to day demands of the palace but not at all interested in retirement.

They arrived in the living room and are greeted by Whotov, who has become accustomed to Brzko's method of travel. "Master Ferocity, you have returned, good evening Agent Brzko. Oh my you look as though you were fighting fires. Would you like me to start the water in the bathing room for you?"

"Yes, thank you Whotov."

"Agent Brzko, will you be staying with us?"

"No Whotov, I'm on my way out. I'm going home to clean up. Ferocity. I'll contact you later, call me if you need anything."

Ferocity nods and heads toward his bathing room, a long hot shower sounds very appealing.

THERE'S NOTHING BETTER THAN YOUR OWN SHOWER

"Where? Where would you like to go?" The Muse of Mischief and Agent Brzko are freshly showered and sitting on their deck overlooking the Pacific Ocean in Lincoln City, on Earth. Agent Brzko has just made a surprising suggestion.

"I'm not sure that I *want* to go anywhere, I don't want to give this up. This is where we met, and I love it here. We could keep this place as a private getaway. But after our recent encounter with the VReoria I'm starting to think that whoever hid us here on Earth won't be back. But if they do want to find us it's not that hard. We're known throughout the Universe. Beings that need help manage to reach out to us all the time. And, I think there's one other thing we should consider." He pauses to let this all sink in.

"Go on…"

"For some reason the VReoria attempted to capture us on Trella. The Dragons think they were successful in eliminating them, but they thought that once before too. If the VReoria find us here on Earth, we won't be able to save the planet and there's no way Earthlings can defend themselves. I don't want to see Earth enslaved by the VReoria. I think we should consider setting up a main residence where the inhabitants know they are not alone in the Universe and have the infrastructure to defend themselves from interstellar attacks. And if we live on a planet like that then Lelelu, Ferocity, Zri, and even Bartala can actually visit. We might be able to work more efficiently. Well, not with Bartala. When he's around we don't always get a lot done."

This makes M laugh. "I see your point and I can't disagree. I like having a place to stay in the palace on Ploosnar but it's not the same as *home* and sometimes I worry that our presence is an inconvenience to the Empress."

"Not the Emperor too?" Brzko teases.

"Nah, he deserves the inconvenience for some of the stunts he's pulled. I think your reasons are completely logical, and I've been considering the same thing. So far we've managed not to attract undue attention to Earth but I'm sure it's just a matter of time. Do you have a place in mind?"

"Three possibilities, yes. I think we should consider a private residence on Ploosnar, Gaznzul, or the Planet of Portals. They are all reasonably safe and well situated to be convenient for the others."

"I like all of those places. Ferocity would have more freedom on Gaznzul or the Planet of Portals than he does on Ploosnar. What about an island? If we had an island on the Planet of Portals, we could have several different structures. How would you feel about having an island?"

"I can see that." A grin spreading across Brzko's face as he considered having an island all to themselves. "Ferocity could have his own place, Lelelu probably wouldn't want to give up her home, I know she loves her place it's been in her family for a long time. But she could have a second place on the island. I think that could work M."

"So I guess we need to go island shopping."

"Shopping? I'm not sure it's called shopping when you're looking for an island M."

They sit quietly for a while, listening to the waves, watching the sun drop below the horizon.

Brzko breaks the silence, "Are we going back to Ploosnar to see G'saar tomorrow?"

"I don't think the Empress would ever forgive me if we weren't there to help them deal with it. I have to distract her, try to keep her from laughing. Although I'm sure when we see G'saar in person he won't look as shocking as his pictures."

"There's something else I want to mention." Brzko said. M just looks at him, waiting for him to continue. "I think we should go back to Trella. It bothers me that we don't fully understand that place, and it seems like it was created for us."

"I agree. When do you want to go?"

"Soon, if we can get away, let me talk to Ferocity first. He lived there alone for a long time. I'm sure he'll have some suggestions about how to explore Trella."

M nods in agreement.

They sit in silence, enjoying the breeze as it comes in off the Pacific Ocean. M feels her tablet vibrate and takes it out of her pocket and unrolls it. Brzko's tablet is on his side table, he also looks at his. They've received a message from Lelelu:

I know you two are enjoying a quiet evening at home, I think this can wait until tomorrow but I wanted you to see this message that I just received from someone named Nyeeq'r. Evidently, he's the official concierge to the King and Queen of Utkrora. It's a small planet in the Cosliuq Galaxy, mostly covered in water. There are two species on the planet - the Spubfurnia who are completely aquatic and the Blenia who are terrestrial. The Spubfurnia are the ruling, or noble, species and it seems the Blenia evolved to 'care' for them. I'll do some more research tonight and hopefully have more details for you tomorrow. Nyeeq'r is a Blenia, and his family has been in service to the royal family for many generations. His message is attached, I'll see you tomorrow at the palace.

They both open the first of Lelelu's attachments.

I am initiating contact on behalf of the King and Queen of Utkrora, as the reputation of the Muse of Mischief and Agent Brzko finding the lost, and helping those in need is well known to them. Princess Cluthea has been missing for several rotations now. The noble inhabitants of Utkrora are Spubfurnia - completely aquatic, they breathe through gills. So you see, the Princess could not simply be misplaced. There are some Blenia that are resentful of the Utkrora and the expectation that they will devote their lives to serve them. With each passing rotation, the King and Queen's fear increases. They fear that Princess Cluthea may have been taken hostage or harmed. Please, on behalf of King Plyke and Queen Eyjdra, I implore you to send the Muse of Mischief and Agent Brzko to assist in the search for Princess Cluthea.

Nyeeq'r Vupromia Flivus
Concierge to the King and Queen of Utkrora
Thirty-second Generation Vupromia to the Nobles

"Hmm, this sounds interesting. Are you up for getting wet Brzko, maybe a little scuba diving?"

"Hell yeah, I'd love to check out Utkrora. Did you see the images she sent?"

"I'm just looking at them now. Ummmmm…. The Spubfurnia look a lot like, well salamanders!"

Brzko chuckles, "You're right, they look like those pink walking fish from the caves in Mexico… um, I think they're called axolotl."

"This is going to be interesting. I guess Trella can wait, we'll go right after we meet G'saar tomorrow?"

PROUD PARENTS

"He's already the size of a five-year-old Earthling!" The Muse of Mischief exclaims when she sees G'saar.

G'ist and Rogs have landed their refurbished Myaad ship in Lecur, a short distance from the Ploosnar Palace. An aircoach was waiting to bring them to the palace. Emperor Bartala, Empress Nalau, the Muse of Mischief, Agent Brzko, and Lelelu are waiting to greet them when it pulls up to the palace entrance. There is an escort in the front seat and three beings in the second seat, the one in the center looks far too large to be a baby. The aircoach comes to a stop and one of the palace guards opens the door for them.

Like the flip of a switch, Bartala turns on. He approaches the visitors with his arms wide, "Friends! Welcome back to Ploosnar, I see you've brought us a new friend." He bends down to G'saar who is standing between G'ist and Rogs, each holding one of his hands. "You must be G'saar, I am honored to welcome you to my palace. Will you come inside and join me for refreshments?"

M turns to Brzko and projects, "*I love seeing him like this. It cracks me up.*"

"*I know, he's so damn good at being a diplomat.*"

"It's what he was born to do."

G'saar looks up at Rogs, seeking permission to answer, Rogs's gentle face gives him the assurance he needs. G'saar turns back to Bartala, "If it please you sir."

At his point Nalau swoops in and reaches for the child's hand, he eagerly let's go of G'ist and Rogs, and takes Nalau's extended hand. "We have some special treats ready for you, would you like to come and see?"

"If it please you ma'am." G'saar answers as he's whisked off by Bartala and Nalau. They look like characters in an Earth fairytale - the tails of Bartala's long black formal coat flutter as he walks and Nalau is followed by the long train of her formal gown. Also black.

Brzko greets Rogs and G'ist, "You're both looking well. It looks as though raising a child agrees with you."

G'ist reaches for Rogs's hand, "We are very well, thank you. Raising G'saar has certainly changed things for us, we are enjoying every day in a new way."

"He has changed our perspectives about many things." Rogs said. "We consider ourselves to be very lucky."

"I didn't expect him to be so well developed, is that typical of Xinoods or Myaads, or both?" M asked.

"Both." G'ist answers. "We are born larger and with more advanced abilities than some species, for example the ability to communicate using vocabulary. And due to the extensive development time of Myaads, they are quite large when they emerge from the hive."

"G'saar was lucky enough to inherit the traits of rapid development from both of us." Rogs said. "I see myself in him in other ways but I also see some of G'ist in him."

"Is he excited to see Myaad, to see where you're from Rogs?" Brzko asked.

Rogs looked at G'ist and they both laugh. "There isn't anything that doesn't excite our G'saar. By the time we get inside he will have asked close to a hundred questions and sampled every food he was offered!"

"Well then, let's go see how Bartala's holding up." M said as she turns and heads toward the entrance, her own long coat flutters as she walks.

The group walks down the main hall, M is in the lead. She can see a butler standing outside of the green sitting room, so she heads that way. As they near the room they can hear Bartala bellowing loudly, "Stand aside ye scallywag, lest ye be tossed overboard and eaten by sharks!"

M doesn't wait for the butler to open the door and announce them, she rushes into the room, Brzko and Lelelu right on her heels, followed by Rogs and G'ist. Just as they enter the green sitting room from the front hallway, Nalau enters from the back hallway. The room is in total chaos - two of the sofas have been overturned and the third is standing straight up on its end. Bartala stands on one of the overturned sofas, and G'saar is standing on the table. Each of them has a poker from the fireplace. Pretending they are swords; they smack them into each other as though they are having a duel. G'saar is giggling hysterically.

Before M can say anything, Nalau speaks. "Kufeter Whakeclyte Wissswara Bartapulnye what is going on?! Why are stabbing that child with a poker, have you lost your sense?"

"Uh-oh. We're in trouble G'saar." He walks to the table, sits his poker down and takes G'saar's, placing it on the table next to his. He helps G'saar down. "My dear, we were recreating an ancient Earth battle between the scallywags and the pirates. It was purely a history lesson, ask M, she'll tell you about the pirates of Earth." He turns and looks at M, waiting for her to bail him out of this trouble.

"Well the pirates are a part of Earth's history. But I'm not sure that upending sofas is the best way to educate G'saar about them. Although I'm sure it was an exciting lesson." She walks over toward Bartala while she speaks. When she's close enough for him to hear her she whispers, "I'm doing this for the kid."

She stops in front of G'saar, "So what did you learn about pirates today G'saar? Anything exciting?"

"Oh yes." Even though he's young, he's intelligent enough to know that he can help Bartala out of this jam. "The Emperor was kind enough to teach me about the giant ships they used to travel the seas. And that they were really just criminals that would steal things and throw each other overboard. Similar to the League of Mongers." He turned toward G'ist and Rogs, "I would like to go to Earth and see the artifacts of the pirates, is that possible?"

They were clearly stunned to see that their son had been involved in something that displeased the Empress, Brzko comes to their rescue.

"The Muse of Mischief and I still have a home there, maybe we can arrange to take you there once your fully grown." Brzko said, knowing this is not likely. With skin the color of obsidian, bright green eyes, and white hair, G'saar will likely never be safe during a visit to Earth.

By this time Nalau has gotten over the shock of walking in on a pirate duel. She's far too gracious to allow palace guests to feel uncomfortable about anything. "Well I'm sure you worked up an appetite during your pirate duel with the Emperor. Why don't we move into one of the other sitting rooms and enjoy some refreshments?"

"A wonderful idea my love." Bartala said with relief, as he realizes he's off the hook for his pirate escapades. "Shall we gather in the grey sitting room, right across the hall?" He slips his arm around his wife's waist and begins walking toward the door. "Come young G'saar, you can tell us what you plan to do when you get to Myaad." He said placing his hand on the child's shoulder, intent on directing him toward the door. But G'saar didn't budge.

"Thank you sir, but..." He looks around at the disarray they had caused.

"Ah, the sofas, yes. I see your point G'saar. But one of the advantages of being the Emperor of Ploosnar is that I get to turn the sofas upside down but I don't have to right them. I have butlers that will do that for me."

G'saar crossed his arms and gazed at G'ist and Rogs. "Thank you for introducing me to the Emperor, I find him most enjoyable."

Bartala answered before G'ist and Rogs could. "Thank you G'saar. You're not bad yourself. Now let's go get something to eat. I worked up an appetite with all this pirate history." Again, he put his hand on the child's shoulder, directing him to the door. This time it works. G'ist and Rogs follow them across the hall, then M, Brzko, Lelelu.

The amazing palace staff already has the room ready for them. On the coffee table there are platters with various fruits and vegetables, a few bowls of lusimis, and a pitcher of something cold, probably a locally grown tea.

"Please, help yourself to refreshments and sit wherever you like." Nalau said as the group entered.

Bartala takes a seat in the only winged chair - grey of course, like all of the furniture in the grey sitting room. Nalau stations herself next to him, standing - they look like an old-fashioned portrait. As soon as they are settled one of the palace staff delivers a glass to both him and Nalau. The blue steam gives away that it contains their new favorite beverage, espidrun.

M and Brzko hang back, letting the guests take in the delights that have been laid out in their honor. G'saar can hardly contain his excitement. Recognizing that, Rogs immediately sets to work assembling a plate of the delicious foods for him. Once he settles in to enjoy his refreshments, Rogs and G'ist seat themselves on one of the sofas. M, Brzko, and Lelelu take the other. They are all immediately presented with a glass of espidrun.

Before anyone has time to even take a sip G'ist stands. "I would like to offer my, well our deepest gratitude to you, Emperor Bartala and Empress Nalau. The work you have done, and the gifts you have bestowed upon not just the Myaads, but also me, is beyond anything we have experienced before. Your kindness has helped us create a new life for ourselves and we are in your debt." He lifts his glass, as do they all, and sips the hot pink liquid with blue steam rolling off of it.

"Please, there is no need to thank us. As a good friend of mine often says, *eh it's what we do*." He looks over at M, she smiles back. "And really, I cannot take the credit for this. The Muse of Mischief and Agent Brzko set things in motion and there were many others that helped, as there always are. Like Lelelu, she kind of holds us all together. What will you do while you're on Myaad?"

"As far as business is concerned, I will attempt to set up a trade relationship with Myaad. We aren't sure if they have had enough time to recover yet, but Xinood 5 is very interested in establishing a relationship with them." G'ist looks to his partner Rogs, letting him finish.

"And I want to introduce G'ist and G'saar to my home and my culture. Myaads are unlike any other beings in the Universe, and I think it's difficult to understand us until one has spent some time immersed in our culture. Everyone assumes that we are thoughtless beings because due to the way we reproduce, but once they spend time with us, they realize that we are in fact individuals. Because we are raising G'saar on Xinood 5 he is already being exposed to that culture. Even though he doesn't look like a Myaad, we can see the exploratory traits of a Rogsaar in his personality, and we want to make sure he has an opportunity to understand cultures." Rogs slips his hand into G'ist's and settles back into the sofa.

They pass the remainder of the visit leisurely chatting, and snacking. When G'saar starts to get sleepy, the new parents make their exit and continue on their way to Rogs' home planet, Myaad.

LET'S GET WET

After meeting G'saar, the Muse of Mischief and Agent Brzko are free to investigate the situation on Utkrora. Lelelu has arranged for them to meet Nyeeq'r at his residence - a floating houseboat type structure above the receiving area for the King and Queen. His residence is a small, single story structure that sits to one side of a large dock. The roof on the side of the house extends out over the open part of the dock. The covered area contains a table and chairs and a few clusters of potted flowers in each corner, giving it a homey feel. M and Brzko usually prefer to arrive a short distance from their intended target and approach on foot, but with a floating structure that isn't possible. Lelelu has explained the situation to Nyeeq'r, she explained that they would just appear.

"Oh, oh, you are here. I knew you would be, but it is still a bit surprising. I am Nyeeq'r Vupromia Flivus, Concierge to the King and Queen of Utkrora, thirty-second generation Vupromia to the nobles." The curious being steps forward and looks up at M. "You, I presume are the Muse of Mischief. It is a pleasure to make your acquaintance." He extends an appendage toward her. This was the first time either one of them had seen a Blenia.

Nyeeq'r is not tall; the top of his head only rises to M's shoulder. His skin is mottled and brownish. He has a very pleasant, although unusual face, with small, pointy ears that stick straight up and a small tuft of hair between them. His eyes are on tentacles that lift them away from his face. And the appendage that he extends ends in a hand of sorts, he has an opposable thumb and a pad, sort of like he wears a mitten.

M extends her hand and accepts his. "Hello Nyeeq'r, it's a pleasure to meet you too. I hope our arrival wasn't too much of a surprise."

Brzko steps forward and extends his hand at the same time he checks in with Ferocity telepathically. *"Ferocity, are you here yet?"*

"Yes Lord Brzko, I'm in orbit, monitoring your situation."

"Good, please stand by."

Ferocity frequently follows Brzko and stays in orbit until needed. Not everyone is comfortable with Dragons, and there's no need to reveal Ferocity unless a specific situation warrants it. Because Dragon ships are sentient beings with cloaking abilities, Ferocity's presence is usually only known to M and Brzko.

"And you have to be Agent Brzko." Nyeeq'r said accepting Brzko's extended hand. "I am honored to receive you, please come, we have much to discuss." He motions toward the covered sitting area. M and Brzko take the cue and head over to the table. "May I offer you refreshments?"

"No, not right now Nyeeq'r. We're fine." M said taking a seat at the table.

"Very well, where to start, where to start? Do you know of Spubfurnia and Blenia?"

"Not yet. You are the first Blenia we've met." Brzko answers.

"Ah. Then a small history is in order. Many generations ago both the Spubfurnia and Blenia were water dwelling beings. But the Blenia evolved to be land dwelling, some say this evolution was forced, others say it was natural. No one can be sure and so there is controversy amongst the Blenia. Our main purpose is to care for and function as the agents of the Spubfurnia, and there are Blenia that reject this. They are without honor, the Blenia have been caring for the Spubfurnia since we emerged from the water. It is who we are."

"What does caring for the Spubfurnia involve?" M asked.

"Very little. You see, it is not too much to ask. Spubfurnia breathe through gills so they cannot survive out of water. They have everything they need underwater, beneath the surface resides an extensive and complex society. Blenia are really just their representatives, a point of contact if you will. The Spubfurnia society possesses and uses a variety of technology, and they continue to advance. That of course means that they need to establish and maintain trade relationships with other beings - a difficult task to do from underwater."

"Hmm, so you're sort of like their land-based representative." Brzko said.

"Yes, exactly. Perhaps similar to how Lelelu works with you. Not every Spubfurnia has Blenia, it is only the.... shall we say, more influential that have a need for a representative as you called them."

Straight to the point M asked, "Are you owned?"

Nyeeq'r turns toward her and angles his eye tentacles to meet her gaze. "No, we are not slaves. We are compensated for our services. My ancestors have been serving the nobles for many generations. I am proud of my heritage but I am free to leave my position at any time."

"So what do you need us to do?" Brzko asked.

"Princess Cluthea has not been seen for some time now. Her parents, King Plyke and Queen Eyjdra, are concerned. They fear that something has happened to her."

"How old is she?"

"She is an adult, a young adult. And she is free to move about on her own, she has her own life and her own interests."

"Is there any evidence of a third party?"

"Third party? I do not know this term."

"Has anything been observed that would lead one to conclude that she was taken against her will? That someone has kidnapped her?"

"No, nothing. There has been no demand for ransom either."

"Was she acting any differently before she disappeared?"

"That I do not know, the King and Queen will be able to tell you more."

"Oh, we'll be meeting them?"

"Yes. I assume you can swim?"

"Swim yes, breath underwater... not so much"

Nyeeq'r's eye tentacles move, looking toward a small table that is next to his house. M and Brzko follow his gaze. "The rebreathers will work for you. Have you used them before?"

"Yes." M said.

"No." Brzko said, looking at M and raising an eyebrow. He wonders where she's had an opportunity to use a rebreather. He assumes it was while she was training with Zri on Gaznzul, she never really speaks about that time in her life.

On the table there is an assortment of diving masks and mouthpieces with cylinders attached.

"How long will the air last?" M asked.

"About an hour, but it depends of course on how rapidly you breathe."

"And what about communication? I don't imagine we'll be understood if we're speaking while using a mouthpiece." Brzko said.

"*Oh. No, no, Spubfurnia are telepathic. As are Blenia but it takes effort for Blenia to communicate this way. You're assistant, Lelelu, said that you are also telepathic?*" Nyeeq'r projected.

"Yes, we are both telepathic." Brzko assures him switching back to speech, there was no need to make things difficult for Nyeeq'r. "What about the water temperature? Will we need a suit of some kind?"

"The Spubfurnia can withstand a wide variation in temperatures so this area of the sea is heated. Below us is a shallow area, you won't have to dive deep or swim far, you should be very comfortable. Are you ready to proceed?"

M stands up, "I presume we can leave our shoes on other delicate items here?"

"Yes, yes, of course. There is a ladder there," Rather than point Nyeeq'r motions to the swimming pool style steps with his eye tentacles, "Or you can jump. Once you are under the surface you will be able to see the receiving area below us. The water is very clear."

Both M and Brzko remove their hats, jackets, and shoes and place them on the chairs where they had been sitting.

"I don't remember the last time I dove into the water." M said.

Brzko doesn't respond, he's already at the edge of the dock. He pauses long enough to sit his mask on the edge of the dock, he bends his knees and executes a perfect dive. The surface of the water is not disturbed. He pops back up and comes up to the dock to retrieve his mask.

As he swims, he projects to Ferocity, *"We're heading underwater now Ferocity."*

"Understood."

"Wow, that was impressive Brzko. Where did you learn to dive like that?"

"Oh just a little something I picked up along the way." He said beaming.

M decides to go for the slightly tamer approach, she uses the ladder. After she submerged herself to wet her hair, she dons her mask.

She reaches for Brzko with her mind. *"Ready?"*

"Let's go."

They both drop below the surface and take a second to test the seals on their masks and adjust their rebreathers. They begin to descend. The receiving area is just a series of railings forming a square. Just outside the square are two stunning beings like they've never seen before. The Spubfurnia are pale pink in color, with small black eyes. They look to be about as long as M and Brzko are tall. Their mouths are low and wide without any visible teeth. They have four legs and long flowing tails. But most impressive is their gills. On each side, long feathery external gills protrude from the back of their heads. There are jewels attached to their gills. They shimmer as their gills sway in the water, creating an amazing rainbow-like glow around them.

"Welcome. I am King Plyke and this is Queen Eyjdra, we are honored to receive you." When he mentioned the Queen, he turned his head slightly toward her. An important trait of most telepaths. Without such clues it would be impossible to tell who was *speaking*.

M and Brzko change their orientation, they had been swimming straight down. They reverse and bring themselves upright, grabbing the railing to fight their natural buoyancy.

"Hello, I am the Muse of Mischief and this is Agent Brzko."

"Good afternoon, it is a pleasure to meet you both."

"We are grateful to you for coming so quickly; we didn't know where else to turn. Your reputations are known to us. We understand that you may be able to help us find our daughter, the Princess. She has been missing for many days now."

Grief emanates from Queen Eyjdra.

"How old is Princess Cluthea, is she fully grown?" Brzko asks telepathically.

"She is fully matured but she is not fully grown. You see Spubfurnia do not attain their full size until many rotations after maturity. She is perhaps two-thirds the size of her mother."

"Did she reside with you, or near you?" M projects.

"She was always near us, but… we do not live in structures. Our resting place is that forest you can see there." King Plyke lifts his head and gazes off to his right. M and Brzko realize that they can see a great distance due to the clear water. He had pointed to an area that is filled with tall strands of grass, gently swaying in the water. It is so tall that the Spubfurnias would be completely hidden from view while there. Far in the distance they can see structures of some kind - but King Plyke said they didn't live in structures. Curious.

They return their attention to their hosts and M continues gathering the details. *"Have there been any disagreements or quarrels lately? Was Princess Cluthea upset about anything?"*

Queen Eyjdra raises her head as though she's about to answer. But King Plyke responds instead. *"They do not mean to upset you my darling Eyjdra, in order to find her they need to know everything we can tell them."*

"I understand." Queen Eyjdra projects. *"Please forgive me, I know you do not intend to cause us any discomfort. Your question upset me because Princess Cluthea does not agree with our ways. Recently she has begun to question the role of the Blenia. There are some that believe it is wrong for the Blenia to serve the Spubfurnia."*

"Is the group that feels this way organized? Or have they taken any action?" Brzko projects, making sure to conceal his remaining question in his own mind. He couldn't help but wonder if there had been any violence.

"No, they have not taken any action. It is really just a small group of young Spubfurnia that are trying to find their place. When we are young, we question the ways of our parents, it is how we grow." King Plyke projects.

"Are there any Blenia that feel this way?" M asked.

"Yes." King Plyke answers. *"Serving the Spubfurnia is a choice. The Blenia are not slaves to us; they are cared for, and well compensated. We think of them as an extension of our own family. Many Blenia families serve the same Spubfurnia family for generations. But some Blenia choose not to. How they make their living is up to them."*

"Do you know if these Blenia have been in contact with the Spubfurnia that are questioning the practice?" Brzko asked.

King Plyke and Queen Eyjdra look at each other, their surprise could be felt. *"We had not considered this, it is possible."*

"We don't have much time left with the rebreathers, is there anything else you feel like we should know?" Brzko asked.

"No. If we think of something else, we will have Nyeeq'r contact you. He can always reach us if you need anything. Please find her, we just want to know that she's OK."

"We will do our best. Nyeeq'r can contact Lelelu if you need to reach us."

King Plyke and Queen Eyjdra turn toward the grassy forest, and with a single flick of their tails they were at the edge of the grass. They walked into it and disappear from view. M and Brzko head for the surface.

~~~

After the meeting with King Plyke and Queen Eyjdra, Lelelu gets to work researching the Blenia that were adversaries of the traditional Spubfurnia Blenia relationships on Utkrora. The Muse of Mischief and Agent Brzko decide to hear the results of her research in person. They arrive at Lelelu's home on the Planet of Portals in the mid-morning. Lelelu has a Gaznzulian transporter installed in her home, that means that Ferocity can easily transport himself to the surface keeping him from having to land his ship.

"How long has it been since you've been here M? A few years?"

"Yeah, that sounds about right."

"OK, so what's up? With both of you and Ferocity here, there is definitely something going on. Spill it."

"Spill it?" Ferocity said leaning his head forward and cocking it to one side.

"Earth slang - spill your guts - meaning tell me everything." Brzko explains.

"Crude." Ferocity said, leaning back.

The group is gathered in Lelelu's garden, with huge butterflies, the same shade of blue as Lelelu, drifting about from one amazing flower to the next, occasionally landing on her bare shoulders. M looks at Brzko to see if he wants to make the announcement. He gestures for her to proceed.

"We've decided to take up a new residence, someplace where we can openly receive you, Ferocity and other guests."

M pauses to see if there were questions, but they both stayed silent, waiting for her to continue.

"We're thinking of an island, someplace where we can set up some serious security, but also have several structures. For example, a private dwelling for you Ferocity, and one for you, when you visit Lelelu, and of course guest quarters. Our recent close call with the VReoria made us realize that we don't want to draw attention to Earth. They aren't ready to deal with anyone as advanced as the VReoria. We'll be keeping our place on Earth so that we can visit it, but it won't be our main residence."

"Where? Where are you thinking of living?"

"Here, on the Planet of Portals, or on Gaznzul. Those are the top two choices." M leans back in her chair and waits for a reaction from Lelelu and Ferocity. Surely she wouldn't have to ask for their opinions.

Ferocity shares his opinion first, "This is very good news. I will enjoy residing nearer to Lord Brzko."

Lelelu stays focused on her tablet. M is just about to ask her to share her opinion when she turns the display toward the others, "What do you think of this island? It's reasonably priced and it's not far from Luchybos although still remote enough that it would be easy to secure."

M and Brzko both laugh.

"So, I take it you would vote for the Planet of Portals instead of Gaznzul?" Brzko asked.

Lelelu smiles. "Well sure. I mean it would make some things easier. And I think you're right about protecting Earth. When you had Ciic stay with you, a Viiv managed to break through your security. Luckily they were confined to your house and not able to wreak havoc on the naive public, but it's probably just a matter of time. Gaznzul would certainly be a secure location, but it wouldn't be as convenient for me and besides, it just isn't as fun as the Planet of Portals - the Gaznzulians really like rules and regulations."

"Those are all valid points Lelelu. But you missed one." M said. "The oceans and sunsets are much prettier here than they are on Gaznzul."

This makes them all laugh.

"OK, so what have you found out about the Blenia that object to serving the Spubfurnia?" M asked, getting them back to work.

"There doesn't seem to be an organized resistance movement yet. Right now, it seems like the small group of Blenia have objected to the system and have set up a small community near an old landing port. Which doesn't seem like it would be an issue, but they are having trouble supporting themselves at the level they were accustomed to."

"How many are living in this community?" M asked.

"About thirty."

M continues to seek more details. "And does it seem like they could become violent or irrational?"

"Well there's always the potential for violence, especially when your standard of living drops suddenly. But so far there's been no reports of violence."

"What about the Spubfurnia that object to being served by the Blenia? Are they connected in some way to this community?" Brzko asked.

"I think so. But that's more difficult to determine. Satellite images don't reveal what's below the surface of the water. I've talked to Zri and he said that he does have an aquatic drone that would provide us the intel. But I'm sure you'd want to discuss that with King Plyke and Queen Eyjdra, I mean that would be like flying a drone right through Emperor Bartala's palace."

"Hopefully it won't come to that. Do you have images of the community? Is it on land or is it floating?" M asked.

"They've attached their *docks* to a small island. The island used to be a landing port for visiting ships. And actually, from what I've learned, it seems like the Spubfurnia own the dock structures and the island. But in an effort to keep things peaceful they are not enforcing any type of ownership. They've shifted their traffic to another port and let the Blenia use the docks and the island." She calls up the images of the community on her tablet and props it up facing M, Brzko and Ferocity.

They scroll through the images; the community looks just like Lelelu described it. A series of docks attached together, forming a small network around an island.

"Is there a leader of this group?" Brzko asked.

"Yes, it is a Blenia named Thlethlut. She is rumored to be the oldest living Blenia."

"And how old is that?"

"123."

"Can you arrange a meeting for us?"

"I already did." Lelelu grinned, she was rightfully pleased with herself for anticipating the next step in the search for Princess Cluthea. "But it's not until tomorrow morning so I guess you'll have time to go look at that island."

~~~

"You must forgive me that I do not rise to greet you, I am old." Thlethlut said from her seat under the canopy of her dock. "Please, come and join me here in the shade." The back of her dock is connected directly to the island. She is surrounded by other docks on all three other sides.

The Muse of Mischief and Agent Brzko step away from her assistant and go to her.

"Hello, I'm the Muse of Mischief, thank you for agreeing to meet with us." She extends her hand and Thlethlut reciprocates. "This is Agent Brzko."

"It is an honor to meet you Thlethlut."

"Please sit." She slowly blinks her eyes and then uses them to point to the chairs she expects them to use. Both her speech and movement are slow with age. Even her eye appendages are wrinkled. "You are here about the dear Princess, Princess Cluthea. I remember when she emerged from her egg sac. Oh, everyone was so excited to have such a perfect little princess."

"Did you know her?" M asked.

"Oh yes, oh yes. I still do. She has never been like her parents; she has always been all her own. I was in service to the King's brother and Princess Cluthea would often visit with him and his children. She was so curious and outgoing."

"Do you know where she is right now?" Brzko asked.

"Yes."

They wait for her to continue but she doesn't, so M does.

"Is she OK, is she safe?"

"Yes."

Again, they paused but she does not elaborate.

"Why did she leave her home, her parents? Is she upset about something?" Brzko asked.

"She is no longer upset, she is at peace now."

"But why did she leave her home?"

"Love. A love that King Plyke and Queen Eyjdra will not understand."

"Do you think she'd be willing to meet with us?"

Thethlut closes both of her eyes and leans her head back. It almost looks as if she's gone to sleep but she hasn't. Telepathy is taxing for the Blenia, and probably especially when they are 123.

She opens her eyes, but instead of tilting her head back up she rotated her eyes toward M and Brzko. "She will speak to you. On the island there is an underground chamber, you will be able to take the stairs down to get below the water level, she will be there behind the glass. The path behind the dock will take you there. Now, please forgive me but I am tired."

They quickly thank her and make their exit so she can rest. The path behind her dock is paved, it leads them around the edge of the island, staying just above the sandy shores. They come to an intersection. As instructed, they take the stairs descending underground. There is low level lighting along the edges of the stairs, their eyes adjusted to the semi-darkness as they descended. At the bottom of the stairs is a large room, the side nearest the sea is made of glass. It was like being at a giant zoo aquarium, only instead of caged fish behind the glass there is a smallish, beautiful

Spubfurnia with jewels on her gills. Standing just behind her is someone else, a Blenia.

"Hello, I'm the Muse of Mischief and this is Agent Brzko. Are you Princess Cluthea?" M projects.

"Cluthea, yes. But I am no longer a princess. This is my partner Xaycarro. I understand that my parents have sent you, they do not understand why I left."

"They seem genuinely worried about you. Are you OK Cluthea, are you here of your own free will?" M asked.

This makes her laugh. *"Yes, of course. I love Xaycarro, we only want to be left alone to live our lives together. That is not possible if I remain the Princess of Utkrora. I willingly choose my husband over my position in the monarchy."*

"Cluthea may we have your permission to share what you've told us with King Plyke and Queen Eyjdra?" M asked.

"Yes, you may tell them why I left. And please tell them that I am happy, this is what I want. They may not believe you though."

Instead of asking another question M and Brzko wait for her to continue.

"They will not understand how Xaycarro and I can be together, they think that all Blenia breath with lungs and must live on the surface. But long ago the Blenia and Spubfurnia lived together underwater. They were equals living in harmony. At the time, all Blenia had gills just as Spubfurnia do. Some of us believe that their evolution to live on the surface was somehow caused by the Spubfurnia so they could take advantage of the Blenia. Without the Blenia, the Spubfurnia society would not have advanced to be what it is today. Because the evolution was the result of manipulation rather than a natural process, it is beginning to reverse. Many Blenia now have lungs and gills, as Xaycarro does. But because they are unsure of how that will be received by the Spubfurnia they keep it hidden, they resist the life of servitude, and they reside here where they are free to live above or below the surface."

Xaycarro drifts forward and slides his arm around on of Cluthea's front legs, he moves his tentacle eyes from looking at

Cluthea to M and Brzko. "*Please tell the King and Queen that Cluthea is safe, she is happy, she is loved. She does not want to see them. But if they want to express their anger at someone, I will meet with them.*"

Cluthea quickly turns her head toward Xaycarro. Their gazes locked while they have a brief private conversation. They turn back toward M and Brzko.

"*Thank you for taking the time to meet with us it was a pleasure to meet you, although I wish the circumstances had been more favorable.*" Cluthea projects. She and Xaycarro turn and swim back out into the open water.

M sends Brzko and Ferocity a single word, "*Home.*" And once again the room at the bottom of the stairs is empty.

~~~

"I'll go." Agent Brzko and the Muse of Mischief are sitting at the front windows in their home overlooking the Pacific Ocean on Earth. But they can't see the ocean today; the rain is coming down sideways and pelting against the windows.

"Are you sure you want to go alone?"

"Sure, Ferocity will be with me and it won't take too long. Besides, I know Emperor Bartala is eagerly awaiting you. I could hear how excited he was, it sounded like he was talking really fast. You should be there for him and Empress Nalau."

"OK Brzko, if you're comfortable with meeting with King Plyke and Queen Eyjdra alone I'll take you up on your offer."

"I'll be fine. Besides, I dive better than you do." He turns to her and grins.

"Yes, you do. Where did you learn to dive like that?"

"I don't know, it's like I just knew how to do it. What I want to know is where did you learn to dive with a rebreather? Was it on Gaznzul?"

"Yep."

"That's it? Yep?"

M smiles at her partner. "OK, OK, I'll tell you about my time on Gaznzul. But not here. Let's go back."

"Great idea!" Brzko said and he stands up grabbing their coats and hats, handing hers to her. Then he takes her hand, and they're gone.

The first time they actually met was at the mouth of the D River in Lincoln City, Oregon, May 27, 1912. This is their special place, a place where they can just chill out with no one around. There were very few people along the Oregon Coast in 1912.

In this time there were several large boulders at the mouth of the river, and there was no Highway 101 across the river so it hadn't been altered to run under a bridge yet. They climb up on the boulders, looking out at the ocean.

"So you went to Gaznzul with Zri after he came to Earth to find you, which was after you almost killed Bartala with a Haplogawa on Chyke 2C95?" He says teasing her, knowing he will get a feisty reaction from her.

"I didn't almost get him killed! I could have moved him in time to avoid being eaten, but c'mon you know him well enough to know that he sometimes deserves a little excitement that's beyond his control. Especially when he was an adolescent." She turns and looks at him, and realizes he's been just ribbing her to get a reaction.

"Oh, I see how you are Brzko! Uh huh OK. So yes, when Zri came to Earth to find out what I was, he was shocked at how strong I was and that I could defend myself. I was pissed that I couldn't take him down, he looked like any other human and at that point I already knew I wasn't human and that I could overpower most of them. As soon as he explained that he was Gaznzulian and that they are reflective, that I was only seeing a projection, I was really intrigued. You know I took Zri up on the offer to help me train to better defend myself. Physical training is part of the education process that all Gaznzulians go through, but when alone they don't always generate reflections - they are in their true forms. Zri got hit with some serious attitude for bringing an alien into the *inner-circle* of Gaznzul. One of his mentors, a

35

member of their ruling council, understood his motivation and what he was trying to do. He was able to convince the council that my training was necessary. As a being that doesn't know what she is, I had the potential to become a destructive force. It was better for them to allow me in, and offer training - and no doubt test me - than to allow me to advance on my own. He assured them that I could be trusted to never speak of my time on Gaznzul. It was so important to them that I just put it out of my mind and honored their privacy. I just don't speak about it."

"So you haven't just seen Zri in his natural state, you've seen all the Gaznzulians in their natural state? Wow! I had no idea."

"Well not ALL of them, but many of them. I lived with them, trained with them, after a while I was accepted as one of them. It was a long time ago and I was pretty young at the time. After I learned some self-defense and tactical skills I just went back to my regular life and didn't really dwell on it."

"So that's what bonded you and Zri, he let you into the *inner-circle* of Gaznzul, he let you see them as they are. That seems like a serious honor M, I've never heard of them exposing themselves like that. Not with anyone."

"It bonded me to all Gaznzulians, but especially Zri. After getting to know me they realized I was going to devote my life to being an advocate for others, and they wanted to be a part of that, because that's their main focus too. And yeah, it was an honor and it taught me so much. Not just how to fight off an attacker, or how to subdue a loser like the Brusher, but it taught me about myself and how to push myself past what I think my limits are."

"So there was underwater training?"

"Yep, and high altitude, and extreme heat, and extreme cold, and low gravity, and dense gravity. Their training methods put me in different environments to practice once I had the basics of self-defense mastered. It was the same training they put themselves through."

"No wonder you can kick ass like you do." He grins at her.

"Ha! Yes, that's how I learned to focus my strength and energy, how to pay attention to and trust my instincts. And like you said earlier, it's what bonded Zri and I - he put his reputation on the line to give me access to his world. I know some Gaznzulians assumed that I would violate their privacy and expose the things they keep private; but of course I have integrity and Zri knew it. I'm really grateful to him, as a frustrated adolescent with superhuman strength, without guidance, I could have ended up in a bad situation. And like you, I certainly wasn't going to get that guidance from the pretend parents. But unlike you, I needed help, help to master my own strength and not let it get out of control. After their experience with me, the Gaznzulians realized it could benefit them to provide training to others. So they set up training facilities - but since they now use specialized facilities, the privacy of the individual Gaznzulians is protected. In other words, the trainees don't get to mingle with Gaznzulians in their natural state."

"That explains why the Gaznzulians are always so quick to respond whenever we need something. They think of you as one of them... in a way."

"Sort of, I guess. I think at first they were just keeping an eye on me. But now they realize that we're all working for the same thing."

"So I have a Dragon and you have a Trelod and all of the Gaznzulians, I never thought we'd end up like this when we met." Brzko said, taking her hand.

"Neither did I, but it's awesome and I wouldn't change a thing Brzko. You were so adorable when we met, leaving me notes back here in 1912. But..."

"I know, it's time to go. I'm going back to now before Ferocity and I head to Utkrora, are you heading straight to Ploosnar?"

"No, since this is an official Ploosnarian event I want to be dressed appropriately. I'll go home with you."

And they did, back to their home, back to their current time.

Brzko reaches for Ferocity while M goes to change. *"Ferocity, how soon can you get to Utkrora."*

"Less than an hour."

"OK, head out when you can and let me know when you're there. I need to update King Plyke and Queen Eyjdra."

"Understood."

Brzko activates his earcom link, "Lelelu, are you on?"

"Yes, I've got you Brzko."

"Please contact Nyeeq'r and let him know I'll be there in about an hour. I have an update for the King and Queen."

"Will do."

M walks out of the back hallway, she's wearing a new design from Schatorren. Her legs are covered in a black spandex looking fabric with a purple stripe running down the outside of each leg. Over that she wears a skirt of sorts, it is triangular, opening in the front, so it really only hangs down on the sides and in the back. The shirt she wears is black with a fantastic purple paisley pattern.

"Damn! Is that new?"

"Yes, I've been keeping Kilome busy."

"Well keep it up! That is a kickass outfit."

She grabs her hat and coat, kisses the love of her life, and is on her way to Ploosnar.

M IS TO BE AN AUTUANIA

The Muse of Mischief arrives at the bottom of the palace stairs and begins ascending them. She can tell right away that things are different - there are red flowers everywhere. That's odd, almost all of the flora on Ploosnar is some shade of blue due to the roinad. At the top of the stairs she's greeted by the palace guards.

"Good afternoon Muse of Mischief. You will find Emperor Bartala in his private sitting room."

"OK, thank you." She makes her way through the maze of palace hallways until she comes to the door of his sitting room. She knocks.

Emperor Bartala called from within, "Come!"

She slowly opens the door and peaks around it, "Hey old man, I hear you're a daddy now!"

Bartala lights up when he hears her voice and runs to greet her. He scoops her up in a bear hug and twirls her around. "M you're here! I can't wait for you to meet him! He is perfect. I am so excited to be a father." He finally sits her down.

She removes her hat and coat, hanging them on a hook next to the door. Purposely staying silent because she knows it will agitate her old friend.

"Aren't you going to say anything?" He pleads, raising his hands in the air.

She looks at him and smiles. "Of course, congratulations old friend. I'm happy to see you so excited. How is Empress Nalau?"

"Fantastic. She is of course with him now, she adores him."

"And have you two decided on a name yet?"

"Well yes, and we will announce it at the ceremony later today. But..."

"But?"

"Yes, we need to talk, please sit, let us enjoy an espidrun while we chat."

"It sounds like you're up to something Bartala." She said taking a seat.

"Well, I have a favor to ask of you."

"It's too soon to ask me to babysit." She just looks at him waiting to hear it. He takes his time and pours them each an espidrun, but rather than drink right away he sits the glasses down on the coffee table and then sits on the table right in front of her.

Now she gets a little worried. Why was Bartala acting so oddly? She quietly waits for his explanation.

"We would like your permission to name our son after you."

"What? Name him after me? How could that work? And isn't there more to it than that? A custom of some kind that comes with responsibility?" She asked perplexed.

"Yes, it will make you his Autuana. If anything should happen to me and Nalau, you would then become his guardian. M, there is no one else I trust with this responsibility."

"What about Nalau, how does she feel about it? Surely she has some family that would be a more appropriate choice."

"No she does not. She has family but she is not close to them. We both trust that you would ensure that he was raised with our values. And that you would not exploit his position in the monarchy for your own gain."

"Well OK. I understand and yes you can trust me to do those things IF something were to happen to you and Nalau. But really Bartala? You can't name the future Emperor of Ploosnar the Muse of Mischief!"

"No! That we cannot do." He turns, reaches behind him for the glasses and hands one to her just as the last of the blue steam spills over the side of the glasses. "We will name him Ezopica Mischievous Wisssdartai, after both of our fathers and you. But we will call him Wisssi."

She presents her glass to him. "To Wisssi." They clink the glasses and sip. "That's a long name. Oh but don't you have like six names... None of which are Bartala." She teases.

"Six no, four. And remember when we used to anger my father, he would try to scold me using my entire name and couldn't. By the time he got to Bartapulnye he'd be laughing."

"I do remember that. Kufeter Whakeclyte Wissswara Bartapulnye doesn't exactly just roll off the tongue. He was a great father, and you will be too."

"Thank you M." He is touched that his oldest friend still knows, and is able to pronounce his entire formal name.

"So tell me about this ceremony."

"It will be a small gathering with us and the liaisons. Nalau and I will make a formal announcement of Wisssi's name and that you are the Autuana. Those things will be recorded in the official record, and that's it."

"OK."

"Where's Brzko? I would like him and Ferocity to be here."

"They're on Utkrora telling the King and Queen that their daughter has relinquished the title of princess and married a Blenia."

"But isn't she Spubfurnia?"

"Yep."

"And Spubfurnia live underwater breathing with gills, while Blenia live on the surface and breath with lungs. So how can they be together."

"Well it turns out that the evolution of the Blenia may have been forced by the Spubfurnia. And the Blenia are evolving again - or is it de-evolving. I don't know, but there is a small group that have both lungs and gills. The Princess fell in love with one of them and married him."

"You and Brzko never have a boring day do you"

"No, not really."

"I envy that."

"Well it's not like you have a bad life Bartala! Jeez. You're the Emperor of one of the most advanced planets."

"I know, I know. And I am grateful. Sometimes I just miss the excitement of…"

"Thinking you were going to be eaten by a Haplogawa?"

"Haha! No not that." He leans his head back and laughs while slapping his own knee.

The old friends sit in silence for a few minutes, reflecting on what was to come.

Bartala breaks the silence. "I'm going to go check on Nalau and Wisssi. The ceremony is scheduled to start in two hours, will you contact Brzko and see if he and Ferocity can make it back in time?"

"Sure."

Bartala heads to the door. "Thanks M."

Once he's left the room she goes to her rooms, but she didn't have to walk. The rooms that Bartala keeps for her and Brzko are perfect, always just as they've been left. She sits down on the large round, purple bed and reaches for Brzko.

"Have you made it Utkrora?"

Instead of an answer, she received the live images from him. She lays down and allows herself to watch the situation unfold in front of her. Brzko is underwater, facing King Plyke and Queen Eyjdra in the same receiving area where they had originally met them. Queen Eyjdra seems to be crying.

"She is my only child; I will never see her again." She wails.

"Darling please, restrain yourself. Cluthea has made her choice. She has married a Blenia, she has no place here now."

The Queen ignores her husband. She turns toward Brzko. *"Will she see me?"*

"I cannot say. We didn't ask her that. You could have Nyeeq'r contact Thlethlut, she will be able to reach her and find out."

"Thlethlut? What has she got to do with this? She used to serve my brother. Surely she's not still alive, she must be very old."

"She lives in the community with the Blenia that have developed gills. She was our point of contact for Cluthea."

"I will have Nyeeq'r contact her, thank you Agent Brzko. You and the Muse of Mischief have been very helpful. We are indebted to you."

"We will not contact her." The King insists.

"You have already lost your only daughter, do you want to lose your Queen too?" Surprisingly the Queen lets this projection out where Brzko can receive it rather than projecting it only to the King. She doesn't wait for his answer, she swims up an over the King and disappears into the grass forest they called home.

"Thank you Agent Brzko, thank you for finding Cluthea." He turns and swims after the queen.

As Brzko heads for the surface he reaches for M. *"Did you get all that."*

"Yes. They actually took it pretty well. I suspect that Queen Eyjdra will eventually be able to get King Plyke to accept Xaycarro."

"I hope so, it's the only way they'll be able to see Cluthea again. Speaking of children, how are Nalau and Bartala?"

"They're fine, they've planned a ceremony for their son's naming and they'd like you and Ferocity to be here. How soon can you get here?"

"I just need to return the rebreather to Nyeeq'r and dry off. Ferocity, how quickly can you get to Ploosnar?"

"Immediately."

"OK, head out now, I'll see you there."

~~~

"I thought you said this was going to be a small ceremony." The Muse of Mischief said peeking around the door, looking at the crowd that is gathering in the palace theatre.

"It will be. I meant small as in duration, not necessarily the number of attendees." Emperor Bartala said. They are huddled in the small backstage room, Agent Brzko, Ferocity, and Zri are with them. "Nalau should be here with Wisssi any second now."

Bartala is pacing about the room nervously.

"Are you nervous?" M teases him.

"Me no, no. I just…" Empress Nalau saved him by walking in with their infant son.

"Darling, you're here. Oh you look absolutely stunning!" And she does. She's wearing a long formal gown, a golden color with a black lace neckline and black lace along the bottom. As usual, it is a perfect match for Bartala's black coat and slacks. His coat is trimmed in the same golden color of her dress. Wisssi is dressed in a tiny version of his father's suit.

"Thank you darling." She allows Bartala to kiss her cheek before she turns to M, and holds Wisssi out to her. "Wisssi, this is your Autuania, the Muse of Mischief." M accepts the infant and he instantly begins to fuss. He isn't really crying, just sort of verbalizing.

Brzko greets Empress Nalau, taking her hand and offering a bow, kissing her hand. "Empress, motherhood agrees with you, you are more lovely than ever today."

She giggles, always delighted by Brzko's charm. "Thank you Brzko."

"Where would you two like us? Should we head out through the hall and take seats in the theatre?" Brzko asked on behalf of himself, his Dragon and Zri.

"Stage." Both Bartala and Nalau answer in unison.

Wisssi really starts to fuss, getting a little loud.

"M what are you doing to my son?" Bartala teases. "You'll have to work it out before we go out, you'll be holding him during the ceremony."

"What?!" M exclaims, she didn't anticipate that. Her reaction startles Wisssi and he starts to cry.

Surprisingly Ferocity comes to the rescue. He bends down and puts his snout right up to Wisssi's ear, he makes a low purring sound. Instantly Wisssi starts to giggle and coo.

"OK Ferocity you've got some secret talents don't you?" M asked. "You better stay close to me out there."

"Pleasure." He said.

"Impressive Ferocity." Zri said. "You can breathe fire and calm infants."

"Here's how this goes." Bartala said. "My lovely wife and I will take the stage, M you follow and stand centered, behind us until presented, Brzko you stand to the side and step back from the Empress, and Ferocity and Zri, you two stand with me."

Nalau turns to Ferocity. "Are you sure you're comfortable with being on stage? We really want you to be there but would understand if prefer to keep a low profile. Not everyone knows that Dragons are real."

"Thank you Empress Nalau. Agent Brzko and I have discussed this at length. It is time for me to come out of hiding and take my place with him and the Muse of Mischief."

There is a knock at the door, a butler steps in. "Your Majesties, Lelelu has just arrived." Lelelu steps out from behind the butler, she's wearing a fantastic black dress. The blue trim matches her skin color.

Nalau rushes to her and embraces her. "Lelelu! You made it in time!"

"Yes, sorry. I got stuck finalizing the purchase of an island, the seller was not very organized."

"An island? Are you moving to an island?" Nalau asked.

"No, not me." Lelelu said looking toward M.

Nalau looks to M, but she just smiles.

"Well we're happy you could make it. You look fantastic! Is this new?" Nalau asked, inquiring about Lelelu's fantastic form fitting dress.

"Yes! It's a Schatorren, of course."

"The three of us must be keeping him very busy." Nalau said, admiring the outfit.

Bartala stands at the door leading to the stage. "My darling, please, can we discuss fashion later? Lelelu just follow Brzko. You can stand with him."

Their entrance is flawless. They stand on the stage just as Bartala directed them to. There are roughly fifty Ploosnarians sitting in the theatre and many of the palace staff quietly come in, packing the standing only area in the back. The front two rows are filled with liaisons. They are all dressed in blue suits that match their eyes. It takes a few minutes for the crowd to quiet. None of them have ever seen a Dragon before.

"Friends, colleagues, fellow Ploosnarians, we have asked you here to introduce you to Ezopica Mischievous Wisssdartai, heir to the monarchy of Ploosnar." He and Empress Nalau step apart and motion for the Muse of Mischief to come forward. "We are proud to present to you Wisssi and his Autuania, the Muse of Mischief!"

M turns the infant toward the crowd and shifts him so that they can see his face. He's a perfect little duplicate of his father Bartala. The crowd begins whistling - the custom on Ploosnar instead of clapping or stomping. Luckily it doesn't seem to have an effect on Wisssi, he continues to wave his little fists up and down and coo.

As the whistling dies down, Bartala continues, "Please share in our joy and welcome Ezopica Mischievous Wisssdartai. We are most grateful to the Muse of Mischief - should the need arise; she will become guardian to Wisssi."

Again the crowd starts whistling. The palace staff quietly slip out of the room, they have a reception to prepare for.

"Thank you for coming today, your attendance here means a great deal to us. We invite you to join us for a small reception on the patio."

The small crowd begins to file out of the room.

Ferocity walks up to M. "May I?" he asks, holding his hands out toward Wisssi.

She looks past Ferocity to Nalau, sees her approving look and gladly hands him over to Ferocity. Again, Ferocity put his snout next to Wisssi's ear and makes a purring sound, again Wisssi begins to giggle and wave his fists.

"Ferocity if he becomes fussy during the night I will be calling upon you. It's a good thing you live here at the palace." Bartala teases.

The Muse of Mischief, Agent Brzko, Lelelu, Ferocity, and Zri all look at Bartala.

"What? What are you up to?" He asked.

"We have some news." M said.

"Oh I see, I'm the last to know! OK, let's go hide in my study and drink espidrun while our guests gather on the patio."

"Bartala!" Empress Nalau scolds. "We can't avoid our guests... entirely... we have to make an appearance... at least a brief one. But only after at least three espidruns." She says almost running for the door.

They all crack up. That was so unlike the Empress. The trip to Trella had changed her.

"My dear you have changed, and I like it!" Bartala exclaims, chasing after her.

With so many guests milling about the palace they choose the most secluded sitting room - Bartala's private sitting room. Only his closest friends make it this deep into the palace and today there are palace guards stationed at the intersection of all palace hallways with additional guards outside the entrance to the sitting room.

There is a beautiful titanium bottle on the table with glasses around it. The palace staff has anticipated the group's desire to gather alone before facing the crowd.

"That's a different bottle. Is that espidrun?" Brzko asked.

"Yes, I found a distributor that uses these tall bottles, I think they are more beautiful than the short squat bottles we used to purchase." Bartala explains as he begins pouring the hot pink liquid into glasses, allowing it to expel its blue steam.

Ferocity seats himself on the stool that Bartala keeps in the room just for him. He's still holding Wisssi. The others, with the exception of Zri, settle in on the facing sofas.

"You're not joining us today Zri?' the Empress asked.

"No Empress, with so many guests here I would prefer to stay sharp." He says from the sentry position he's taken next to the door.

Empress Nalau walks over to him, "Zri, we have a full complement of palace guards, and I'm sure you have at least one Gaznzulian ship in orbit monitoring the palace..."

"Three actually." He mumbles, looking down at the floor like a toddler that has been busted swiping a cookie off the table.

"If you don't participate in the toast to welcome our son I will take it as a personal insult." She continues.

They stand there staring at each other for a few seconds, it seems like an eternity.

Zri, realizes he's been outranked and concedes. "Yes your Majesty."

She walks back to the sofa and settles in next to Bartala after she hands Zri his glass. He takes a seat next to Lelelu.

As usual Bartala offers the first toast. "To the best friends we have ever known, we thank you from the bottom of all three of our hearts for sharing this momentous day with us. To friends!"

They all toast. "To friends!" The moment the glasses hit the table, they are refilled.

There's a knock at the door.

"Come!" Bartala bellow.

One of the nannies peeks around the door. "Your Majesties, do you require anything?" She quickly scans the room and notices the infant is cradled in the arm of a Dragon while his free hand holds a glass of hot pink liquid with blue steam rising out of the glass. She faints, her body crumples to the floor.

The friends think this is hilarious and all of them laugh, even Ferocity. The palace guard stationed outside the door kneels over the nanny and awakens her. He helps her to stand.

"My most sincere apologies your Majesties. I... I can offer no explanation for my inappropriate actions." She said with her eyes completely downcast. She thinks she's about to be fired.

Nalau goes to her side. "Please relax. There is no need to apologize, I'd like you to meet our dear friend Ferocity." She looks to Ferocity, he sits his glass down and walks over them, still holding Wisssi. "It turns out Dragons have a special way of calming Ploosnarian infants."

Once the nanny sees that Wisssi was waving his little fists and staring up at Ferocity while he drools and coos, she relaxes just a little. Ferocity hands her the infant and returns to his seat. The nanny quickly ducks out of the room without saying another word.

The glasses are refilled but the nanny had interrupted the friends from making a second toast. Nalau lifts her glass before she takes her seat. "To Ferocity and fainting nannies!" She is the only one that drinks, everyone else is laughing to hard.

She sits down and looks toward the Muse of Mischief. "Tell me a story about an island M."

The Muse of Mischief

THE ISLAND

The Schwarth Sea is bordered to the north by Unilond, Luchybos to the west, Qoshnides to the east and open land to the south. It's by far the largest sea on the Planet of Portals, it covers at least a quarter of the planet's surface. There are numerous islands scattered near Unilond and Luchybos, some are vacant, some are privately owned. It's here that the Muse of Mischief and Agent Brzko have decided to build their new home. The Planet of Portals is an advanced planet with outstanding security and self-defense capabilities. They have been welcoming travelers for so long that the population has become completely diversified. Trelods are native to the Planet of Portals but they only make up about 40% of the resident population, the remainder are immigrants such as M and Brzko.

The Planet of Portals is governed by a ruling council, which is also quite diverse. There are very few laws, because there doesn't need to be with advanced beings. For the most part everyone here behaves with dignity and respect.

M and Brzko have decided to combine their names and call their island Misko. When they purchased Misko there was one ancient stone structure - a castle that was built centuries ago. All that was really left of it was three walls, one of which was a great three-story stone structure that looks out over the rocky cliffs above the Schwarth Sea. They had intended to remove it and start with all new buildings but when Ferocity saw the grand stone walls it reminded him of the structures on Dragona. So they kept it. They had the existing walls and roof repaired, rebuilt the fourth wall, and updated the infrastructure to the latest technology. A landing pad and hangar were built next to the castle for Ferocity's ship. The interior now consists of a few standard rooms, a bathing room, sleeping quarters, and library and a kitchen with butler quarters. But the main area has been left wide open - it's more than adequate for Ferocity to spread his wings.

M and Brzko have not revealed the details of his new home to him, he only knows that they agreed to renovate the old castle walls for him. In fact no one but Zri has seen Misko since it was purchased. Zri oversaw the installation of all of the security and technology systems, he spared them nothing. Misko is literally a fortress. M and Brzko have a home built for themselves from the native stones of the Planet of Portals, it's large enough for all of their interests. Their books alone take up the walls of a room that's as large as Ferocity's hanger. It sits near Ferocity's renovated castle, but not too near. It too sits above the cliffs on the edge of the sea.

There are two other structures, also overlooking the cliffs. They are smaller versions of M and Brzko's residence, but each has an attached hanger with a landing pad. One is intended for Lelelu and the other for other guests as needed - likely Emperor Bartala and Empress Nalau, or Ciic and Muum from Suus.

These four structures sit in a semi-circle on the high side of the island, the other side of the island gently slopes down to fantastic black sand beaches. There are several trails, gazebos, and sitting areas built into the landscape which is as nice as any botanical garden.

Zri and his team have been checking and double checking all of the security systems to make sure that everything is functional.

"Have you found any issues Zri?" Brzko asked.

"No, everything is functioning properly."

"Good. Because M will be here with Lelelu any second."

Just as Brzko said this M appeared with Lelelu in tow.

"Hey Lelelu, welcome to Misko." Brzko said.

They are outside in the gardens near M and Brzko's residence. Lelelu slowly turns a complete circle, taking it all in. "Oh that must be Ferocity's old castle. Wow! I love the way you had them keep it looking old. Has he seen it yet?"

"No, you're the first." M said.

"This house over here is the one we had built for you. We know you don't want to give up your main house but we thought it was important for you to have private quarters here, for anytime you stay over." M explains.

"You had a house built for me? Zri! You knew and you didn't even tell me." She walks over to Zri and punches him playfully, and then kisses him on the cheek. He embraces her.

M and Brzko watch this with surprise, they probably looked like idiots with their chins hanging down. They had no idea that Zri and Lelelu were partners, they'd been so focused on Misko for the last few months that they hadn't really paid attention to anything else. They were both trying to think of something to say but luckily Zri rescued them.

"You're not surprised are you?" He teases.

"Well, yeah a little." Brzko said. "But we should have known."

"We wanted to keep it to ourselves until we were sure. We all work so well together and if things didn't work out we didn't want it to create any tension. So we figured it was best to keep a low profile until we made it official."

M embraces Lelelu. "I'm happy for you Lelelu, he's a good one."

"What about me?" Zri pretend whines.

"OK, I'm happy for too." M said embracing one of her oldest friends. "And really it's about time. You're lucky she waited for you. Wait, what do you mean official?"

Lelelu holds out her left wrist so they can see the thin silver band she wears, as is the custom with Trelods to signify that they have a partner.

Before Brzko can comment on their new status he hears Ferocity.

"*I'm here Lord Brzko.*"

"*Great, you have the landing coordinates correct?*"

"*Affirmative. Am I clear to land?*"

"*Yes.*"

M was also able to hear Ferocity telepathically, Lelelu and Zri had been around them enough to know when they were communicating with him.

"Is it Ferocity? Is he here?" Lelelu asked.

"Yes, there he is." Brzko points to a small ship quickly descending to the landing pad next to Ferocity's castle.

They wait for him to power down the ship and then walk over to greet him. The ramp in the rear of his ship descends and Ferocity walks out. They were all surprised to see Whotov, who had served as his butler while he lived at Bartala's palace, follow him out of the ship.

"Whotov! I thought you had decided to stay on Ploosnar." Brzko said, shaking his hand.

"Lord Brzko," He said accepting Brzko's hand. "Upon reflection, I realized that my life would be far too boring should I stay on Ploosnar. I am too old to serve in the palace and I do not want to retire. So if it is still acceptable, I should quite enjoy continuing to serve as butler to Ferocity the Dragon."

"Of course, of course Whotov. We're happy that you've decided to stay with Ferocity. Are you ready to see your new home Ferocity?" Brzko asked.

"Why don't you show them around Ferocity's house and I'll show Lelelu and Zri around hers." M said.

It didn't take them long to settle into their new homes. And while Lelelu has no intention of giving up the house that has been in her family for generations, she does enjoy having another house that she can escape to. Especially one in a stunning location like

Misko. Ferocity is delighted with his new home, but not just the home. The Schwarth Sea to the south of Misko is vast, he finds this wide-open area a great area to fly. It reminds him of his home world, Dragona. After spending so many years alone on Trella, with only his sentient ship for company, he is relieved to be near his bond, Lord Brzko. The two enjoy each other's company..

The Muse of Mischief

WHO IS GOING TO MYAAD

"Good morning." The Muse of Mischief said sleepily. She and Agent Brzko are early risers, so it was unusual to hear from Lelelu before their coffee had kicked in and made them fully functional. "What's wrong Lelelu?"

"Nothing's wrong M. We received a message from Kiik and Bivoor, there's activity in the hives on Myaad. The eggs are about to hatch."

That woke M right up. "Really? Did we lose track of time or is it a little early?"

"It's a little early, but Kiik said there's nothing to worry about, the eggs all seem to be fine. There is no sign of aberidus."

"OK, I guess we need to go to Myaad. Are you planning to go? Is Kiik already en route?"

"Yes, we're both going to Myaad." Zri said, popping into frame behind Lelelu.

She chuckles to herself. "OK Zri, who's ship are you guys taking?"

"Mine." Zri and Lelelu say simultaneously.

Now M wasn't holding back. Holding her hand in front of her mouth, she says, "Oh OK both ships then. We'll see you there. When will you arrive?"

"We should be there by tomorrow evening. Kiik said that she will arrive in a few hours." Lelelu continues. "Do you think Emperor Bartala or Empress Nalau will want to be there?"

"I'll call him but I doubt it. I don't think they're ready to travel with Wisssi yet, and I doubt if either of them would leave him with a nanny. You two be careful, I'll see you on Myaad tomorrow."

M closes her tablet and reaches for Brzko telepathically. *"Hey Brzko, where are you at?"*

He answers immediately. *"Oh, good morning sleepy head. You're finally awake."* He teases.

"It's not even light yet! Where are you?"

"In the garden, teaching Ferocity how to fly the hive drone. What's up?"

"Lelelu called, the eggs are about to hatch on Myaad."

"OK, we'll wrap this up and get ready to go. Who all is going?"

"Lelelu and Zri are leaving today, and Kiik is already en route. I'll call Bartala and see if he wants to be there, but I doubt it."

"I doubt it too. He won't want to leave Wisssi yet." Brzko said out loud, after returning to the inside of their home.

"Hey, did you leave Ferocity to pick up your toys?"

Brzko laughs. "No, the drones are already put away. He's getting his ship ready for Myaad."

"Did you ever ask him about naming his ship? It seems weird to call a sentient being 'his ship', it seems like it should have a name."

"It does have a name. It's 'Ferocity's Ship'." He said grinning.

"Funny." M said, playfully punching him. "So when do you want to go to Myaad?"

"After breakfast."

"OK, I'll find out if Bartala wants to go while you cook breakfast."

"Oh, I'm cooking?"

"Yep, it was your idea."

Brzko went out to the kitchen to see what his options were for breakfast, while M went to her office. Sitting in front of the communication portal she initiated a call to Bartala. He picked up right away. The screen was filled with an image of him holding Wisssi up toward the camera.

"Say hi to your pesky Autuania Wisssi. Why do you think she's calling us so early?"

M cleared her throat, pretending to be annoyed.

"I mean, good morning dear friend. What can do for you today?" Bartala said sarcastically.

"Did you hear about Myaad? The eggs are ready to hatch."

"No! That's excellent. So everything seems to be OK. There are no signs of aberidus?"

"No, no signs of it. They have developed a little early but so far the scans haven't detected anything concerning. Are you interested in going, or would you rather stay home and play daddy?" She asked her oldest friend sarcastically.

"While traveling with you is always exciting - remember last time when the VReoria attempted to capture us - but I think I'll pass this time. I'm not ready to leave Wisssi yet."

"That's what I figured but I wanted to…" There was a commotion to Bartala's left, M couldn't see what was happening.

He turned to someone else and said "OK, OK." and then got up and moved out of sight. To M's surprise Empress Nalau sat down in front of the communication portal.

"Good morning Muse of Mischief. It looks as though your new home agrees with you because you look lovely this morning."

"Thank you Your Majesty." They were not usually this formal, but M still reciprocated for Nalau using her full name.

"M, what if I wanted to go to Myaad with you?"

"I think the Myaads would be honored to have you there, and I think we could have some fun. Maybe even get into a little trouble."

"Hey, don't corrupt my wife! I know what you're capable of M!" Bartala hollered from out of sight.

M and Nalau both laughed at his reaction. "I think he's actually just concerned that I will tell you about some of the parties we went to when we were adolescents. There was this one party on Foskpruchu and…"

This time he physically butted into the conversation by pushing himself up next to his wife. "Hey! Stop that! Or I'll tell Brzko about a few parties myself."

"OK, OK deal." M said, pretending to be insulted. In reality, neither of them had secrets from their partners. But they had spent so much time together as adolescents that they were like rival siblings, they couldn't help teasing each other. "Now go away and let me plan a trip with your wife." He obeyed.

"So Nalau, I know a full complement of palace guards is required for the Emperor, but as Empress how many escorts are you required to have? In other words, how many ships will be going to Myaad?"

"Actually for me, none are *required* because I'm not the actual heir. But it is strongly recommended that I not travel without at least one palace guard. And due to the way my husband is now gesticulating I will of course honor that suggestion."

"Great. So with one or two of the palace guards you can get away with taking Bartala's personal ship. If you leave today, you should get there tomorrow. Which is when Lelelu and Zri will arrive."

"Oh perfect! This is going to be fun. I need to go pack. I'll contact you when I leave Ploosnar."

"OK, Nalau, take care." M closed the communication and went to find Brzko.

"What's for breakfast?" M asked as she walked into the kitchen, a little confused because she didn't see any food.

"Shhhh." Brzko said raising a finger to his lips. "You'll make it fall." Before she could say anything he turned and opened the oven door. He took out a perfect mushroom souffle.

"Wow! Is that made with niptdyn?"

"Of course! Grab some plates and meet me at the table."

She gladly obliged. Niptdyn is a mushroom like fungus that grows on Drolla O0, and is one of their favorite foods.

"I figured we should use the niptdyn before we leave so..."

"So you just whipped up a souffle!" M finished for him, digging in to the souffle.

Before he could answer, their earcom links came to life.

"Good morning again." It was Lelelu. "Hey I just heard from Ciic. M, do you have time to give her a call?"

"Yeah sure, is everything OK?"

"I think so. She'd like to be on Myaad when the eggs hatch. But she didn't leave with Kiik, and if she leaves now, her ship can't get her there in time."

"OK, I'll call her right after breakfast. Thanks Lelelu." She turned to Brzko. "This is really good. You could make this again anytime. I'd help you clean up but, well, I have to go call the leader of Suus. You know how it is." She said smiling as she got up from the table.

"Right. Hey have you noticed how complicated things are sometimes? It seems like we never just take a simple trip anymore."

"Hmmm well let's see…. Our core group is made up of a Dragon, a Trelod, a Gaznzulian, the Emperor and Empress of Ploosnar, and the leader of Suus. Huh? I can't imagine why anything would ever be complicated." She teased.

"Good point." he conceded. "But I'd still like the two of us to go to Trella with Ferocity sometime soon."

"I agree."

Once again, seated at the communication portal, M initiated a call to Ciic. She answered immediately.

"*Thank you for calling Muse of Mischief. It is always a pleasure.*" She projected.

"Your welcome Ciic. What can I do for you?" She projected back, as they were both telepaths and not in mixed company, there was no need for M to speak. Ciic of course, could not speak. Suus do not have mouths.

"I did not think that I could take the time to travel to Myaad, and to be there as the eggs hatch, so I sent Kiik. But now, as the time draws near, I feel I must go. But I don't have a ship that can make it in time..."

"No worries Ciic. I can take you. When were you thinking of going? I understand Kiik is due to arrive tomorrow."

"Tomorrow would be perfect. I will have access to Kiik's ship for sustenance and rest once I'm there. And of course I can return with her."

"Will it be just you or does Muum want to come too?"

"M, we don't want to inconvenience you to that degree."

"I might have a way for you to go together. Ferocity has a ship with a jump drive. If he's available, he may be able to get to Suus and then to Myaad in the same day. I'll check with him."

"Ferocity?" Ciic slightly tilted her head, as tried to figure out who that was.

"Oh right, you haven't met him yet. Ferocity is Agent Brzko's Dragon. They were recently bonded."

"So it's true? We thought it was just a rumor. Our database contains several entries about Dragons, but that was many generations is the past. With no new sightings we thought it may be folklore rather than fact. It would be an honor to meet him."

"Dragons were almost wiped out by the VReoria. But their population has almost recovered. I suspect you will begin to hear more about them."

"We would be honored to travel with him M."

"OK, let me see if I can arrange it. I'll be in touch soon."

After closing the communication portal, M reached for Brzko and Ferocity with her mind. *"Hey guys, I need to ask you something... where are you?"*

~~~

The logistics of getting two time traveling superheroes, one Dragon, one Ploosnarian, one Trelod, one Gaznzulian, and two Suus to Myaad in less than a day was a little complicated, but nothing that the group wasn't used to. Ferocity jumped over to Suus and picked up Ciic and Muum - riding with him to Myaad was a momentous occasion for Ciic to say the least. And vice versa - Ferocity being charged with transporting the ruler of Suus and her spouse was equally momentous. Lelelu, Zri, and Empress Nalau, all made it on time in their own ships. The Muse of Mischief and Agent Brzko of course didn't need ships.

In the early hours of the morning everyone, with the exception of Kiik and her team, gathered in the garden area near the Bivoor administration building. The same Bivoor that had taken the lead on organizing the return of the Rogsaars was in charge today. But something had changed, M detected more confidence, better communication, and a desire to lead. She wondered what other changes were in store for a species made up of clones. The devastation of aberidus had really taken a toll on all of the Bivoors, Dumeers and Rogsaars. Everyone here had played a part in helping them overcome it. Today was the final piece - the eggs were about to hatch. Kiik and her team have been monitoring the development and are sure that there is no sign of the disease. But after watching so many die, the Myaads are of course nervous. They need to see for themselves that aberidus no longer infects their hives.

Bivoor addressed the group, "Friends - both old and new, all of Myaad is grateful to you. Without you the Myaad would have ceased to exist. We are once again honored by your presence. I have just been informed that the first three Rogsaars have emerged. They appear to be fine."

Everyone voiced their relief. Once it was quiet, Bivoor continued, "Kiik and her team will complete a medical scan of each of them. Once that is done, their caregiver will take them to their residence."

"So they'll be raised separately, in individual residences instead of a traditional nursery?" M asked.

"Yes, initially we considered our traditional nursery methods for raising the newest Myaads. While that is more efficient, if there is a recurrence of aberidus, or any other problems it would also be more devastating. The Bivoor also agree that because of what we've been through, we have the potential to over-shelter these new Myaads, and that could have detrimental effects on their development. They will each be raised in a separate home. Their guardians will be bringing each of them through the garden on their way home. In fact here they come now."

Everyone turned in the direction Bivoor was looking, walking toward them were three pairs of Rogsaars - each pair consisted of an adult and an identical looking child. The children were about the size of a five-year-old human. The first pair stopped at the edge of the garden, Nalau was the closest to them. She gracefully knelt down, with her long blue skirt fanning out behind her.

"Hello young Rogsaar. We are all so pleased to meet you." The child just gazed at her, not frightened, but clearly not able to comprehend her words. Nalau stood back up and addressed the adult Rogsaar, asking what everyone but Bivoor was wondering. "How long will it take for language skills to develop?"

"We don't know for sure. Learning begins immediately but full comprehension could take three months."

The Muse of Mischief and Agent Brzko recognized this Rogsaar as soon as he spoke. It was the Rogsaar that had been abandoned on Jinn. The one that had introduced them to Afrit the Great.

Brzko stepped forward with his hand out, "Rogsaar! It's a pleasure to see you! It looks like you are adjusting well to being back on Myaad."

Rogsaar let go of the child and accepted Brzko's extended hand, "Hello Agent Brzko. Yes, yes, I am very pleased to be back on Myaad. And I am honored to be able to raise one of the first Rogsaars."

The child began to wander as soon as Rogsaar's hand accepted Brzko's. It only seemed that the young Rogsaar wandered through - stopping in front of Zri the young Rogsaar looked up at him, pointed and grunted.

Kneeling next to the child Bivoor did not scold or correct the young Rogsaar, but instead turned this into a teaching moment. "This is a Gaznzulian." Young Rogsaar turned and looked at Bivoor. "Gaz-n-zu-li-an."

The young Rogsaar attempted to say Gaznzulian, it was really just grunting. Now satisfied at knowing what Zri was, the child returned to its guardian.

"I didn't realize the positive impact that having you all here would create. For these young Myaads, to see so many different species within hours of emerging from the hive, I suspect this will create a curiosity within them." Bivoor said.

"Myaad is going to evolve." Nalau said.

"Yes, and we are ready for it." Bivoor replied. "These Myaad will be different than any others."

By now there were several young Rogsaars with adult Rogsaars in the garden. The positive energy was unmistakable. In all, it took a little over two hours for all thirty of the young Myaads to leave the hive. Once they were all settled with their guardians the group lingered in the gardens. There were a few Bivoors, Dumeers, and Rogsaars with them. It had been such a momentous day, no one wanted it to end. As the conversations began to wind down, M noticed Kiik and her two assistants coming toward them from the hives.

"*Hello Kiik.*" M projected to her.

"*Muse of Mischief, hello.*" She projected back.

When she, and her assistants arrived both Ciic and the lead Bivoor went to them.

"Kiik, thank you. With your help we have successfully cured the hives. We could not have done it without the help of the Suus." Bivoor said.

Kiik deferred to Ciic, and let her answer. *"It was our pleasure. We all owe our gratitude to Kiik, her determination and commitment to restoring the hives has honored all Suus. This is why she will no longer be Lead Researcher of Suus."*

Kiik's confusion could be felt by everyone.

Ciic continued, *"She is now our Interplanetary Excursionist AND Lead Researcher. She will command a small fleet of ships, with the freedom to come and go from Suus as needed. Her accomplishments have demonstrated that more can be accomplished with a strong leader as our point of contact for working with other beings."*

Kiik was quiet for a moment, speechless, as if she weren't telepathic. *"Thank you for this honor. I will serve Suus to the best of my abilities."*

This was a big change for the Suus. Because they maintained the largest database of any beings, they often helped others by providing information when asked. But adding excursionist to the researcher's role meant that they would now be looking for opportunities to help others, rather than waiting to be asked. One by one everyone offered their congratulations to Kiik.

When it was M's turn, Kiik projected a private message to her, *"Muse of Mischief I am indebted to you. Thank you."*

"Me? Why would you be indebted to me? This was all Ciic." M projected back.

"Surely you had something to do with this."

"No, nothing more than asking for help. But you can bet I'll be calling on you for more help in the future. Especially now that you command a small fleet of ships. Are you ready for all that adventure?"

"As long as I can consult with you and Agent Brzko, I'm ready."

The Bivoors had arranged for a meal to be prepared and offered to the visitors. This turned out to be a good thing because none of them really wanted to leave. As the leader of Suus, Ciic rarely gave herself the opportunity to leave her home planet. The meal didn't appeal to any of the Suus because they only ingest vapors, but they were enjoying everyone's company. Lelelu and Zri always enjoyed being on assignment together. And while they did get to see each other frequently, their responsibilities sometimes made it challenging. The most enjoyment was had by Empress Nalau. After a conversation with Bivoor she came to find M.

"Why didn't you tell me M?" Nalau said taking a seat next to M at the table where she was sitting.

"Sorry, tell you what?"

"That having a child would actually give me more freedom! I have so enjoyed this trip. It will not be my last."

M laughed. "Honestly Nalau, I didn't see that coming. But it makes sense. I mean if Bartala is committed to being the main parent, then you gain freedom. Uh-oh. You might need some larger closets. I have a feeling you'll be doing some shopping."

"Could I pass for human on Earth?" Nalau's question surprised M. The shock showed on her face. "Oh sorry, M. I didn't mean to shock you."

"Oh no worries Nalau, you just surprised me. But I guess I shouldn't be surprised. Why wouldn't you want to see new places, places you've heard about but not been? Yes, with the right wardrobe you could pass for human on Earth."

"Splendid! Can we plan a trip?"

Brzko caught that just as he walked up to where the ladies were sitting. "A trip where?"

"Earth, Brzko. I'd like to see Earth."

"Oh! OK. You might enjoy some things about it."

"I'm sure I will. Well, when we have time maybe we could plan a quick trip. Right now I need to depart, I want to get back to Bartala and Wisssi."

After thanking the Bivoors, and saying their goodbyes everyone headed home. Of course for the Muse of Mischief and Agent Brzko, it was instant.

The Muse of Mischief

LELELU GOES MISSING

Later that day, the Muse of Mischief was in one of her favorite spots. With a cup of jasmine tea she had settled into a chaise lounge on the balcony overlooking the Schwarth Sea. Even from high above, she could hear the waves crashing against the cliffs. She was reviewing a recent batch of messages that Lelelu had forwarded. Lelelu would sift through the requests for help and forward the legitimate ones. As always, M had her earcom link in and activated. She was a bit startled when it came to life.

"M help! I can't outrun them." It was Lelelu and she sounded insane with fear.

"Lelelu where are you?" Nothing, no reply. "Lelelu, can you hear me? Zri, are you on com?"

"Yes M, I'm here. Is Lelelu with you?"

"No she hasn't made it back from Myaad yet. I need her last known location immediately. Ferocity…" Brzko appeared on the deck with Ferocity at his side.

"Ferocity, can you take off right away, as soon as Zri can get us Lelelu's last known coordinates?"

"Yes. I can leave now." He grew silent for a second as he telepathically contacted his ship. They could hear the engines fire from inside the house. He used his Gaznzulian transporter to transport aboard his ship as it was taking off. "Zri, do you have the coordinates yet?" he asked via earcom link.

"Yes, I'm sending them now. She was way of course. Why would she have veered off course on the way home?"

Because Ferocity's ship used a jump drive, unless Zri was already closer he'd be able to get to Lelelu's ship sooner.

"I found her ship. I'm going aboard." Ferocity said.

"Ferocity be careful, someone may be on the ship." Brzko said.

"She may be hurt Lord Brzko, I can't wait."

"Show me." Brzko said.

He closed his eyes and accepted the telepathic images from his bonded dragon. He was on the bridge of Lelelu's ship. It was empty and there were signs of a struggle. He silenced the proximity alarms and continued to look around. "She's not here. Zri, how far away are you?"

"It will take me two hours or more to get that far out in the Zenbliuq Galaxy. If you can get her ship back to Misko before that. I may as well meet you there."

"Affirmative."

"*Do you need any help Ferocity?*" Brzko asked telepathically.

"*No. I will be able to transport Lelelu's ship within my shields. I'll be there shortly.*"

"Shit! What the hell happened? Who would want to harm Lelelu?" M asked Brzko.

"We'll find her M. Don't worry. We'll find her."

"Hey don't do that calming thing to me. I'm pissed and I want to stay pissed."

"OK, I know. As soon as Ferocity gets here we can start trying to piece together what happened from her sensor logs."

"Until then. I think we should also alert Bartala and Ciic. They both have large networks of ships that could be on the lookout for any information about Lelelu. And there's a chance that they may be in danger."

"Good idea. I'll contact Ciic, you contact Bartala."

They both decided to deliver the bad news in person, temporarily leaving Ferocity's butler, Whotov, as the only being on Misko.

~~~

The smell was wretched. It smelled like the time she'd been walking along the beach with her father. They'd come across a dead igao, it looked like its belly had exploded. There were rotting guts oozing out of it - much to the delight of the sea birds that were making a meal of the rotting carcass. "Baba, why did the igao die all the way up here, away from the water?" She was raised by both parents, but her father was by far her favorite. These times alone, exploring the natural wonders on the Planet of Portals with her father, had ensured that she too would be an explorer.

"This isn't real Le, you need to wake up. You're in danger"

"What are you talking about?" She looked up at his kind blue face. He looked worried.

"Le, you know you can't be here with me, you're not a child anymore. Le WAKE UP NOW, you're in danger."

Why was her father yelling at he? He never raised his voice, especially not to her. She started to realize something was very wrong, her hands were restrained. And... her eyes were very heavy. She continued fighting her way to consciousness, her head felt thick. Lelelu finally managed to open her eyes, just a slit at first. She was in a filthy room, there was no furniture, only walls that look like they're made from steel. Struggling, she managed to sit up. Her hands were tied but she wiggled enough to be able to loosen and then remove the cord. As she stood, she felt everything around her shift, she was light headed. Placing a hand on the wall, she closed her eyes and focused on her breathing, it was coming back to her now.

After a visit to Myaad she was on the way back to the Planet of Portals - her sensors had detected a ship approaching her position. But then they went silent, non-responsive. In fact her entire ship seemed to stop responding to her. She could feel her ship traveling very fast but in what direction she couldn't tell. Then she was boarded. The memory made her wince. It was the VReoria. Two of them had gotten past her shields and transported to her bridge. She tried to fight them off, managed to call for M, and then they released a gas of some kind. That was where her memory ended.

Her stability had returned. Lelelu checked for her earcom link, it had been removed. She patted her hip, looking for her pulse weapon, gone of course. She started scanning the walls for a door. She either had to escape or be ready to attack her captors if they entered this cell. She found what looked like a doorway in one of the walls - she positioned herself next to it and waited.

~~~

Ferocity stayed on Lelelu's ship all the way to Misko on the Planet of Portals. He maintained a constant telepathic link to his sentient ship; so once in orbit, he separated the ships and manually landed Lelelu's ship in its usual space, allowing his ship to land on its own. He dropped the side ramp and exited the ship. The Muse of Mischief, Agent Brzko, and ShyUst were waiting for him.

"Ferocity, I'm sure you remember ShyUst." Agent Brzko said, reintroducing them.

"Yes, of course. Hello ShyUst."

"Hi Ferocity. I was closer than Zri so I came to see if I could help. Were you able to find anything in the logs that could help us?"

"I'm not familiar enough with Lelelu's ship to attempt accessing the logs. I would not want my lack of knowledge to destroy any information."

"Good thinking Ferocity. Muse of Mischief, if you don't object I'd like to have both my technology officer and science officer attempt to figure out what happened."

"Please, I'm sure they are far more capable at retrieving information than any of us."

Within seconds two Gaznzulians transported down from his orbiting ship. They immediately boarded Lelelu's ship and went to work.

"How far out is Zri, ShyUst, and how is he?" Brzko asked.

ShyUst checked his armband before responding, "He is less than an hour away and he is not doing well. I think he's blaming himself for letting her travel alone."

"I can understand that but it's not his fault." Brzko said.

"And there's no way Lelelu would allow anyone to tell her she couldn't travel alone. She is seriously independent." M added.

One of ShyUst's officers appeared at the top of the ramp, "Sir, we've been able to identify the energy signature from the ship that overtook her. It's the same as the ship you encountered leaving Trella. It was the VReoria."

"Damn it." M said. "What the hell do they want this time?"

"Probably the same thing they wanted last time. US." Brzko said. He reached for Ferocity with his mind. Out of respect to Dragona's insistence of privacy, they never spoke of Ferocity's home aloud, in mixed company. *"Ferocity, can you contact Dragona, tell them what's happened and ask them to help in the search?"*

"Yes Lord Brzko." He immediately left the group to contact Dragona.

Zri had arrived. As soon as he was close enough he transported himself to the planet. "Where is she? What do you know so far?" He looked back and forth between ShyUst and M.

"Sir, my officers have found the energy signature from the ship that overtook her in the logs, it was the VReoria." ShyUst said, looking concerned.

Zri literally roared in frustration. He was about to erupt. M reached for Brzko, *"Please take ShyUst and see if you can help on the ship."*

Brzko stepped toward ShyUst and motioned toward the ship's ramp. He understood and follow Brzko aboard the ship. M and Zri were left alone.

"Walk with me Zri." He didn't budge. "Now." She said, gently taking his arm and tugging.

He broke down as they began walking toward the beach on the far side of the island - his reflection began to shimmer as the extreme emotion overtook him. "M, I shouldn't have left her alone. This is my fault."

M let him continue to beat himself up as they walked. She didn't say anything, just kept walking with him letting him curse himself until he was ready to get to work.

"What are we going to do? What's the plan and what steps have you taken so far?" He asked as he regained control.

"Oh there you are Commander." M said.

"My apologies I just…"

"Love Lelelu like you've never loved anyone in your life. There's no need to apologize Zri, I understand. And you know as well as I do that Lelelu is, and will always be independent. You will never change that, and this is in no way your fault, so get off it."

"You're right. That was a completely emotional response."

"It's OK, I'm the only one that saw you break down. There was no harm done." He nodded. "So far Ciic and Bartala have been alerted that Lelelu is victim to what we assume is a kidnapping. Ferocity is contacting Dragona as we speak, and…"

"They thought they had neutralized the VRreoria after they attempted to kidnap you and Brzko on Trella."

"I suspect that they did neutralize the VReoria that were involved in that attack. After being enslaved by the VReoria I doubt if anyone has more of an interest in annihilating the entire population. But the VReoria are surely not all in the same place at the same time, they must have a good hiding place."

"Good point. OK, so what else can we get from Lelelu's logs and why did they take *her*?"

"I suspect they'll demand me or Brzko in exchange for Lelelu. But it doesn't make sense, the VReoria are known for occupying and enslaving entire planets but attempting to kidnap me or Brzko… I don't see the connection."

"You're correct, it doesn't make sense. And why attempt to kidnap you or Brzko, you can't be confined." He paused; he was receiving a communication via earcom link. "I understand. Yes, I'll inform her."

"What's up?"

"Ciic contacted Gaznzul, she's sending her entire security force. As is Emperor Bartala. Rather than searching for the VReoria on their own they'll join us."

"How many ships?"

"Around 200 from the two of them, we have at least that many Gaznzulians available."

"Seriously? I think we should contact the Ruling Council, they are going to wonder why so many ships are heading toward the Planet of Portals."

No sooner had she said this than a low flying ship approached. It was almost identical to Lelelu's ship. It landed in the open area near M and Zri. The ramp descended and a Trelod walked down the ramp toward them. M and Zri went to greet him.

He stopped before them and offered a shallow bow, his loose-fitting suit billowing in the ocean breeze. "You must be the Muse of Mischief. I am Vustia, liaison to the Ruling Council of the Planet of Portals. We understand that one of our citizens has been kidnapped by the VReoria."

M extended her hand, "Yes, I'm the Muse of Mischief. This Zri, Security Commander of Gaznzul and a very dear friend of Lelelu's."

"The Ruling Council has asked me to inform you that you have their full support. The resources of the Planet of Portals are at your disposal. Just tell us what we can do."

"Thank you Vustia. We are expecting a ransom, but have yet to be contacted. Zri will coordinate all resources. At the moment we have one request."

"Please…" Vustia said gesturing for her to continue.

"Please inform the Ruling Council that there are several hundred ships on the way here, Ploosnarian, Suus, and Gaznzulian.

We wouldn't want anyone to think that the Planet of Portals is under attack."

"Some of them are already showing up on our scanners. We will take the appropriate action to accommodate them as they arrive."

"We're going to need a base of operations. I'd like us to all work out of the same location, we can use this residence here." M gestured toward the empty guest house. "Right now I need to run an errand. Zri is in command until I return."

M left Zri with Vustia and walked toward her own house. She had no intention of going to the house, she just didn't want to disappear in front of Vustia. Before she left, she reached for Brzko, *"I'm heading to Ploosnar, I'll be back in a few minutes."*

"OK, be careful M."

~~~

The Muse of Mischief almost always arrived at the bottom of the palace stairs when she visited Ploosnar. A habit she had developed when she was young in order to prevent the palace guards from being startled. Today, there was no time for that. She arrived on the landing, outside the entrance. The palace guards were momentarily startled. M was well known on Ploosnar and once they recognized her they relaxed.

"Sorry, I'm in a real hurry today." she said.

"We understand." one of them answered.

M rushed inside and asked the first butler she encountered, "Where is Empress Nalau?"

Before he could answer the Empress rounded the corner. "Oh M, I'm so sorry. How can we help?" She said embracing her.

"I need a big favor Nalau." The Empress just looked at her, waiting to hear what it was. "I need a coordinator, someone that can handle incoming and outgoing communications for me. Brzko and I can't get bogged down with the details but I'm afraid we may miss something without someone managing communications."

"Of course, it would be my pleasure. Do I need to bring anything?"

"No, we should have everything you'll need. We're going to set up the guest house as a command center."

"This would be the guest house you built for us on Misko?" Emperor Bartala said as he rounded the corner with Wisssi lounging in his arms.

M realized she rarely saw the Emperor and Empress this relaxed - Bartala wore green slacks and simple white shirt with the sleeves rolled up and Nalau was wearing an almost identical outfit.

"Hey Bartala. Yes. Don't worry, Nalau will be safe."

"I have no doubt! Please contact me if you need anything and keep me informed when you can."

Empress Nalau took a second to kiss her child and embrace her husband, and then turned to M. "OK, let's go." And they did.

They arrived near M's house. She kept her grip on Nalau's arm to steady her.

"Which house?"

"That one." M said pointing to the guest house and walking that way.

"I don't need an escort M. You have more important things to do. Have someone get me an earcom link and I'll take care of the rest. Where's Whotov?"

"Probably there." M said pointing to Ferocity's house.

Nalau was off. She went to Ferocity's house first, intent on securing Whotov's help with gathering supplies - she intended to have sustenance and other supplies available for everyone on Misko.

Whotov answered when she knocked on the door. He was shocked to see her, "Empress Nalau! To what do I owe this honor." he said as he bowed.

"There's no time for formalities Whotov, I need your help." She said stepping into the house.

M clearly didn't need to babysit her. She had made the right choice getting her to help. Nalau may be an Empress but no one can organize and mobilize better than she can. "Zri," M called via earcom link.

"Go ahead M."

"I need you to get Empress Nalau an earcom link and set up a full communications center in the guest house."

"Brzko told me where you went. Everything is ready for the Empress."

"Thanks. Brzko, Ferocity, where are you?"

"We're all at the guest house." Brzko answered. "We need to start working on a plan."

BABA LIVES

Lelelu could not get used to the death smell. It hung in the air like a thick fog. At first she thought it must be actual dead beings that created the smell, but she began to realize that it was the smell of a barbaric species. The VReoria sustain themselves on flesh. Is that why she'd been taken, was she to be eaten? It didn't take her long to get past that idea, she assumed she'd been kidnapped in an attempt to gain access to the Muse of Mischief and Agent Brzko, after the failed kidnap attempt on Trella.

She couldn't figure out why she kept having visions of her father. After disappearing on a mission to the Glion Galaxy he was presumed dead. Debris from his ship had been found far from where he was supposed to be, but she couldn't remember where. She'd been just a child and that part of his death wasn't important to her. All that mattered was that her Baba was not coming home.

After standing for hours she grew weary and slid down the wall until she was sitting. She dozed off and immediately saw him. *"Hello Le."*

"Hi Baba." Lelelu said to an empty room.

"Le, you've got to stay awake, stay ready."

"OK Baba, why do I keep seeing you? You're dead."

"I'm not dead Le, I'm here."

Before she could process what he'd said, she heard something outside the door. Instantly, she was fully awake, standing, and ready to attack.

The door slid open and two cloaked VReoria entered. Even when they attempted to look like Trelods they were hideous and slimy looking. Their appearances shimmered and the falsified appearance disappeared, revealing creatures that are slimy and bulky, with elongated heads and large eyes, long appendages, covered in tentacles hanging down from the front of their faces.

She stepped toward them, ready to attack. But they were surrounded by some sort of energy field, it pushed her back. She went at them again, and again it pushed her back.

"Oh, more tenacious than the other after so many years. Perhaps we should keep her." The VReoria nearest the door said.

"No, we already have one of them. This one is bait." The other said, they made a hideous high-pitched sound and seemed to jiggle. They were laughing.

The one closest to the door slid a tray along the floor, kicking it really. "Sustenance."

They both turned and left. She rushed the door, but she wasn't strong enough to hold it back. If she hadn't removed her fingers they'd have been snapped off.

She looked at the tray they had left, it contained a bowl with some foul-smelling liquid in it. She kicked it and it flipped over, letting it spill through the holes in the floor. That at least reduced the smell.

"You have to eat Le."

She just about jumped out of her blue skin. She turned a complete circle almost expecting to see someone else in her cell. But she was alone. It was one thing to have dreams about her father, but to hear him in her head when fully awake. Lelelu thought she'd lost her mind.

"Le, listen to me. They're going to trade you, trade you for someone you know."

"Oh get out of my head! Is this some desperate attempt to get information." She thought, assuming she was under mental attack by the VReoria.

"Le, it's Baba. I'm here. I've been here for a very long time."

"Baba's dead. If you paid better attention to the details you're stealing from my mind, you'd know that."

"I'm not dead Le. I've been imprisoned here all this time. This is specimen ship. The VReoria are attempting to collect one of every species. I don't know what they're planning but I'm sure it's not good."

"Shut up! Get out of my head already." She yelled aloud.

"Le, do you remember the name of your best friend in early school? Wasn't it Zestrilia?"

"Nice try, anyone could know that. My father's dead."

"OK Le, ask me a question. Ask me something only I would know."

She leaned her head against the wall and closed her eyes, thinking back to her childhood, trying to recall a secret that only Baba would know. *"Why did I refuse to go sailing with Zestrilia when I was a child."*

"Because you said that her feet stunk, and if she couldn't keep her feet clean then she couldn't be trusted to keep you safe on the water."

Lelelu had never told anyone but her father the truth about why she didn't go sailing with her friend, not even her mother. The realization that she was really communicating with her father hit her hard. It defied logic. Even if he was here, she wasn't telepathic.

"I've lost my mind." She said out loud to an empty cell.

"No Le, you haven't. I'm really here."

"Baba?" She broke down and wept, wept for all the time she'd missed her father; wept for fear of her current situation; wept for fear she was losing her mind.

~~~

Luckily Dragons are very disciplined. Otherwise heated debates, such as the one the Great Assembly was in the midst of, could end in flames. They had gathered in the great hall to discuss a proposal that had been made by their newest, and youngest member.

"Yes this seems drastic, but we must take action. It is time to emerge from our seclusion. We can offer assistance without opening Dragona to strangers." Hasira said. "There is no honor in staying hidden while others fight the VReoria."

The Great Assembly of Dragona was seated at a round table in the center of the great hall. The walls were lit with the red flames burning in the sconces. Haurangi, the second eldest, fondled his medallion while he took a moment to consider his response.

"We barely survived the VReoria. It has taken us many years to recover from their enslavement."

"But we are recovering, and no beings have more experience fighting the VReoria than Dragons. We owe it to all beings in the Universe to come out of hiding and help put an end to them."

"If the VReoria enslavers return to Dragona, we may not survive another attack from them."

"There may not be enough of the enslavers remaining to attack us again."

"What if we draw attention to ourselves, the attention of the collectors?"

"If we do not help the others put an end to this, they surely WILL return, and probably more powerful than they were last time. We cannot live our lives in fear, there is no honor in that."

This last comment made many of the Dragons at the table begin clicking, communicating in one of their ancient languages.

Kwaai raised his scepter, commanding their attention, "A vote."

To Hasira's surprise, all but Haurangi stood and vowed "With Hasira." Even Kwaai.

Kwaai looked at Haurangi, "Haurangi, the Great Assembly of Dragona has voted to end our seclusion. We will no longer live in hiding, we are to take our rightful place in the Universe. Will you consider changing your vote, making this a unanimous decision?"

They all looked at Haurangi, waiting for his response. He stood, "We are stronger together, I will support this decision."

Kwaai nodded to Haurangi, "Thank you Haurangi, the Great Assembly benefits from your presence, your concerns will help to keep us cautious." He turned to Hasira, "Inform Ferocity that you will attend the meetings on the Planet of Portals as our representative. When there is a plan in place the Dragons will be ready to assist."

~~~

There are two main features of the guest house on Misko; a huge dining room that can seat up to 24 and an equally large sitting room. Empress Nalau was doing a fantastic job of making sure the head of each group involved was kept in the communication loop. She had borrowed Whotov, Ferocity's butler, to help with the tangible things - making sure there was food and beverage available and gathering and dispersing supplies. The guest house has only two bedrooms, but that is of no consequence, all of the visitors have ships available to them. Nalau was the only one that needed to actually reside at the house.

After receiving the ransom message, the Muse of Mischief requested everyone's attendance at the massive dining table to share the VReoria's demands and come up with a plan. The table was so large that she and Agent Brzko were both able to sit at the head of the table. Immediately to her left was Nalau, ready to take any action requested. Immediately to Brzko's right was Ferocity, but surprisingly, he wasn't the only dragon at the table. Hasira had made it in time for the meeting. He had confidently positioned himself between Zri and Vustia. Also at the table were Waaw and

Xiix, commander and sub-commander of the Suus fleet, Pruglar, commander of the Ploosnarian fleet, and of course ShyUst.

Agent Brzko opened the meeting, "We've received the ransom demand from the VReoria." He looked at his tablet, laying on the table in front of him he read the message aloud.

"We the VReoria have your precious Trelod. We will only exchange her for the Muse of Mischief. You will meet us on Cazoova at the following coordinates one rotation from now."

"That doesn't make sense." Zri said. "The VReoria know that you and Brzko can travel at will, they can't detain you."

"They must think they've found a way." M said slowly. "Or… they think they have a way to instantly kill me. Why the hell do they want me?"

"Specimen logging."

Everyone turned toward the voice. Hasira took a second to gather himself. "Please forgive me if I have spoken out of turn. We have kept ourselves secluded for so long that I am unfamiliar with your protocols."

"Honest communication is the only protocol here, Hasira. Please continue." Ferocity said aloud, putting the other Dragon at ease.

"When Dragona was enslaved we observed many things about the VReoria. They looked upon us as though we were lower life forms so they spoke freely around us. But we listened and remembered every detail we heard. They spoke of another classification of VReoria, the collectors."

"More than one kind of VReoria? I don't like the sound of this." M said.

Hasira continued, "The collectors have a small fleet of specimen ships. These ships are said to travel around this Universe, and others, collecting perfect specimens of higher life forms. The beings are suspended in state of existence that is neither living nor dead. They experiment with using the genetics from the collected species to alter their own genes. Some said they were attempting to create a master race of warriors by adding the strengths of every species they encounter to their own DNA."

"Is that how they were able to cloak their appearance when they attempted to kidnap us on Trella?" Brzko asked.

Hasira considered his response carefully, sharing information with other species was new to him. "Possibly but I don't know for certain. It was the other classification, the enslavers, that occupied Dragona. I don't think they ever cloaked their appearance, but that doesn't mean they couldn't have."

"They sound ruthless." M said.

"Mmmm. They are. They poisoned Dragona, altering the atmosphere in order to dominate us. It took us a very long time to figure out why we could no longer fly or breathe fire."

Hasira's comments weighed heavily on them all. It was such a barbaric thing to do. The room stayed silent while everyone thought about a fleet of VReoria collectors on specimen ships.

ShyUst broke the silence, "Muse of Mischief, I don't understand. You and Agent Brzko can time travel, is there a reason you don't travel back in time and prevent this, or leave a warning for Lelelu?"

"I wish it were that easy but it doesn't work that way. If we change something in the past it doesn't stop it from happening in this Universe, because it already did happen. Changing history just creates fractures in the timeline, or what some call parallel universes." M explained.

"You can't exchange yourself for Lelelu, we can't allow the VReoria to capture you. Can you imagine what they could accomplish if they actually were able to use your genes to obtain the ability to travel through apertures?" Zri said. "Once we hear the details of the exchange we'll need to find a way to make them think you're exchanging yourself for Lelelu, just long enough to get her back."

"*A clone.*" Everyone turned toward Waaw, and Xiix, unable to tell which telepath had projected the thought. It was Waaw, he continued, "*We all know that members of the Universal Coalition have agreed not to participate in cloning activities. But given the circumstances, they may be willing to hold an emergency vote and allow a single deviation from the agreement."*

"That could work." Zri said. "I'm sure that Gaznzul would give their approval."

"As will Ploosnar." Nalau said.

"I think the ruling council of the Planet of Portals will also agree." Vustia said.

"Although Dragona is not currently a member of the Universal Coalition, we also support the idea, as long as we are assured that the equipment used is to be destroyed afterward." Hasira said.

Brzko looked across the table to Waaw, "You must think that Ciic will approve of the idea?"

"I do. You and the Muse of Mischief have served Suus on many occasions. She will not approve of the Muse of Mischief exchanging herself for Lelelu."

Brzko turned to M, "So what do you think?"

"Uhhh, other than being a little creeped out by the idea of cloning myself I think it could work. Waaw, who has the technology and how long will it take? We don't have long to prepare."

"Please allow me to return to my ship and consult with Ciic. The Suus database contains the details of successful cloning processes. The practice was common for cloning diseased organs long ago. I will need to review the data in order to give you an accurate answer." Waaw projected.

"While you're doing that, we need someone to contact the Universal Coalition and inform them of what's going on." Brzko said.

"I already have." Nalau and Vustia said in unison.

Vustia gestured to Nalau, suggesting that she continue. She did, "They were already aware of the situation, the kidnapping. They have approved of the plan to use a clone, as long as it's a single clone, destroyed after the rescue, and the equipment is also destroyed."

"Wait, so it's a clone of me, then wouldn't it have my abilities?" M asked.

"*No.*" Waaw projected. "*It will only look like you, we will not clone your entire brain.*"

"Wow, this just keeps getting creepier. OK so Waaw, while you return to your ship to get started on the clone idea, the rest of us need to come up with a plan for taking down these VReoria specimen ships once and for all." Brzko said.

"It won't be that easy." M said. "We have an obligation to rescue all of the *specimens* that are still alive."

~~~

Lelelu lost track of time; she struggled to stay awake but she kept dozing off. Finally she gave in and let her body, and mind, rest. She woke up sitting on the floor, right where she'd fallen asleep. Her body ached from the struggle, the stress, and the complete lack of comfort in this cell. Slowly inching her way up the disgusting, cold wall she stood, tilting her head from side to side she started her morning stretching routine.

Now that she was fully awake and had relieved some of her physical discomfort Lelelu was ready to work on a plan for escape. Out of habit she touched her ear, still no earcom link. If she made it out of this alive she was going to have Zri install some kind of subcutaneous link that could not easily be removed. She checked her pockets to see if she had anything that could help her. There was nothing. Her thoughts drifted to her father. He'd been dead since she was a child, what was causing her to hallucinate about him now.

"*You're not hallucinating Le. I'm here, stuck on the same ship.*" Again she started hearing her father's voice in her head.

"*That's not possible, my father is dead. And he wasn't telepathic... so whatever!*"

"*Le, think about the stories you heard as a child. The stories of the ancient ones.*"

"Some of them had wings and could fly. Yeah I heard those stories, what's the point?"

"How did they communicate?"

She paused and searched her mind for stories she'd been told as a child. *"Some of them were telepathic..."* She said starting to think her father may actually be real. *"But even if Baba was telepathic, I'm not."*

"Maybe you always have been, but the ability lay dormant because you didn't need it. And now, you need to use everything you've got to survive and your mind knows it."

"Baba? It's really you?"

"Yes Le, it's really me."

"Why are you here? I want to see you."

"I was captured, just like you. The VReoria are relentless in their efforts to capture one of every species they encounter."

"How have you survived here all this time?"

"I'm in stasis Le. I can't move, only my mind works."

"Is that what they are going to do to me?"

"No, you're bait. They intend to trade you for something called a Muse of Mischief."

"It's a someone, not a something. How do you know that?"

"The VReoria have shallow minds, they are not capable of telepathy. They don't realize that I can hear them; they often speak about their plans as they tour the gallery. There are others here in the gallery that are aware too."

"Gallery?"

"I can't send images via telepathy but I know someone who can. Stabilize yourself, sometimes telepathic images can be disruptive. Standby."

"OK Baba." Lelelu positioned herself in the corner of her cell. She was standing but supported on each side by a wall. She leaned back, closed her eyes and waited.

The image came, at first she couldn't focus on it, it made her head hurt. With her eyes closed she took a deep breath and focused her mind. She was in a huge, well lit, round room. The floor and walls were white. There were rows of yellowish looking tubes. She tried to focus on the one right in front of her, but she couldn't control the focus. This wasn't a live image, it was someone's memory. She could feel the viewer being pulled forward, she felt them resist. As they got closer to the tube in front of them, she could see that someone was in the tube, it looked like a Ploosnarian. The tube was full of liquid. Her body flooded with the Trelod version of adrenaline as her flight or fight response kicked in. She could feel the viewer begin to struggle hard now. As the struggle ensued, she caught a glimpse of the flailing arm of the viewer. She was seeing this memory through the eyes of a Suus. It ceased, and she was relieved. She leaned over, put her hands on her knees and worked on calming herself.

"*Le, are you OK? Did you see the gallery?*"

"*Yes Baba, I'm going to get you out of there.*"

"*Oh Le, I've been here a very long time. Many of us have. I don't think there's any hope for us. But you could escape, when they exchange you for that Muse of Mischief.*"

"*Don't worry Baba, you don't know the Muse of Mischief like I do. She and Agent Brzko will find a way to get us all out here.*"

~~~

When the VReoria attempted to capture the Muse of Mischief and Agent Brzko on Trella, they had escaped; and instead, they captured the VReoria. As is the way of the VReoria, they activated their death glands and extinguished themselves before they could be interrogated. The Dragons arrived at Trella with the intent of obliterating the VReoria once and for all. After years of oppression and enslavement by the VReoria, the Dragons found a weakness and overthrew them, taking Dragona back. That was long ago, and there were many Dragon casualties. After that, they secluded themselves, they needed time to recover from the decimation of war. But time has given them an opportunity to rebuild themselves - their home, their fleet, their lives. Now it is time for them to emerge from their seclusion, the Universe needed their help. And they are back with a vengeance.

Once M returned from providing a sample of her DNA to Kiik on Suus, the planning continued. The group had once again gathered in the dining room of the guest house on Misko.

"Hasira, your information was accurate. Our scanners are able to locate the VReoria ships using their energy signatures even when they're cloaked. We're going to continue scanning, to make sure we have them all." Zri said.

"How many specimen ships have you found?" Hasira asked.

"Two, at least we think they may be specimen ships based on their size and the variety of life forms on board. Each one is escorted by two smaller ships." Zri answered.

"Where are they, are they near each other?" Vustia asked.

"One is very close to us, it's near Cazoova of course. But the other is in the Glion Galaxy."

"Where in the Glion Galaxy is the other specimen ship Zri?" Hasira asked.

"Not far from the Black Sea Planet, and our scans indicate that there are Trelods on both ships. Two on the ship near Cazoova and one on the other." He answered, and then continued, "They know that the Muse of Mischief can open an aperture and transport herself if she's conscious so they'll need to subdue her immediately and keep her subdued. That means they either have to handle the exchange on one of their ships or very near it."

"Hasira, do you think they will attempt the exchange on board a ship?" M asked.

"No. They are smart enough to know that you will have a plan in place to try and overtake them - to rush them when they drop their shields, they won't risk it. We need to have ships close to theirs so that we can disable them when they drop their shields to transport to the exchange site."

"How can we get close to them? If they see more than one ship coming near them they'll know what we're up to." Vustia said.

"Dragon ships are able to cloak themselves. Zri, I need the exact coordinates so I can have our ships begin surrounding the VReoria."

Zri slid his tablet across the table to Hasira. After looking at the coordinates he transmitted them telepathically to Dragona. Kwaai would take care of coordinating the Dragon fleet.

"OK, so the Dragons disable the ship's shields, then what?" M asked.

Ferocity jumped in, "Agent Brzko will be with me near Cazoova. As soon as their shields are down he can board their ship and leave a transport receiver. That will allow our combined forces to board the ship. They can simultaneously work on keeping the shields down and subduing the VReoria. Zri, can you outfit the Ploosnarian, Trelod, and Suus ships with transporters?"

Instead of answering directly, Zri looked at ShyUst. "I'm on it." ShyUst said and transported himself back to his ship to begin replicating and distributing transporters.

"What about the other ship?" Zri asked. "Do you have a plan for them?"

"Agent Brzko can only be in one place at a time, and we expect the Muse of Mischief to be busy with the exchange, so as soon as he leaves the transporter on the first VReoria ship we can jump to the second and follow the same process. By the time we get there, the Dragons will have their shields down and the combined fleet will be en route or there." Hasira said. "Unless there is another option that I've missed."

"I don't see a better option, does anyone else?" Zri asked. When no one said anything he continued. "Xiix, will you provide the combined fleet with their instructions? Divide them in half and provide them with the coordinates where they are to rendezvous. ShyUst will contact them to provide the transporters. Each team should be led by the fastest ships. Make sure they understand the entire plan thus far."

Xiix stood to leave the table, "*It is my honor.*" He headed for the door to take his shuttle back to his ship. Once his ship had a Gaznzulian transporter, and he had an individual transporter strapped to one of his arms, he'd be able to move between the surface and his ship instantly.

Once he had left, Empress Nalau questioned the group, "So what is the plan for rescuing the specimens? I understand our intent is to destroy the VReoria ships, but we cannot do that until we've rescued everyone. Hasira, do you have any knowledge about how they're held?"

"We've only heard rumors Empress." He paused as if that was all he had to say, but clearly rumors or not, everyone at the table wanted to hear them. "They VReoria collectors place their victims in a type of stasis tube. It's filled with liquid that prevents them from aging or decomposing, but it prevents them from moving."

"Are they conscience?" Empress Nalau asked.

"Yes. We've heard that their minds are fully functional."

Vustia was the first to speak. "Ahhhh." He sighed. "So they are kept alive and aware while unable to move?"

"Yes they are alive, technically. Each being is fitted with an appropriate breathing tube. If they attempt to stop breathing then the function is performed for them. Some of these beings have probably been kept this way for far longer than their expected lifespan, they will be insane."

"OH! This is just horrid. What... How..." Empress Nalau was shocked and frustrated beyond words.

The Muse of Mischief reached for her hand and quieted her. "Zri, can Gaznzul accommodate any of the beings that are damaged mentally and unable to adjust to freedom?"

"Yes M. We will make whatever accommodations they need. There's a facility on Gaznzul where they can live the remainder of their days in peace." Zri said. "Since our intent is to destroy all of the VReoria ships, we'll need a team to transport them as quickly as possible and a ship, at each location, set up to care for them. Waaw, can the Suus handle that?"

Waaw nodded in affirmation.

This helped to calm Nalau. She was new to this work, it would take her some time build a tough exterior and help without taking the pain personally. After she recovered she moved them on, "When will the clone be ready M?"

M looked across the table to Waaw, assuming that she'd been in telepathic contact with Kiik. "*It is ready now.*"

"So how do we keep the VReoria from seeing two Muse of Mischief's? I assume they will monitor her arrival at the site of the exchange." Vustia wondered.

"*The clone and the Muse of Mischief will be wearing cloaking shields. They will make it appear as though the Muse of Mischief's life signs are coming from the clone, while keeping its life sign hidden.*" Waaw projected.

"Will you bring the clone here while we wait for the details of the exchange?" Vustia asked, looking at M.

"No. I'd rather not." She answered. "I think it would be better to go from here to Suus, and then from Suus to the exchange site with the clone."

"Good, I don't think any of us really want to see the clone." Brzko said.

Zri countered, "I'm a little curious about it. But it is a little… what's that word you use M?"

"Creepy? Gross? Disgusting? Take your pick!" She said making them all laugh, at least they could still laugh.

~~~

"*Le! They're coming for you. Le?*"

She was instantly up and ready to defend herself when she heard her father in her head. "I'm ready Baba."

The smell of the VReoria was so strong that she could smell them before they even opened the door. When the door opened they did not enter. Four VReoria stood just outside the door, looking at her. "Extend your arms." One of them commanded. She had no intention of making this easy for them and wanted to resist, but there was no point. Four VReoria could easily overpower her, she extended her arms.

"*Don't fight them Le, it will make it worse. They will gladly hurt you to make you comply.*"

"*I know Baba.*" she thought, wondering if he could hear her thoughts.

A shackle of some sort was placed around her wrists, there was a chain attached to it so she could be led like a dog. The VReoria began to walk away from her, giving the chain a yank. She stumbled and barely kept her balance, following them. Two more VReoria fell in behind her. They walked down a long hallway and then turned into an open area, it was some sort of a transport. They led her into the center of the room, she heard something start humming and the VReoria in front of her began to turn transparent, as did she.

Lelelu could tell by the gravity and air pressure, they were on the surface of Cazoova. She started scanning the area, looking for the Muse of Mischief or some clue as to what was about to happen.

THE CLONE DOES ITS PART

The exchange was to take place on Cazoova, in a remote, forested area. The Muse of Mischief went to Suus to check on her clone.

"*So how do I control it?*" She was in Kiik's lab, looking at an exact replica of herself. It was very disturbing.

"*You only have to think commands to it - use your telepathic abilities.*" Kiik projected. "*Try it now. Tell it to walk forward.*"

The Muse of Mischief looked at herself that wasn't her and thought about it walking forward. She almost jumped when it did. It didn't stop, she realized she had to tell it to stop. She thought about the clone stopping and it did.

"*How does that work? Do we have some sort of link or can anyone control it?*"

"*It is possible because the only area of the brain that we allowed to develop was the telepathic receivers. It has been conditioned to accept commands from only two beings... you or me. I am a safety net, just in case.*"

"*I understand. We need to go. I want to be on Cazoova before the VReoria transport to the surface. Are the scan jamming shields active?"* She asked looking at the small device strapped to her bicep.

Kiik picked up a handheld scanner and first scanned M from head to toe, then scanned the clone. *"Yes, your life sign is being transmitted from the clone. You are undetectable to scans."*

"OK, then I guess we're ready."

"Good luck M, if there is anything I can do..." Kiik didn't know how to finish that so instead she stepped forward and embraced M with all four of her arms.

When Kiik released her, M reached for Agent Brzko and Ferocity, *"Is everyone in position."*

"Affirmative." Ferocity answered.

"Yes M, everyone is ready. If anything goes wrong reach for me. I'll be there."

"OK Brzko. But it's going to be a breeze. I'm female but not..."

"feeble." They finished together.

She took her clone's arm and left Kiik's lab. They arrived near the coordinates of the exchange, but not quite close enough to see it. M quickly surveyed the area, finding a grove of whapus trees near the exchange site. With their thick wide trunks, they provide the cover she needs to stay out of site. Still holding her clone's arm she walked to the far side of the grove, keeping the exchange site visible. M had the clone step past the tree line, out into the open to wait. After a few minutes she watched four VReoria materialize, Lelelu was sandwiched between them with her wrists bound. M moves her clone toward them and tells it to speak.

"Release Lelelu!"

"Not yet." One of the VReoria responds. "Keep walking toward us."

M move her clone forward a little more, but once again it stopped. It stayed silent and motionless, waiting for the next command. But the VReoria were intimidated, the lack of emotion from what they thought was the Muse of Mischief confuses them. They don't want the Muse of Mischief to change her mind, Lelelu has little value to them, and suddenly they second guess themselves and wonder if she may not have as much value to the Muse of Mischief as they thought.

One of the VReoria in the front turns to Lelelu and unlocks her restraint. It drops to the soil beneath with a sickening thump. "Walk toward the Muse of Mischief. If either of you attempt to escape you will be shot." The point was emphasized with the raising of a weapon.

Lelelu walked slowly toward the Muse of Mischief, M moves the clone forward very slowly. As soon as Lelelu is near enough, she directed the clone to speak. "As soon as you pass me, run to the trees. Do not stop."

"M, wait I...." Lelelu protests. By this time she was right next to Lelelu.

M turns the clone's head to face Lelelu, "RUN!"

Lelelu was shocked and frightened, her dearest friend had never been so cold. But she knew there was no choice, she followed the instructions. M moved the clone forward as Lelelu neared the trees.

Something was wrong, the VReoria seemed agitated. Two of them transported back to the ship. They must have been informed of the attack. One of them ran forward and grabbed the clone, M had it go limp and fall to the ground. This confused the VReoria, he looked up at the sky and let out a blood curdling scream - it's long tentacled appendages sticking straight out as it screamed. Their plan was falling apart. The other VReoria rushed to his side to assist in lifting and carrying what they thought was the Muse of Mischief.

Lelelu hit the tree line and kept running. She ran right past the real Muse of Mischief. That was fine, M didn't want to stop her yet - she wasn't sure what kind of range the VReorian weapons had.

M peeked around the tree that had been providing her cover. One of the VReoria had picked up the clone, the other stood nearby. They were about the return to their ship. She activated the small explosive hidden inside the clone, it and both of the remaining VReoria were vaporized.

"Lelelu!" The Muse of Mischief yelled as loudly as she could as she took off running in the direction Lelelu had gone.

~~~

Agent Brzko sat silently next to his bonded Dragon, Ferocity, waiting for the VReoria to drop their shields. The shields would only be down long enough for a transport to the surface, there was no margin for error. They were right next to the VReorian ship, but they were undetectable. They were cloaked.

Ferocity's sentient ship understood the situation. It was maintaining a constant scan, waiting for the ship to drop its shields. Finally it happened. The ship fired three rapid energy pulses, dead on target. The shield emitter and engines were damaged beyond use. The ship instantly became visible. Aiming for the center of the ship, Brzko opened an aperture and went aboard the ship. As he did, he initiated his earcom link.

"The transporter is on board. You're clear to board and begin the evacuation now."

Zri answered for the combined fleet. "Roger that Brzko."

He hadn't even finished saying Brzko when the gallery where he had arrived began filling with Dragons. Their first task was to clear the ship of all VReoria while they waited for the remainder of the combined fleet to arrive. Brzko couldn't stay and help, there was another specimen ship that he needed to deal with. He went back to Ferocity's ship.

Out the front of Ferocity's ship, Brzko could see the other Dragon ships uncloaking and engaging the two VReoria guard ships. First one exploded, then the other.

"Raaaaaaaaaaaaaaahhhhhhhhhhhh!" Ferocity let out a roar that made Brzko's ears ring.

"How far out is the fleet?" No sooner had Brzko asked then ships began appearing - Gaznzulian, Suus, Ploosnarian, Trelod. It was an amazing site - a mixed fleet of more than 200 ships. Brzko wished he could be fighting with them as Ferocity prepared to jump to the Glion Galaxy.

"*M, can you hear me?*" Brzko reached for the love of his life, worried about how things had gone on the surface below them.

"*I'm here Brzko. I have Lelelu, are you still in orbit?*"

"*Yes, preparing to jump.*"

"*Jump will initiate in twenty seconds M.*" Ferocity projected.

The Muse of Mischief didn't waste any time speaking, she took Lelelu's arm and opened an aperture to Ferocity's ship in orbit above them. Brzko jumped out of his seat and went to her, scooping her up in a tight hug, kissing her neck. "M!" He released her just as the ship jumped and they all three fell to the floor when the ship lurched. Jump drives created a little turbulence so they stayed put. Brzko leaned forward and embraced Lelelu.

"Lelelu, are you OK?" he asked.

She just looked at him and shook her head yes, then no.

"What's wrong? Are you injured?"

She just stared at him, in a state of total shock.

M answered for her. "The VReoria have her father on that specimen ship."

"What! How?"

The ship lurched again. "We're here." Ferocity said, standing up. He walked over to M and Lelelu and offered his hand to help them up. Brzko went to the front and looked at the scene, the VReoria specimen ship was visible, it had been immobilized, and the shield emitters destroyed. The debris field behind the ship suggested that the two guard ships had already been destroyed. The VReoria specimen ship was surrounded by Dragon ships. Lots of Dragon ships, it was going to take a few more minutes for the rest of the combined fleet to get here. "They will be waiting for you on this ship. You need to take me with you this time." Ferocity said.

"OK, let's go. You hold them off with fire, or ice if you prefer, and I'll start trying to deactivate the status tubes."

"As you wish Lord Brzko."

Brzko turned to M. "I know you want to come, but stay here with Lelelu until the rest of the fleet arrives."

"Yeah, I will. I don't want to leave her alone."

Brzko kissed her cheek, picked up the transport receiver, took Ferocity's arm and they left Ferocity's ship.

M rummaged through a storage bin and found something that would function as a blanket. Lelelu was in shock and needed to be kept warm. She activated her earcom link and tried to reach Zri. "Zri, what's your eta?"

"Less than a minute until I'm close enough to transport. How's Lelelu?"

"Before shock set in she said she was uninjured." M answered.

Zri transported to Ferocity's ship. "Lelelu, Le…" He lifted her off the floor and just held her.

She looked up at him like she wasn't sure where she was. "Zri?" She desperately grabbed onto him, "Zri! Oh Zri!" She began to sob.

M put her hand on Zri's forearm, "Take care of her." and went to the VReorian ship.

Zri was anxious to join the fight, but Lelelu was his priority. He would stay on Ferocity's ship with her until she regained herself.

RESCUES IN THE GLION GALAXY

Agent Brzko and Ferocity arrived in the gallery of the second VReoria specimen ship. The VReoria were waiting for them. With Brzko behind him, Ferocity swept the room with his icy breath. Ice was sometimes safer than fire, especially in unfamiliar surroundings. The icy breath of a Dragon had the desired effect, the VReoria were immediately immobilized.

Brzko activated his earcom link, "The transporter is in place." The gallery immediately began filling with members of the combined fleet, including the Muse of Mischief.

They could all hear ShyUst via earcom link. "Clear the room of all VReoria and station a guard at each entrance. I want a perimeter established in the gallery now."

Soldiers continued to transport in - Gaznzulians, Ploosnarians, Trelods, and Suus. As they arrived ShyUst directed them out into the main ship. They could hear the commotion but they had other work to do.

"We want to take the VReoria live if possible, but once captured they will activate their death gland and extinguish themselves. Be ready." ShyUst commanded to everyone.

Xiix arrived to help with the stasis tubes.

"Xiix, do you know how to safely deactivate the stasis tubes?" M asked.

"*Yes.*" He approached the nearest tube and opened a panel at the base. "*Like this. Someone be ready to catch the inhabitant - you're going to get wet.*" He pulled out a cluster of wires, singling out the two red wires, he yanked until they were disconnected.

The clear tube began to descend into the base, as it did the stasis fluid began to gush out, drenching all of them. The head of a male humanoid became visible, it looked like it might be a Ploosnarian. He began to fall toward Ferocity. The Dragon reached up and took the being securely by the shoulders as the remainder of the fluid spilled out.

"*Lean him down so that I can reach the breathing tube.*" Ferocity complied. Xiix removed the clear piece that covered the being's mouth and nose, and then slowly began to pull on the breathing tube. "*Remove the tube slowly, and be ready to provide rescue breathing.*"

As soon as the tube cleared the being's mouth he began coughing. Ferocity gently laid him on his side, on the floor next to the tube, bending over him, he attempted to wake him. "You're going to be OK, you're free again."

The being's eyes fluttered, then opened. He looked around disoriented and then realized a Dragon was leaning over him. He screamed. Brzko went to his side and projected calmness, it worked.

Suddenly they were surrounded by Suus. "*We have a ship setup to receive the evacuees and attend to them. Work in teams and start freeing them from the stasis tubes. This team will transport them as quickly as we can free them.*" Xiix projected, referring to the Suus that had just arrived, they all wore blue armbands to signify their role. The strength of the four-armed Suus made them the perfect candidates for transporting the evacuees. One of them stepped forward and easily lifted the first being that had been rescued, immediately transporting him to the evacuee ship.

Empress Nalau transported into the gallery, not quite looking her usual self. Her hair was tightly bound and she was donning work pants and boots. "How can help?" She asked walking over to them.

"Empress! How did you get here? It may not be safe." M said.

"I don't have time for safe M. There's work to do. And to quote a dear friend of mine, *I might be female but I'm not feeble.*"

M smiled. "OK let's go." She led Nalau to the next stasis tube and showed her the process.

Brzko and Ferocity took the next tube. And so it went for quite some time. They cleared tube after tube, freeing species they were familiar with as well as some they'd never seen before.

After M and Nalau had cleared several tubes she heard Zri. "M." He called. She could tell by the way that her earcom link had activated that this was a private conversation, the earcom links of the others were not activated. M motioned to a Suus, and for Nalau's benefit she spoke to her out loud, "Fill in for me for a second. I'll be right back." The Empress didn't even look up from what she was doing, she kept working falling right in sync with her new partner.

After stepping aside M replied. "I'm here Zri, is Lelelu OK?"

"Yes, she's OK. But we're going back to the other specimen ship. She needs to see if her father has been rescued yet."

"How will you get there?"

"My ship is here."

"But that will take a few hours won't it?"

"Yes.

"Hold on, I have another idea." M reached for Ferocity using telepathy. "*Ferocity, Zri and Lelelu need to get back to the first specimen ship to see if her father has been rescued. But it will take his ship a few hours to get there...*"

He interrupted her, "*My ship will take them and then return here. Tell them to sit down and prepare for jump.*"

"*Understood.*" She activated her earcom link to reach Zri privately. "Ferocity's ship will take you, it can get there in minutes. Sit down and prepare for jump. Once you get there and transport off of the ship it will return here."

"Will do. Please give Ferocity our gratitude."

The Muse of Mischief rejoined Empress Nalau, there were still stasis tubes to clear.

The rescuers worked nonstop. The scene was slimy chaos - the floor was covered in thick stasis fluid with breathing tubes and wires scattered about. It wasn't until the four of them approached the last tube that they realized they had cleared them all. M stepped back and let Brzko and his Dragon handle the last tube. Ferocity was focused on the wires, pulling the red ones. As the tube began to descend, and the liquid began to spill Brzko saw that the being was a Dragon, a very small one.

Brzko positioned himself to catch the dragon, "Ferocity look."

Ferocity stood up and saw the Dragon. He gasped and took over the retrieval, gently laying the dragon down and removing the breathing tube. Everyone stayed silent, hoping that this was not going to be one of the few deceased specimens they had encountered. The Dragon didn't move. Ferocity leaned down, and with his snout next to the small Dragon's face he made the same purring sound that had calmed Wisssi. One of the Dragon's toes twitched. Ferocity continued to purr. The Dragon became more animated, eventually becoming fully awake. If Ferocity hadn't been there, the team would not have been able to resuscitate this small Dragon. One of the Suus with a blue armband came toward them, ready to transport the Dragon to the ship with the other evacuees.

"I will take her." Ferocity said quietly, as he stood, lifting the small Dragon.

"*As you wish.*" The Suus projected.

Ferocity manipulated his Gaznzulian armband and transported off the ship.

M activated her earcom link, "ShyUst, what's your status? We have evacuated everyone from the gallery."

"We have three VReoria in holding, the rest have been dispatched. We are making a final sweep of the ship, searching for anyone we may have missed. We'll meet you in the gallery."

"Copy that." M said.

Empress Nalau approached one of the Suus that had been helping to transport the evacuees. "Will you please show me how to adjust this transporter? I want to go to the ship with the evacuees." She held her arm out.

"*It would be my honor Your Majesty.*" They both transported to the other ship.

Luckily the Muse of Mischief and Agent Brzko were alone in the gallery, they needed a few minutes to catch their breath. This had been a rescue operation like no other.

"You look like shit M. You're soaked with that nasty stasis fluid." Brzko teased as he embraced her.

"Hey I'm not the only one! Ewwwww…." she said pushing him away. "Do I smell like that too?"

"Ummm yeah. You stink."

"We could jump home real quick and shower…." she said knowing that they would never do something so selfish.

Brzko just laughed. "So did everything with the clone work like it was supposed to?"

"Yeah pretty much. They thought it was me until it was too late. By then Lelelu had gotten away and I detonated the clone."

"So was it weird to blow yourself up?"

"It was a relief… having a clone of yourself is really creepy Brzko, really creepy."

ShyUst entered the gallery, "The ship is clear. We are ready to destroy it."

"Good." Agent Brzko said. "Ferocity, what's your location?" he asked using his earcom link for the benefit of the nontelepaths.

"Aboard my ship, awaiting instructions Lord Brzko."

Brzko turned back to ShyUst, "M and I will watch the destruction form Ferocity's ship. How long will it take for the evacuees to get to Gaznzul?"

"From here, almost a day. They have already departed with a full security escort." ShyUst answered.

"OK, we'll meet them at Gaznzul. Thank you ShyUst. You led the combined fleet through a difficult mission." Agent Brzko said, shaking his hand. "How are the evacuations from the other ship progressing?"

"The VReoria ship is clear and ready to be destroyed. The evacuees are already underway to Gaznzul even though there were more beings held on that ship. They had about the same survival rate. And interestingly, that ship seemed to have several species we've not seen before. Maybe that ship had been in other universes - we'll be able to meet the new species when we get to Gaznzul." ShyUst said.

"Excellent. We'll catch up with you there." And with that M and Brzko left the specimen ship for Ferocity's ship.

"How's the young Dragon, Ferocity?" M asked as soon as they were aboard.

"She is expected to make a full recovery." He answered solemnly. "Where are we going now?"

"Home." Agent Brzko said taking a seat. "As soon as they blow up that ship let's go home. I want to shower before we head to Gaznzul to meet the evacuees."

~~~

The cargo bay of the Suus ship had been modified to serve as a modern triage hospital. There were three small clean rooms available for seclusion or emergency procedures; but mostly everyone is in one large space with organized rows of beds, each with a medical monitoring system. The bed linens are color coded to indicate the condition of the patient. White for those that seem OK and only need rest; yellow for those that need closer evaluation; and orange for patients that were either critical or at risk of becoming critical. Empress Nalau had never seen anything like this in person. She turned to the Suus that had escorted her here, "How many? How many are here?"

The Suus she spoke to seemed to pause, but Nalau knew that she was consulting the Suus that had been stationed on the ship during the rescue. *"127."* She projected telepathically.

"How can I help?"

Again the Suus consulted the others telepathically. *"The young, the infants. They are in need of comfort from a being more similar to them than a Suus. Follow me."*

Empress Nalau was led to one of the clean rooms, it had been converted into a nursery for its six inhabitants. Three of whom, were indeed infants. Nalau picked up a very small humanoid, it looked like a human to her and it was crying hysterically. It instantly calmed when it felt her warmth. She sat down on one of the beds and looked toward her escort. "Please hand me the remaining children, I want them all near me here on the bed."

Without comment the Suus followed her direction, handed her the remaining two infants, and helped the three toddlers climb up on the bed. Nalau was literally covered in frightened little ones. They needed rest, and so did she. She resigned herself to just sit quietly.

Sometime later a Suus entered the room, she could not tell if it was the same one that had escorted her here until she heard her voice in her head. *"Your Majesty, I have come to inform you that we are about to depart for Gaznzul. There is a medical facility there that is ready to receive all of the evacuees. It will take us quite some time to get there, if you would like to leave the ship before we depart..."*

"That won't be necessary." She said. "I'll stay with the children until we get there. Do you have appropriate sustenance available for them?"

"Yes Your Majesty. I will have it delivered immediately."

"Thank you."

Nalau settled in for a long journey. She was glad to be alone, she needed time to process everything that had happened - to attempt to come to terms with horrific images of the rescues that were now a part of her. And to consider the changes she was about to make to her life.

~~~

Lelelu had fully recovered from shock before they left for the specimen ship where she had been held captive; but she still wasn't herself. First she's never experienced anything as dangerous as a kidnapping. She thinks, or thought, of herself as an independent and capable being. But now, she has to accept that she is more vulnerable than she thought. And then there was her father. She wondered if she had invented his voice in her head. Maybe it was her own survival instincts that had created that voice, knowing it would mobilize her. This was all racing through her mind as Ferocity's ship took them back to the VReoria ship near Cazoova, the ship where she had been imprisoned.

Zri could feel her stress and discomfort, he reached for her hand. "Lelelu I'm here. We're in this together."

The ship lurched, as the jump drive disengaged. They were above Cazoova, surrounded by the ships of the combined fleet. In front of them was one of the largest Suus ships. Just as Zri was trying to figure out how he would determine which ship held the evacuees, Ferocity's ship spoke to them.

"You are clear to initiate transport to the Suus ship." The ship said in a voice that was neither male nor female sounding.

Zri has never interacted with a sentient ship before, "Uh OK. Is it the ship directly in front of us?" He asked aloud, assuming the ship was listening.

"Yes. I have contacted them, you are expected."

"OK then." He and Lelelu stood up, he activated the transport and transported them to the cargo bay. The scene was almost identical to the other Suus ship, but there were even more evacuees here.

Lelelu immediately took off to search for her father. "Lelelu wait." Zri called. It was no use. He couldn't stop her.

"Zri! I was informed of your arrival. We have cleared the VReoria ship and are ready to destroy it."

Zri turned and saw Waaw approaching him. "Waaw! I'm relieved to see you. Before we deal with the VReoria ship we need to deal with something else. Did you find a Trelod in gallery?"

"Yes, her father is here. He is waiting for her in this room." Waaw gestured toward one of the private rooms near them. Through the clear glass in the center of the door, Zri could see a Trelod lying on the bed. He looked around for Lelelu, she was walking toward him with a Suus. It was evident from the look on her face that she had been told her father was rescued. She hadn't imagined the whole thing.

When she got to Zri he didn't say a word, he just opened the door for her. Before he closed the door, he heard her father's relief when he saw her. "Le!" They needed some time together, some time alone.

Zri turned to Waaw, "Let's go take a final look at that VReoria ship and then destroy it." Waaw nodded, they both transported to the ship.

The gallery of the VReoria specimen ship looked like it had been the site of a riot. The floor was wet with stasis fluid, and there was well over 100 destroyed stasis tubes. "This is disgusting… what those beings must have endured being held here for so long."

"Indeed. Some were held for well over their expected lifetime. We have also recovered species that we've never seen before, species from other universes we suspect."

Zri turned toward Waaw quickly, he was shocked. "What? Species from other universes? So the VReoria ARE able to travel back and forth in the Multiverse?"

"That seems like the logical conclusion."

Zri heard a new voice in his head. *"Commander Waaw, the ship has been cleared. We are the only beings aboard."* He turned to see a Suus subcommander enter the gallery.

"Very good. Zri, unless you have more to do here I propose that we return to the evacuee ship and commence with the destruction of this one. The other specimen ship has already been destroyed."

"Waaw, what do you think the odds are that there are more specimen ships?" Zri asked.

"Odds? When one is certain, there is no need to consider the odds."

Once he was back on the evacuee ship, Zri went to check on Lelelu. She was still with her father, of course, he quietly knocked once. She looked up and her face lit up when she saw him. She rushed to the door and opened it.

She jumped into his arms, "Zri! I'm so glad you're here. I want you to meet my father." She took him by the arm and led him across the room, "Baba, this is my partner Zri. Zri, this is my father, Iysuno."

Iysuno attempted to stand, but he was weak from decades in a stasis tube.

"You don't have to stand sir, it is my honor to meet you." Zri extended his hand.

"Le, help me up." Iysuno said, ignoring Zri's outstretched hand and lifting his left arm toward her. Zri immediately knew where Lelelu got her stubborn streak. He turned back to Zri, "I insist." He said as he managed to stand, leaning on Lelelu. He extended his hand, "The honor is all mine Zri. Without you neither my daughter nor I would be here now. Thank you."

Zri paused, the past few days were catching up with him. He didn't know what to say, there was just too much going on in his head at the moment. He was afraid he'd break down again.

Lelelu rescued him, "As our friend the Muse of Mischief said, *eh, it's what we do!*"

"When will I meet this creature?" Iysuno asked. "Please sit." He motioned Zri toward a chair next to the bed.

"Thank you." he said taking a seat. "She and Agent Brzko will meet us on Gaznzul."

"How long until we arrive at Gaznzul, Zri?" Lelelu asked.

"We will be there before morning."

A QUICK TRIP HOME

Thanks to the jump drive in Ferocity's ship, it only took a few minutes to get home from the Glion Galaxy. After the intensity of the rescue mission, they didn't want to use aperture travel to get home and leave Ferocity to make the trip alone. The Muse of Mischief and Agent Brzko had never been so glad to see Misko.

At the sound of Ferocity's ship, Whotov came rushing out of Ferocity's house. "You have returned! What news do you bring, was there success?"

"Yes Whotov. Lelelu is safe, the captives have been rescued, and the VReoria specimen ships have been destroyed. Come, I'll tell you all about it." Ferocity said, extending his wing around his butler and escorting him toward his home.

"Dibs on the first shower." M said picking up the pace as she headed to her own home.

"Why? I don't see why you should get the first shower, I smell just as bad as you do!" Brzko said following after her.

"Because I want to go see Emperor Bartala on the way to Gaznzul."

"Oh, OK then. Be my guest."

Showered, and in fresh clothes - low boots, tight black leggings, a short skirt, a corset, and of course her derby - M went to Ploosnar. Arriving at the bottom of the palace stairs she began the ascent. Bartala was waiting for her on the landing when she got to the top.

"Where is my wife M? Was Empress Nalau harmed?" He demanded nervously.

"No, not at all. She's fine Bartala." He immediately relaxed. "Where's Wisssi?

"Inside with a nanny. I didn't want him to see... to be with me in case you had bad news." He turned and walked toward the palace, M followed.

The nanny was just inside the door. Wisssi reached for the Muse of Mischief as soon as he saw her, making some sort of indiscernible baby sound. The nanny presented the baby toward M, she had no choice but to take him. "Oh! OK then. Hello Wisssi."

He squealed with delight. "Ah you see he already loves his Autuania." Bartala said. "Now, tell me how the rescue went, is Lelelu OK?"

"Yes, we were able to rescue Lelelu and destroy the VReoria specimen ships."

"Specimen ships?"

"Yes, the VReoria travel around the universes collecting one or two of every species they encounter. They plan to either alter their own species or create a new species, with bits and pieces of their collection."

"Wait, universes? They can travel through the Multiverse?" He interrupted.

"We think so. We rescued species that none of us have seen before, not even the Suus."

Bartala was silent, letting this sink in. "Where is Nalau?"

"She's on one of the evacuee ships with the young beings that were rescued in the Glion Galaxy. She wouldn't leave them, insisted on staying with them until they get to Gaznzul, which will be sometime tomorrow."

"Ah, that sounds like her. How many beings were rescued?"

"Around 300, and it seems most will survive… physically anyway."

Wisssi grabbed the derby off of her head and dropped it on the floor, squealing with delight. Bartala reached for him. "OK, OK, little Emperor, that's enough torturing your Autuania for today. Physically?" He said wanting M to continue.

"Each being was held alone in a stasis tube. It kept their bodies from aging but their minds were functional. That kind of seclusion is sure to have driven some of them over the edge. They'll be evaluated at a rehabilitation facility on Gaznzul, those that are OK will be found places to live. Those that are not, will be able to live out their lives in the rehabilitation facility."

Bartala looked like someone had punched him in the gut. "I cannot imagine the anguish they must have suffered. And there were young beings? The VReoria are truly vile creatures."

"And one of the beings rescued is Lelelu's father."

"What? No, he was killed when she was a child, was he not?"

"Apparently not, just captured by the VReoria and put in stasis."

Wisssi began to fidget, Bartala let him slide down to the floor. He waddled off, down the hall giggling, one of his nannies right at his heels.

"He can walk already?" M asked.

It took Bartala a second to answer, he was still processing everything M had told him. "Hmmm? Oh yes. He can walk. He's Ploosnarian! Not human or whatever it is that you are!"

M was relieved, her friend was returning to normal. "I think you should consider taking Wisssi to Gaznzul to meet your wife. She's going to need you with her when she begins to process all that she's been through."

"Oh I'm sure she heard and saw things she's not accustomed to while handling the administrative duties, but she's strong, she'll be fine."

"Uh Bartala, she wasn't in an office somewhere. Empress Nalau was on the front line of the combined forces, helping to release the captives from stasis."

"What!? The Empress of Ploosnar, my wife, took an active role in the mission? I don't know what to say." He stood there, with his mouth agape, looking completely dumbfounded.

"Well first, close your mouth. You look like a dork. And then get your butt in gear and have the guards prepare your ship, you and Wisssi are going to Gaznzul. I've got to go."

"Mmm OK. We'll see you there." He turned to go find a butler that could make the arrangements and M returned home.

"How's Bartala?" Brzko asked. He and Ferocity were sitting at the table eating something that smelled divine.

"Fine. I told him to take Wisssi and go to Gaznzul to meet Nalau. What are you eating? More importantly, is there more? I'm starving!"

Brzko smiled, "It's lasagna, there's a plate for you in the oven, salad's on the counter."

M went to the kitchen and got her food before joining them at the table. "Do you want to leave for Gaznzul as soon as we finish eating?"

"I'd like to but I don't think we should." Brzko said. "The first rescue ship won't arrive until the morning; and Ferocity needs some time to contact the Great Assembly on Dragona; and we should contact Ciic, and Vustia. I'm sure they were in contact with their ships, but they may have questions for us. Oh and sleep would be good."

"Oh sleep, right." M said sarcastically, making Ferocity laugh.

"I know how to make you slow down M." Brzko said grinning. She just looked at him, waiting. He reached under the table and produced a beautiful titanium bottle.

"Espidrun!" She exclaimed. "Now you're talkin'!" She jumped up to get glasses.

Ferocity sat his fork down and looked over at Brzko, tilting his head slightly.

"An old Earth phrase... I'm not sure of its origins but it basically means 'now you're saying something I agree with'."

"Earth must be a very difficult place. Why don't they just say what they mean?" He picked up his fork and went to work on his salad, because of course Dragons eat with utensils.

M returned with shot glasses and lined them up. She opened the bottle and filled each with the hot pink liquid, they all three watched the blue steam rise as it was exposed to oxygen. She distributed the glasses and held her up, "To a kick ass mission!"

~~~

The Gaznzulians had cleared the Suus cargo ships transporting the evacuees for landing. It just wasn't practical to transport over 100 beings to the surface via shuttle, especially when many of them suffered from muscle atrophy from being confined for so long. They've converted a training facility into temporary quarters for the evacuees. Originally there had been a very small wing of the facility that served the medical needs of the trainees - they'd tripled the size of the wing as soon as the rescue plans were made. They also brought in a team of medical professionals to help - Gaznzulians could handle the security of almost any species but not the medical needs. In addition to Gaznzulians there were Suus, Ploosnarian, Trelod, Myaad, Dragon, and Xinood medical professionals all standing by, ready to receive and evaluate the evacuees. A few of them were specialists in psychology. Each wore a white band around a forearm to identify them as part of the medical team.

The Muse of Mischief, Agent Brzko, and Ferocity, made sure to arrive before the first ship did. As soon as they heard it land, they went out to meet it. They were all three anxious to see Lelelu and Zri, and to meet her father.

Zri stepped off the ship first and was greeted by the highest ranking Gaznzulian general. With the formalities over, he turned back toward the ship, motioning for someone to come down the ramp. It was Lelelu and her father.

"M! Brzko! Ferocity!" She called as she descended the ramp. She walked slowly, holding her father's arm, supporting him. Lelelu approached each of them, hugging them as she went. Ferocity wrapped his wings around her as they hugged. Once released she stepped back and looked at him, "No one hugs better than a Dragon!"

"Hey…" Zri teased.

"I'd like you to meet Iysuno, my father." They greeted him one by one, approaching him. He was walking, but with great effort. The muscles needed time to strengthen after decades in stasis.

They heard commotion at the top of the ramp and turned that way, first off the ship were those too injured to walk on their own. Always efficient, the Suus had loaded their beds onto hovering cargo transports, two per transport. Life support equipment blocked their view of the first two beings. After six of the hover transports containing invalids had passed, two Suus came down the ramp with a group of young beings. M quickly counted them - there were eleven, including one that was being carried.

One in particular caught everyone's attention. Walking with small blanket wrapped around its shoulders was a yellow being with pointed ears. The facial features looked like most humanoids, with almond shaped eyes. M reached for the Suus telepathically, "*What species is that?*"

"*We can find no record of such a being in the database, they call themselves Keateran.*"

"*Male or female? Do they speak?*"

"*Female, yes she is able to communicate. We have not alerted her to the fact that we have never seen her kind before. There are others on the other ship, adults.*"

By now they were at the bottom of the ramp, passing M and the others. "*Oh, that's good. She won't be alone.*"

"Iysuno, do you want the medical team to attend to you?" Zri asked.

"No, no, I'm fine. Well going to be fine. The Suus gave me a once over on the way here. They did not find anything concerning with my health, it will just take time for my muscles to recover."

"And how are you Lelelu?" Brzko asked.

"I'm OK Brzko. I... "She paused, considering her next words carefully. "I'm OK physically but I have to come to terms with the reality that the Universe is more dangerous than I like to believe, and I either need to upgrade my weapons and shields or stop traveling alone. It feels like a betrayal, a betrayal of my freedom. Right now I just want to go home and sleep in my own bed."

"We can help you with that, which home?" M asked.

"The one on Misko, I look forward to nothing but the sound of the waves."

"Will you be going too Iysuno?" Brzko asked.

Lelelu answered before he could. "I wouldn't have it any other way."

"There you have it, I indeed will be going with her. Do you have a ship here?" He said looking around, expecting to see a small ship somewhere nearby.

"Not exactly." M said. "We can travel a little faster than that. Lelelu can explain once we get there." She stepped forward and gently took Iysuno's arm. "Zri, I'll be right back to get you."

M moved Iysuno to Misko before he knew what was happening. She kept a firm grip on his arm and used her other hand to help steady him once they'd arrived. "Easy now, the dizziness clears in just a second."

Lelelu and Brzko arrived a second later. "Baba, are you OK?"

He didn't answer her directly, instead he turned toward M, "You're one of those beings, no wonder you led the rescue."

"Those beings? Do you know others that can travel like we do?"

"No, no, just stories from childhood, stories of beings called Clyreans."

They both really wanted to question him about these stories but it wasn't the right time.

"I'll get Zri." Brzko said and left, returning with Zri a few seconds later.

"We're going back to Gaznzul, call us if you need anything." M said before she and Brzko left.

Back on Gaznzul, all of the evacuees had gotten off the ship. Waaw was waiting for them with Ferocity outside the converted barracks. *"I'm glad you have returned."*

"Is something wrong?"

"No, no, nothing is wrong. The second ship is almost here, I need to go and I just wanted to thank you. A rescue mission of this size never would not have succeeded without great leadership. It has been my honor to work with the three of you."

"It was our honor to work you Waaw." Brzko said. *"You have represented your home well, and without YOU this would not have worked. We all look forward to the next time we can work with you, but hopefully it won't be a cause such as this."* After addressing each individually, Waaw headed for her ship.

"There you are! You always keep me waiting!" The familiar voice of Emperor Bartala was a welcome comfort, even if he was his usual sarcastic self.

M, Brzko, and Ferocity turned toward him as he walked out of the barracks, followed by two of his guards and a nanny. He was carrying a struggling miniature version of himself. "Now go get your Autuania." He said setting Wisssi down. They were dressed in identical outfits, both of them making serious fashion statement with identical long black jackets trimmed in, purple shirts and a black scarf secured with a jeweled family crest.

Wisssi ran over to M and grabbed onto her legs in a bear hug. "Auta, Auta" he chanted. M picked him up.

"Hey little Bartala, how was your trip?"

"Auta, Auta…." he giggled, reached for hat and almost got it.

"Careful Wisssi, I might feed you to the Dragon."

He tried to say Dragon, it came out more like a grunt. Apparently he'd already had enough of his Autuania and started struggling again. M sat him down and ran over to Ferocity, who gladly picked him up. Ferocity made the purring sound that Wisssi loves, making him giggle again. Then he settled in, completely content to be held by a Dragon that could breathe fire.

"Huh... what's he going to turn out like after being exposed to so many different species as a baby?" M asked rhetorically.

"For real." Brzko said. "He's going to think that Suus, Trelods, Dragons and Xinoods are part of everyone's family."

"Aren't they?" Bartala asked sarcastically.

They heard the second evacuee ship before they could see it. Bartala was overwhelmed with the anticipation of seeing his wife. He started walking toward the ship as soon as it was down.

"Oh it's OK Bartala, Ferocity can watch Wisssi for you!" M called after him.

He turned halfway toward her and waved his hand at her dismissively, knowing that if Ferocity tired of Wisssi the nanny would be right there to attend to him.

The ramp descended and Xiix walked toward them, *"Hello."* He projected to all of them.

"Hello, I am Emperor Bartala of Ploosnar, I don't think we've met."

"Ah, hello Emperor, it is a pleasure. I must tell you, your wife, Empress Nalau was of great service to the evacuees. She is a wonderful person."

"Yes she is, and I can't wait to see her."

"She's coming now."

Empress Nalau somehow managed to look regal as she descended the ramp, even though she wearing pants and work boots, was covered in a combination of dried stasis fluid and baby drool, and was carrying an infant and surrounded by a crowd of little evacuees. She was met at the bottom of the ramp by two of the medical team. They quickly whisked the children away. She fell into her husband's arms and laid her head on his shoulder. They stayed that way for quite some time.

"Ferocity, we are going to need your assistance. The young dragon you rescued had to be secluded. Every time anyone approaches her she attempts to burn us with her fire."

"Of course" Remembering that they were in mixed telepath company he switched back to speaking, "Of course. Right away." He was still holding Wisssi, he was about to hand him back to M when Nalau left her husband's embrace.

"Ezopica Mischievous Wisssdartai, I missed you!" She said as she reached for him. He lit up, squealing and kicking his feet and waving his fists. Ferocity sat him down and he took off, running toward his mother.

Ferocity followed Xiix up the ramp and the debarkation began as soon as they were out of the way. The same process as before, the most infirm were taken to the barracks first.

"Darling, are you ready to go home? There is a full medical team here, they can take care of the evacuees now." Bartala said.

Nalau handed Wisssi to him, "In just a minute darling. I want to speak with M." She didn't wait for an answer, she just walked a little ways away. M followed, as did one of Bartala's guards at a distance.

Once they were out of earshot she spoke, "M, this mission has changed me. It was dangerous, and disgusting…. I mean look at me." She gestured toward the grime on her shirt, "I'm covered in dried stasis fluid, infant puke, and I don't know what else. But I feel stronger than I ever have."

"I'm not surprised Nalau, you kicked ass. You were much more of an asset than I had envisioned. You impressed all of us."

"More, I want to do more."

"What do you mean? More with the evacuees?"

"No, I want to take an active role in helping others. Like you, Brzko and Ferocity do."

"Your husband might not be…. shall we say agreeable to that."

She laughed casually, "I'm certain that he won't be, at first. But if anyone can help him understand that it's what I need to do, it's you. You two go back a long way, he listens to you, he trusts you. That's why I wanted you to know first. So that when he comes to you and tells you he disallows it, you'll be ready to squash his objections."

"You know Nalau, I'm starting to feel sorry for my old friend."

"Why?"

"Because with the two of us working together, he doesn't stand a chance!" They both laughed. "I'll be ready for him, but please, at least wait a few days OK?"

"I don't know if I can, but I'll try."

"Now go home and take a shower, you stink!"

~~~

The Suus had managed to coax the young dragon into a private room. That had calmed her enough that she stopped throwing fire, but as he approached the door to the room, Ferocity could see burn marks on the walls and floor outside the door. He gave the door a single knock and opened it a crack.

"Hello. I'm here to help you get home."

She was standing against the far wall, looking at him.

Not sure if she heard him, he spoke again. "Can you hear me? Can you understand my words?"

"Yes."

He entered the room, a little on edge, he didn't want to get burnt. "I can help you get home."

"I don't know where home is, I don't remember home."

"Close your eyes, and try to accept my thoughts." To his surprise she complied, he projected his memories of Dragona to her. After a moment he spoke again, "Do you remember this place? It's called Dragona, it's the place where all dragons come from."

"Not me. I'm not from there."

He didn't want to argue with such a small being, she'd been through enough. "OK. Do you have any memories from before we got you out of the stasis tube?"

"Yes." She closed her eyes and focused on sending him images. "This is where I came from."

The images he received were of some sort of lab. She was in a bin of some sort, looking at other hatchling Dragons. There was still debris from the eggs in the bin. He could see VReoria on the other side of the room.

"Your egg was stolen before you hatched. I see. Do you know what happened to the other dragons, the ones that hatched with you?"

She sent him another image, there was a hatchling Dragon pinned to a work table. Three VReoria stood around the table, the Dragon was screaming in agony as they did something to it.

"Dead, all dead." She said. "They kept only me."

"I see." He said. "What do you want to do now?"

"What do you mean?"

"Well you can't stay on this ship, it belongs to the Suus and they have other missions to perform. We are on a planet called Gaznzul. You can stay here at the medical facility as long as you want to, or I can take you to Dragona..."

"Is that where you live?" She interrupted.

"No, I am bonded to Lord Brzko. I live on his island, it's called Misko."

"That's where I want to go. I want to live with you." She broke down, ran toward him and grabbed his leg, just as Wisssi had grabbed onto M. The little Dragon was so small that the top of her head only came up to his waist. "Please, please don't let them hurt me." She sobbed.

He reached down and gently picked her up, cuddling her just as he had cuddled Wisssi. He began to make the purring sound, it calmed her. "OK, OK, you can come with me for now. But I need you to make a promise first."

She leaned her head back so she could look at his face.

"I need you to promise that you will not throw your fire again unless I direct you to do so. Dragons are honorable, and we do not, under any circumstances, purposely hurt the innocent. Do you understand?"

"Yes."

"Do you promise?"

"Yes. I promise."

"Good. You are a Dragon, you are strong, you are proud, you are honorable, and you carry the honor of all Dragons with you. You will walk off of the ship with your head held high, and you will apologize to the Suus before we leave for Misko."

"What should I call you?"

"My name is Ferocity."

"OK Ferocity. I will do what you have asked."

"Because you are a Dragon, because you are honorable." He coached.

She caught on right away. "I will do what you have asked because I am a Dragon, because I will be honorable."

Ferocity turned and walked out of the room, assuming that the young Dragon would follow, and she did. Xiix, a few other Suus, M and Brzko were standing at the bottom of the ramp, waiting to see how Ferocity faired with the young Dragon that they could not control. Ferocity stopped just past the group. The young Dragon stopped in front of the Suus.

"I am sorry, I behaved without honor."

"*Thank you little one, we understand how difficult this has been for you. We wish you the best.*" Xiix projected.

The little Dragon accepted this as a dismissal and went to stand next to Ferocity.

By this time all of the evacuees had debarked the ship. Xiix said his goodbyes to the Muse of Mischief, Agent Brzko, and Ferocity, and boarded his ship to ready it for departure.

"I want to check in with the medical staff here before going home. What are you two going to do?" M asked.

"I'll come with you." Brzko said.

"Lord Brzko, if you do not need me with you, I would like to return home. I want to spend some time with..." He gestured toward the young Dragon, not sure what to call her. "...her. She has requested to stay with me on Misko."

"Of course Ferocity, M and I will join you later."

~~~

"Currently there are 279 individuals here. Unfortunately we were unable to resuscitate a few of them. For the most part their physical condition is good, of course their muscles need time to recover from stasis. We encourage everyone to participate in a body movement regime in the morning, and a stretching regime in the evening." Dr. Q'osp is the lead medical professional on Xinood 5. Because his specialty is species other than Xinoods, he is the lead on the medical team serving the evacuees on Gaznzul.

"What about their mental state?" The Muse of Mischief asked.

"Some of them will need some time. As you can imagine, some of them are delirious. Left in stasis for so long, they resigned themselves to accepting that this was to be their eternity. Now that they are free, they have to change their outlook. Sadly, there are almost thirty beings that I suspect will not recover from the dementia. They have been moved to a special facility, where they can be properly cared for."

"How many different species have you identified?" Agent Brzko asked.

"Identified? Seventeen. There are several that none of us have seen before. Most of them are humanoid, but not all of them. Luckily we have some very skilled veterinarians, they are helping to create the proper environments for the non-humanoid beings. We suspect the species we've never seen before are from different universes. Assuming of course that it's true that the VReoria can travel the Multiverse."

"We think it's true." M said. "In fact we suspect they hide there frequently."

"Hmm, that would make sense."

"Do you have a list of the evacuees by species?" Brzko asked. Dr. Q'osp handed him a tablet with the list. "There were humans? The VReoria had humans?" Brzko asked, looking up from the list.

"Yes, as you can see there are four."

"Are you aware of humans any place other than Earth?"

"Actually yes. There is a small colony of them in the Glion Galaxy, I'll have to research exactly where. And interestingly these four all have similar genes, they are related."

"I know there was one young Dragon found on the second ship, were there any others?"

"No, there are no Dragons here, but there are a few Haplogawas. Luckily they are too young to be dangerous." As Brzko scanned the list, with M looking over his shoulder, Dr. Q'osp continued. "We've already begun making arrangements to transport anyone who has recovered to their original home. So far, every official we've contacted has been willing to help the evacuees reestablish their lives."

"I'm glad to hear that." M said. "What about the new species, what's the plan for them?"

"We don't know yet. I think that there are concerns for not only their safety but the safety of others, given that we know nothing of them. That is a decision for the Universal Coalition. Would you like to meet some of the evacuees?"

"Yes! We definitely would." M said.

"Follow me." Dr. Q'osp said. He turned and headed to the entrance of the barracks.

He scanned a key card to gain access, just inside the door is a small reception area, there was someone seated at a desk, reviewing information on a tablet. He looked up, took note of Dr. Q'osp and returned to his work.

The main room is a large day use area. One side of the room opens to a cafeteria style counter with small tables and chairs clustered in front of it. There is a sitting area with sofas and stuffed chairs, and a few gaming areas. There are a variety of individuals scattered about, some eating, some talking, some sitting quietly.

"Come, follow me please." Dr. Q'osp headed across the room toward a sitting area with several yellow individuals. Zri had returned from Misko, he was there with a large tablet spread on the table in front of them.

"Oh, Muse of Mischief, Agent Brzko, I'd like to introduce you to some new acquaintances of mine." He said standing up. "This is Numia, Chuna, Blona, and Scomia. They are Keaterans, we were just trying to locate their home world."

The Keaterans are bright yellow humanoids with pointed ears. Each clothed in bright red sarong type garment. Following Zri's example, they all stood to receive M and Brzko. After the greeting, everyone took their seats again.

"You honor us with your presence, thank you for rescuing us." Numia said.

"You're welcome Numia." M said. "I'm glad to see that you all seem to be faring well. Do you need anything?"

"We are attempting to find our home on these navigational maps but we do not see our planet. In fact we do not see anything we are familiar with. These planets are all different."

"Is that chart from the Suus?" Brzko asked.

"No, it's actually from the Jinn - who have more detailed charts." Zri said.

"How many galaxies have you looked at?" Brzko asked.

"We're most of the way through our Universe."

"Does anything look familiar?" Brzko asked.

"Yes, the position of the planets in this area is similar to an area I worked in, but it is not precisely the same." Numia said, scrolling to a map of the area near Trella with a hand made up of a thumb and two wide fingers.

"What type of work did you do?" Brzko asked.

"Cargo. Chuna, Bloma, and I worked on a cargo ship. We mostly hauled food to and from Keatera. Our captain did not survive the fight, she was killed when the VReoria overtook us."

"I'm sorry to hear that. So was your crew entirely female?" Zri asked.

All four of the Keaterans tilted their heads, and slowly blinked their almond shaped eyes as if Zri were suddenly speaking a language they could not understand.

"Yes, Keatera is a matriarchy. Males do not usually leave their homes." Numia said.

"Interesting." M said smiling. "I can see the benefits of that! What were some of the characteristics of the planets in that area that looks familiar?"

"Tren is a unique planet." Chuna said.

"How so?" M asked.

"It is entirely pastel, with colors that are beautiful but not normal." Chuna explained.

"So what planet on this chart is the closest to where you would expect to see Tren?" Zri asked.

"Here." Numia said, pointing to Trella.

Zri looked up, he M, and Brzko stared at each other for a few seconds. He looked back at the tablet and called up images of Trella. "Does Tren look like this?"

"Yes! That's Tren." Numia said.

"Interesting, this is actually a planet we call Trella. So, it would seem that you are from a different universe." Zri said.

"How do we get back to our universe, to our home?" Chuna asked with desperation.

"We don't know." M said. "The VReoria are the only species we know of that can travel the Multiverse."

"We don't want to rush you into making any decision, but please consider what you would like to do now that you're here." Zri said. They all four just looked at him. "There are many planets that will take you in, help you establish housing, employment, a place in the community." They could see the disappointment on their faces. "We're not suggesting that we will give up on trying to find a way to get you home. But, living here at a temporary medical facility? Well that doesn't seem like a good option."

"You're right." Numia. said. "We are all still in shock about our situation. But we must accept that we are better off than some. We need some time to think about it. Do you think it would be possible for us to work together on a cargo ship again?"

M decided to jump in. "Yes. I have a friend that does a lot of shipping, his planet produces an element called roinad, they ship it all over this Universe."

"That might be a good fit for us. We will discuss it. But a ship is no place for Scomia. She needs to finish her education in a stable environment." Numia said.

"If you decide you're interested in shipping roinad, we may be able to find a home for her on the same planet. What do you think Scomia, are you interested in continuing your education in a home on the same planet where Numia, Chuna, and Bloma work?"

She shrugged, again looking at her feet. "OK."

"If there's a different place that you'd like to live please feel free to tell us. We'll try to accommodate your request." M said.

Again she shrugged. "OK."

"Well, Brzko and I need to check in with some of the other evacuees." M said, standing up. "If you need us for anything, just ask one of the medical staff to contact us. They can reach us anytime."

M and Brzko made their exit and walked a ways away from the group of Keaterans. "Hey, I need to go see Emperor Bartala. Empress Nalau sent me a message while we were chatting. I need to go see them."

"So what did she tell you when she got off the ship, before she left for home?" He asked.

"Well, basically... she wants to work with us."

"OH!" His face displayed his surprise. "I see why you need to speak with Bartala, I'm assuming he'll try to stop her."

"Of course. So you can see why I need to go to Ploosnar, I need to verbally slap some sense into him."

Brzko laughed. "I'd love to watch but..." He hugged her. "OK be careful M. I'm going to visit with a few more of the evacuees before I call it a day. I'll see you at home later."

NALAU GETS A NEW JOB

"No, no, no, no. Go away Muse of Mischief!" Emperor Bartala said, sort of spitting the last word, as he walked out of the palace to meet her. She could hear the espidrun in his voice.

"Oh we're using full names today Kufeter Whakeclyte Wissswara Bartapulnye, you must be really pissed."

"Why did you do this? Why are you attempting to steal my wife?" Bartala said, shaking his fist at her.

"Let's go inside Bartala, I don't want to discuss this here." What she really meant is that she didn't want the Emperor of Ploosnar to air his dirty laundry on the palace steps where guards and other staff could hear him.

He waved his hand, dismissing her, as he turned and walked into the palace. "Fine, but I'm not giving you any espidrun."

"That's OK, I brought my own bottle." And indeed she had. She still had rooms here at the Ploosnar palace, and she kept a supply there. She had quickly visited her rooms before she officially arrived at the palace.

He turned to see if she really was carrying a bottle. When he saw that she did indeed bring a bottle with her, he offered no more than a harrumph. He walked down the long hallways to his private sitting room without saying a word. When they turned the last corner, M could see Empress Nalau standing at the end of the hall in the shadows. She smiled at M and mouthed the words 'thank you'. M just smiled and nodded.

"Sit." Bartala said, taking glasses from the side table and filling them with espidrun. "We can drink from my bottle, and I'll keep yours for later."

"OK." There is no need for toasts or formalities with these old friends, they both tossed back the first drink. He immediately refilled them. And then took her bottle and stashed it on a side table. "So…"

"Ah. No." He held up his hand in stop gesture. "Not until I've had three of these, I like my drinks in three now. Another BAD habit I picked up from you."

She laughed. "OK, works for me. There's two, pour up old man."

He did and they drank the third. He filled the glasses a fourth time but they both just let them set on the table with the blue steam slowly rising and spilling over the side. Espidrun was really strong, and three shots, back to back? M could already feel it. But she sensed it had worked, her oldest friend was now calm enough to discuss his issues.

"So what did Nalau tell you, Bartala?"

"That she wants to work with you, she wants to run around the Universe risking her life for the benefit of others."

"Really? That's how she put it?"

"No, but that's what I heard."

"I bet you were shocked, weren't you?"

"Yes! My lovely wife is the definition of refinement and grace. She came home covered in stasis fluid and baby alien puke. But did that disgust her? NO! It made her realize she has a higher purpose and it's your fault. Because you asked her to help you while Lelelu was held captive by the VReoria."

"You done? If there's more tell me now."

"Damn it M. I had everything just how I wanted it, and now it's going to change."

M raised an eyebrow at him, waiting to see if he realized what he'd just said. He didn't continue. Instead he took his fourth shot, she copied him.

"So let me get this straight. When Nalau had everything in her life just how she wanted it, you announced that you wanted a child. And despite your long lifespan, you wanted the child now. She complied, with the use of a surrogate, but she still complied. Did that change her life?"

"Yes. It changed her life." He said, she detected a hint of shame in his voice.

"So, are your wants more important than hers? Because you're the Emperor? Because you are male?"

"Not when it comes to our marriage, no, I am not more important than her. But M, I'm worried, terrified. I know some of the situations you get into. I mean look at what just happened to Lelelu!"

"OK, so that's what the problem is? Not that she wants to do something but that she wants to do something that could be dangerous?"

"Yes. And I will miss her whenever she's gone. She's my partner, my best friend."

"What about Wisssi?"

"Wisssi? He is not a replacement for his mother!"

"No, of course not. But you do devote a lot of time to him right? You have assumed the role of the main parent?"

"Yes, that was our agreement. Nalau did not want to be a mother."

"Hmmmm so, with a fair amount of your time devoted to your son's development what should someone as intelligent and as capable as Nalau do with her time? Should she take up knitting, underwater basket weaving, or perhaps advanced floral arranging?"

"You're not being fair."

"I'm not being fair? What do you think years of a mindless hobby like that would do for someone such as your brilliant, fearless, lovely wife?"

Bartala took a deep breath and met M's gaze. "It would kill her spirit."

"And we both know you love her far too much to do that to her."

"Yes I do."

"OK then, get over yourself and help us develop a plan that will ensure her safety."

"I hate you." He said as he poured a fifth espidrun for them.

"It's mutual buddy. And by the way. This isn't my fault. You're the one that wanted to go to Trella, and that adventure is what piqued her interest." She got up as she was speaking, extended her hand to him and pulled him off the sofa. "Careful there, that espidrun hits hard."

"Yes, and I started before you got here."

With her hands on his shoulders, she looked him directly in the eyes. "Bartala, you are my oldest and dearest friend. I cherish your friendship above many things. I promise you, I will do everything I can to ensure that the love of your life is safe." She embraced him in a bear hug, as he so often did to her.

"I know, and I'm holding you to that." She released him and he stepped back. "I'll go and find my wife, we have some plans to make."

Nalau opened the door and strolled into the room. "There's no need darling, I've been listening at the door the entire time."

M couldn't help herself, she laughed out loud. Then covered her mouth.

Bartala looked at her. "Your influence on my wife has been…"

"Shut up and pour me a drink Bartala." Nalau said. "You know you love me just as I am."

"You are correct my darling. And I do like it when you take charge!" He said as he complied with her demand. He continued to pour for her until she'd had three shots. "Are you sure this is what you want to do my love?"

Nalau sat her glass on the table and met Bartala's gaze. "Yes."

"That's it? Just yes?"

She reached forward and grasped his hands, he expected her to say something very regal and reassuring, but she didn't. "Darling, I'm female not feeble! Now let's toast to... me!"

"Wow, you've really built up a tolerance for the espidrun Nalau." M said laughing.

"Yeah well, that trip to Trella changed me."

M yawned. "Oh sorry, it's been a long couple of days. I have some ideas that I'd like to share..." She paused, waiting to see if they were ready to get down to business. "First, Nalau I think you should take personal defense and flight training. Both of those skills need to become intuitive. If you're in a crisis you don't have time to think about reacting, you have to just handle it."

"OK. Who would I train with?"

"Zri." Bartala answered for M.

"Yes, Zri, or actually a Gaznzulian training facility. The physical training will be tough, but if you stick with it, you'll gain a lot of strength and confidence. I also think the Gaznzulians have some of the best flight training."

"Will you arrange it or should I contact Zri?"

"I'll take care of it. And Bartala, while she's in training I think you should have a special ship designed for her. Something that's really fast, but also heavily armed. You have access to cloaking and transporter technology now. Instead of installing that on a ship that you already have, build her a new one. And if you ask really nice you might be able to get a hold of the Dragonan jump drive technology. It needs to be large enough for Nalau and a few guards."

"Guards? As in palace guards?" Bartala asked. He clearly approved of the idea of his wife having guards with her.

"I don't know that's up to Nalau. She'll need to select her own team. But whoever you select Nalau, they need to go through the same training you do."

"Oh, I hadn't thought of that. A great idea M." Nalau said as she tossed back another shot.

"You'll want to select the best candidates, figure out what your criteria is and then search for them. Please don't just take palace guards because you have access to them."

"What criteria would you suggest?" Nalau asked.

"First, loyalty, loyalty to you, loyalty to the missions. And also, intelligence, physical abilities, and integrity. For example most palace guards have families here on Ploosnar right?"

"Yes."

"On a mission they may be distracted worrying about or missing their loved ones. But if your team was made up of those that are free from family responsibilities there should be fewer distractions. Do you see what I mean? "

"Yes. What about some of the evacuees? Are any of them suitable candidates?"

"I don't know. You'll have to spend some time with them. I also suggest that your team be comprised of multiple species. A variety of perspectives can help you find a solution in tough situations."

"Brilliant idea. OK, I'd like to start by talking with some of the evacuees. There are so many that need to find a new place in the Universe."

"Yeah, that's something I wanted to talk to Bartala about. Have you ever heard of Keaterans?"

"No. What's a Keateran?" Bartala asked.

"Oh, aren't they yellow? With pointed ears?" Nalau asked as M unrolled her tablet and showed them an image of a Keateran.

"We rescued four of them, three adults and a child. The adults used to work together on a cargo ship. Bartala, assuming they have the right skills, would you employ them in shipping?"

"Of course, But why don't they just go home?"

"Because Keatera is in a different universe. We don't know how to get them there."

"Oh, what about the child?"

"I've suggested to her that she can have input on where she lives. But if she doesn't have a different idea, I think she should live here on Ploosnar so that she can see the other Keaterans from time to time."

"Kilome." Nalau said. Both M and Bartala just looked at her. "The last time I was at Schatorren having clothes designed, I spoke with Kilome. He expressed his desire to adopt someone. As you know there are rarely Ploosnarians in need of adoption, so he was considering a displaced Sarfet from his home on Drolla O0. But he may actually enjoy helping this Keateran. What's her name?"

"Scomia."

"I'll talk to him tomorrow."

"Thank you Nalau. Now if you two don't need anything else tonight, I'm going home to see the love of my life."

The Muse of Mischief

WHERE IS CLYREA X9

"Master Ferocity, welcome home. Who is our young guest?" Whotov asked, meeting him at the door.

The young Dragon was surprised by the appearance of the Ploosnarian butler, still sporting the Londo style hair that was popular on Ploosnar before he left. She edged closer to Ferocity, until her shoulder was touching his leg.

"This is one of the evacuees from the VReoria specimen ships, we will call her Nguvu. She will be staying with us for a short time Whotov."

Whotov stepped forward and extended his hand. "Hello. My name is Whotov, if you are in need of anything while you're here, you have only to ask."

She cringed with fear. Ferocity placed his hand on her shoulder, giving her courage. She extended her own hand. "Hello." was all she could manage.

"If you would be so kind as to follow me, I will show you to a guest room. Are you hungry?" Whotov asked, moving toward the hallway.

She looked up at Ferocity for guidance. "Please follow him. Whotov will care for you, you can trust him." She didn't speak, she just did as she was asked.

Ferocity was exhausted but not quite ready to sleep. He reached for Agent Brzko. "*Lord Brzko, are you on Misko?*"

"*Yes. I'm on the lower terrace. If you're here, join me. The espidrun seems to compliment the waves nicely this evening.*"

After letting Whotov know where he was headed, just in case there was an issue with the young Dragon, Ferocity stepped outside and spread his wings. After a couple of stressful days, flying was relaxing. He headed out over Schwarth sea, then turned and flew back toward Misko. He glided toward the terrace, landing on the railing. He jumped down and took a seat on one of the stools, near where Brzko sat. Brzko poured him a drink.

"Espidrun, although I know it doesn't have the same effect on Dragons, you may still enjoy it."

The hot pink liquid released its blue steam when he poured it. Ferocity stared at it and chuckled.

"What? Did I miss a joke?"

"I lied."

"I'm sorry?"

"The effects of espidrun and other alcohols are not lost on Dragons."

This gave Brzko a good laugh. "Seriously? So you've been enjoying the effects of espidrun and nekmid all this time?"

"Yes." Ferocity said with a smile that reveals his large jagged teeth. It's not really a friendly look.

"And so you lied because…."

"I was intimidated."

"Intimidated? You're a Dragon, you can breathe fire and ice, not to mention you can fly, and you were intimidated? By who?"

"I was the outsider to a tight group of friends visiting Trella. Just being a Dragon was enough to frighten the others, I didn't want to add to their concern."

"Hmm. I see your point. That was probably a wise decision. Well I'm glad to know that we have another way to enjoy each other's company." Brzko held his glass up to Ferocity in toast, and then drank it. Ferocity did the same.

"So how are you? As tired as I am?"

"Yes. I look forward to a long sleep. Whotov is caring for the young Dragon we found."

"What's her story? Did they grab her when they were oppressing Dragona?"

"Her egg, and many others that did not survive their experiments. She was the only Dragon they had."

"So she's never really been to Dragona, she doesn't remember it as her home?"

"No. Her memories begin in the lab of a VReoria ship. And they are horrible and painful."

"What do you want to do with her?"

"I would like to raise her myself, but she needs to be around other Dragons, and she is too young to be left here alone when I'm out. She needs to learn how to be a Dragon. I will take her to Dragona once she's stabilized and find someone to host her."

"OK, let me know if you need anything."

"Thank you Lord Brzko. Where is the Muse of Mischief?"

"Ha! Beating up on her old friend Emperor Bartala." Ferocity tilted his head waiting for more. Before continuing, Brzko refilled their glasses. "It seems that Empress Nalau has decided she wants to work with us. And as you can imagine…. Bartala was not happy to hear that. Nalau asked for M to help her convince him."

"She will be a great addition to the team. I sense that she is much stronger than she seems."

"I agree. She's also highly intelligent and dedicated. I think…"

"Hey, got room for one more?" They turned in the direction of the voice. It was Lelelu, she had come down the stairs so quietly, they didn't know she was there until she spoke. She wore a long flowing sarong wrapped around her. The white color provided a great contrast to her bright blue skin.

Brzko jumped up and went to her. "Of course. Lelelu, how are you?" He said as he hugged her. He hadn't heard Ferocity move but he was right behind Brzko and as soon as he released her, Ferocity embraced her, wrapping his wings around her.

"Lelelu." Was all he said.

She took a seat next to Brzko and he poured her an espidrun.

"Thank you." She said watching the blue steam spill over the side of the glass.

"So how are you Lelelu? How's your father?" Brzko asked.

"Baba's doing OK. It hurt him to know that my mother died a few years ago. Once he realized his freedom was a reality he wanted to see her. I hated telling him but I'm sure he already knew… Anyway, he seems to be doing well. I'm going to give him my house on the mainland and move in here permanently. If that's OK with you and M."

"You know we'd both love to have you here all the time."

"Thanks. It just feels right, my father used to share that house with my mother; and of course Zri would prefer that I live here. He designed the security systems here on Misko."

"How's he dealing with everything?"

"Hmmm, as well as can be expected. He wants to keep me locked up so that I'm always safe, but my independence and strength are the things that drew him to me. He knows that if I lived that way, I wouldn't be me. So…."

"Speak of the devil." They turned toward Zri, walking down the stairs to the terrace.

Brzko stood to greet him. He was laughing. "You got that wrong Zri. It's not the actual devil that says 'speak of the devil' it's the ones that are speaking about the devil that would say it." He shook his hand and welcomed him.

Zri shrugged and sat across from Lelelu, she moved to the other side of the deck, sitting next to him. "Eh, what do I know about Earth sayings. Is there more espidrun in that bottle? I could use about five shots in a row."

Brzko accommodated his request while his mind was with M.

"Have you and M had time to read the message from Ciic?" Lelelu asked.

"Hey Brzko, I'm home. Where are you?"

"On the lower terrace with Ferocity, Lelelu, and Zri." Brzko answered M telepathically, aloud he answered Lelelu, "Yes, M and I haven't talked about it yet but I don't see why we wouldn't honor her request. It will just make us stronger."

M appeared at the bottom of the stairs and walked over to the group. "M and I haven't talked about what?"

Brzko stood and gave her the best Hollywood kiss ever, sweeping her back and giving her a lengthy kiss. He released her, stepped back and said, "You're drunk."

"Shit. You have no idea! I had to get Bartala drunk to calm him down enough to even converse. He was literally spitting mad when I got to Ploosnar." She took the chair next to Brzko's. "Hey guys," she said acknowledging Ferocity, Lelelu, and Zri. "Oh I bet you were saying we haven't talked about Waaw yet. Right?"

"Yep." Brzko answered

"I don't see any reason not to have Waaw work with us." M said shrugging, and looking around to see if anyone had comments.

"Waaw wants to join us?" Ferocity asked.

"Yes." Brzko answered. "Ciic has provided her with a small ship that she can easily handle alone. It seems like a good idea, she'd be a great asset, and give us quick access to all of the Suus knowledge."

"Agreed. And then I won't be the only non-humanoid on the team." Ferocity smiled, revealing his jagged teeth. Where will she stay?"

"Hmmm. Don't know yet." He turned toward M, raising his eyebrows to solicit her opinion.

"I think we'll need to build another house on Misko. We'll just need to get some specifications from her so that we can make sure the design is conducive to a being that sustains itself on vapors. I suspect we should build a greenhouse into it, so she can grow some of the flowers and herbs they enjoy." M said.

"She is welcome to stay with me until her house is ready. I have more than enough space." Ferocity said.

"Thanks Ferocity I'll suggest that, how's the young Dragon?"

"I think she will be OK, M. Whotov is looking after her right now."

"Good, and how's Iysuno?" She asked, turning back to Lelelu.

"He's doing OK. I still can't believe I have my father back. I never dreamed that it was a possibility. I was telling Brzko that I'd like to take up permanent residence in my house here, on Misko, and give him my house on the mainland. After all, it was originally his home."

"That's great news Lelelu, I'd love to have you here all the time."

"So how's Bartala, did he come to terms with the idea of Empress Nalau working with us?" Brzko asked.

"Yep. Under a few conditions." M said. "Pour me an espidrun and I'll tell you all about it." Brzko of course complied by pouring everyone another round. "So first, I've asked Nalau to attend personal defense and flight training on Gaznzul. She's a lot tougher than any of us realized, but the training will give her some new skills and boost her confidence."

"Agreed. I'll make the arrangements." Zri paused, he clearly had something else to say but was considering his words carefully. Everyone just waited.

Lelelu looked at him, "What?.... Oh! You think I should learn personal defense too?"

"Yes." He said carefully because he wasn't sure how she'd react.

"OK, it's a good idea, I think I'll enjoy it." Zri looked relieved when she answered. "What are the other conditions?" She asked, looking at M.

"Bartala is going to have a new ship built for her, something that is very fast, and heavily armed, with cloaking abilities."

"Can he build two? I know I don't travel as much as Nalau probably will, but it would be nice to have an updated ship." Lelelu said.

"I'm sure he will, I'll talk to him tomorrow."

"Anything else?" Brzko asked.

"I've asked her to select a small team to work with her. She's going to consider some of the evacuees. I suspect some of them would love this type of work."

"Good plan, I assume they'll be attending training with her?" Zri asked.

"Yes. That will also give you time to observe them and make sure they are…. Mmmm 'right' for the position. If you know what I mean."

"I understand. We'll test their mental status while they're on Gaznzul." Zri said.

"She also has an idea for a host for the young Keateran, Scomia. She thinks Kilome the designer might enjoy providing her with a stable home while she completes an education."

"That would work well, assuming Bartala was willing to employ the other three Keaterans." Brzko said.

"He is. He might be temperamental but his heart, well hearts, really are in the right place." M said.

"Hmmmm does that sound like anyone else you guys know?" Brzko teased her.

The friends sat quietly for a while, they'd recently been through a lot. The sound of the waves from the Schwarth Sea below was soothing, allowing them to all be lost in their own thoughts. A fair amount of time had passed when they heard Iysuno approach.

"Hello all, may I join you?"

"Baba! Yes please, how are you feeling this evening?" Lelelu asked.

"Better, a little stronger every day. It's just going to take time. The doctors said that stasis prevented me from aging, so once my body recovers I'll feel young again. Can you imagine that?"

Zri stood up and offered his seat. "Please, sit here next to Lelelu, Iysuno."

"Thank you Zri, now what are you all drinking out here next to the ocean waves?" He said as he took a seat next to Lelelu and Zri pulled up a chair on her other side.

"Espidrun, have you heard of it?" Lelelu asked.

"No, but it looks toxic with that bright pink color. Are you sure it's not poison?" He laughed. "Who's going to pour an old young man his first espidrun?"

Brzko was already pouring when he asked. Iysuno's face scrunched up when he saw the blue steam. "This has got to be poison!" He blew the steam away and took a careful sip. "And I don't care if it is!" He tossed back what remained in his glass. "Pour me another would you?"

"M are you still on com?" She heard Bartala call via earcom link.

"Yes Bartala what's up are you OK?" Everyone looked toward M when she spoke, Bartala had called only to her, probably because of the late hour.

"Neither of us can sleep, we were thinking about how much fun we had sitting around sharing stories on the way to Trella. We were just wondering if you and Brzko were still up."

"Yes, Bartala, we're having a party on the lower terrace. Would you like to come?"

"Yes please. We're in my sitting room, if you come here directly the guards won't see me leave." Bartala said.

"I understand. We'll be right there." She turned to Brzko. "Bartala wants to sneak out of the palace unguarded, will you come to his sitting room with me to get him and Nalau?"

"Of course."

They were both gone instantly, only to return to the deck less than a minute later, each with a guest in tow.

~~~

It has been a while since the friends have had a casual gathering, not since their trip to Trella. On the way there they had a wonderful time telling stories and just hanging out together. But after the VReoria had attempted to kidnap the Muse of Mischief and Agent Brzko, a dark cloud hung over the return trip. As it turned out, that dark cloud was farther reaching than they first thought. They were just beginning to come out from under it, and it felt great. Gathered on the lower terrace of Misko, overlooking the Schwarth Sea, the odd group is together again. To say they are an odd bunch is an understatement - the Muse of Mischief and Agent Brzko look human but aren't, they possess powers that not even they know of yet; Emperor Bartala and Empress Nalau, both look regal, he in a formal jacket, she in long gown, but both are far more than the dignitaries of Ploosnar; Ferocity, the Dragon bonded to Agent Brzko, able to breathe fire and ice, and fly; Lelelu, a Trelod blue from her bald head to her nail less toes; Zri, a Gaznzulian, a reflective being that to the observer look to be the same species as themselves, rarely does a non-Gaznzulian see them in their true form (in this group only M and Lelelu have had that honor); and tonight, there is one more, Iysuno, Lelelu's father, also a Trelod, thought to be long since dead but actually held in captivity by the VReoria.

Sensing that Ferocity may be in need of sustenance, his well-seasoned Ploosnarian butler, Whotov, has taken it upon himself to deliver a tray of food and a fresh bottle of espidrun. "Please forgive the intrusion Master Ferocity." He said announcing himself as he came down the stairs. "But I thought you may need something to eat." He placed the large tray on the table, followed by a beautiful titanium bottle filled with espidrun.

Before Ferocity could respond to his butler, Empress Nalau was up and hugging Whotov. "Whotov! How wonderful to see you! We miss you at the palace."

"Oh your Majesty, please forgive me. I didn't see you.... and the Emperor sitting there." He said with the hint of a question because he knew that the Emperor of Ploosnar was expected to travel with palace guards and there were no guards here tonight.

"Hello Whotov." Bartala said. "Is the Dragon treating you well? If not, you are welcome back at the palace anytime." He teased.

"Oh, I should say your Majesty! No, no, Ferocity is a pleasure to serve. And if you will all excuse me, I do not want to be gone long, in case the young Dragon should wake." He headed for the stairs.

"Stop trying to steal my butler, Bartala! You can't have him back." Ferocity teased. When Whotov heard this he grinned from ear to ear. He loved living on a remote island and being the butler to a Dragon, it was like something out of a children's story - spend a lifetime in service at the Ploosnar palace and retire to become butler to a real Dragon.

"OK, OK, don't shoot fire at me." Bartala teased. And that made them all laugh. "So do I know you well enough now to ask you something Ferocity?" Bartala continued.

"Considering how much espidrun I've had this evening, you can ask me anything." Ferocity said, helping himself to an apple off the food tray.

But before Bartala could ask his question Lelelu interrupted. "Wait, you told us on the Trella trip that alcohol doesn't have an effect on Dragons."

"I lied." He said, offering no further explanation, making everyone laugh.

"Wow! You certainly do hold your liquor well." She said.

Ferocity grinned at her, and a grinning Dragon is rather frightening. He tossed the apple up, opened his snout, grabbed it and began chewing the entire thing with his mouth closed.

"OK, back to my question. How does one request being bonded to a Dragon?" This grabbed everyone's attention.

"A request is made to the Great Assembly or to a young Dragon's parents."

"And do females ever bond?"

"Some do, yes. Most stay on Dragona to raise other Dragons, but some do not want to be parents."

"Uh -huh." Nalau said, like this was confirmation of all females having the right to choose not to be a parent, as she looked over at M with a satisfied nod.

Bartala ignored her and continued, "And what criteria is used to determine if a request is to be honored?"

"Are you going to ask for a Dragon, Bartala?" M asked confused.

"No, of course not, but..."

"Wisssi!" Nalau interrupted.

"Yes, Wisssi. What is to become of the young Dragon that was rescued from the VReoria?"

Ferocity held Bartala's gaze for a moment. "This is an interesting idea, Emperor. Preparing to be bonded would give her a purpose. But it is too soon to tell if she will be up to the challenge. She is at a disadvantage, having not been raised by Dragons."

"Or perhaps that is an advantage." Bartala said, snatching vegetables sticks that looked like purple carrots, off of the tray.

Ferocity tilted his head, "Explain."

"If one only learns the ways of their ancestors, they may be ill prepared for our ever-changing universe."

"I see your point and I agree, but the knowledge of our ancestors should create the foundation of knowledge."

"What will she be called?" Nalau asked.

"Nguvu."

"Does that name have special meaning?"

"Yes, it means strong in one of our ancient languages."

Nalau decided to change the subject, "I have a question." Everyone turned in her direction, she looked at Lelelu, "Were the two of you together on the trip to Trella?"

Silence hung over the group, it was a very direct question about an intimate relationship.

"Yes. But we weren't ready to share it with everyone yet." Lelelu answered.

"I told you!" Nalau said as she slapped Bartala's shoulder.

"I should never doubt the intuition of a female!" He said.

Taking a softer approach, Nalau had another question for Lelelu, "So how are you Lelelu? Were you injured during the abduction?"

"Not physically, just a few sore muscles from fighting back. But… my self-esteem." She paused, considering her words before she continued. "I used to think I could handle anything, I didn't think I was invincible but I thought I was better prepared. But it turns out, I'd just been lucky. I'm going to make some changes, I'll be training with you on Gaznzul and…"

"Oh yea!" Nalau squealed, allowing the effects of the espidrun to be heard.

"And I plan to upgrade my ship. If your husband is so inclined, I'd like him to have his engineers build one like yours for me."

"Of course, of course, Lelelu. I've already requested a trio of them, just in case. And they are going to be like nothing we've seen before!" Bartala said.

"Thank you Bartala. I intend to give my ship to Baba. You'll need something to get around in, I know you won't want to stay put for long." she said turning to him.

He'd been so quiet that they almost forgot he was with them tonight.

"Thank you Le. I'm sure it will be a while before I'm ready to travel, and when I do I think I'll employ some of your security team Zri."

"Good, I wouldn't have it any other way Iysuno." Zri said standing up to pour everyone another round of espidrun.

"Is there any specific place you want to see?" Brzko asked.

"Yes. There were a few telepaths in stasis, my contact with one in particular kept me from going insane. Over the years, we managed to keep each other's minds challenged, thinking of something other than our situation."

"Where was he from?' Brzko asked.

"She is from Suus." Iysuno said. "And the knowledge she shared of her home leads me to believe it is one of the most beautiful planets. I'd like to see it with her, if she survived."

"I'm sure we can arrange that for you." Brzko said taking his tablet out and unrolling it, calling up the list of evacuees on Gaznzul. "Do you remember her name?"

"Her name is Faaf, but aren't the Suus uh... selective about who visits their planet?" He asked.

"Yes, they are Baba. We just learned that a Suus named Waaw will be moving to Misko with us, as a member of our team. The Muse of Mischief and Agent Brzko are good friends with Ciic of the Naan family. They saved her life as a child." Lelelu explained.

"The Naan family? Aren't they the leaders of Suus?"

"Yes." Lelelu answered.

"You know the leader of Suus?"

"Yes Baba, she is a friend, an ally. M and Brzko attended her wedding."

This rendered Iysuno speechless for a moment. He leaned forward so he could see past Lelelu, to Bartala and Nalau, "So I suppose you really are an Emperor and Empress too? I thought maybe those were just nicknames."

This made everyone laugh. "Oh no, I assure you Iysuno, we really are the Emperor and Empress of the planet Ploosnar." Bartala said, still smiling.

"Le, you seem to have fallen in to a good crowd here."

"Faaf did survive, Iysuno." Brzko said, putting his tablet back in his pocket. "Her prognosis is good, she has the same muscle atrophy that you do. But she's expected to make a full recovery. Would you like to go see her tomorrow?"

"Oh my, yes. I would like that very much."

"So Iysuno, you're telepathic then?" M asked.

"Yes. Ancient Trelods were telepathic and the children's stories suggest that some Trelods could even fly. I spent a very long time alone, unable to move, only my own thoughts to keep me company. At some point I realized I would go mad, so I started focusing my mind on 'hearing' others. At first I only heard noise, like static on a communications device. Eventually I was able to receive clearly. And later I developed the skill of projecting. I think all Trelods have the ability, but it lies dormant. It's not comfortable for us."

"That's the truth!" Lelelu chimed in. "When I was on that ship Baba had a Suus send me images of the stasis tubes telepathically. I thought my head would explode with pain."

"When we met you Iysuno you suggested that you'd heard of beings that could travel through their own apertures, I think you called them Clyreans?" M asked.

"Yes, that's right. My grandfather would tell me stories about them while we were on seaweed gathering trips."

"Do you remember any of the stories?"

"Oh yes, those were my favorite times. I loved being alone on the water with him. He told me about Dragons too, but I wasn't sure I could believe him. Most other adults thought he was a little 'off' if you know what I mean."

"We do, we do." Brzko stood and grabbed the open espidrun bottle, making the rounds to refill everyone's glasses.

Iysuno continued, "Grandfather told me that something had happened in their homeland and the Clyreans had scattered around the Universe, trying to blend in with others. He thought that no more than two were on any given planet, and the children were hidden with host parents. So was I correct, you two are Clyrean?"

"We don't actually know Iysuno. We were both raised by pretend parents on a planet called Earth." Brzko said. "We know we're not human, as Earthlings are, but we don't know for sure what we are."

"Can you travel back in time?"

"Yes."

Iysuno nodded at Brzko. "Telepathic?"

"Yes."

"Given the magnitude of the rescue operation, I'm sure that you have high levels of strength and endurance. What about invisibility?"

"Invisibility? I wish!" M said.

"Ha! Really!" Brzko added. "No, we aren't able to make ourselves invisible, at least not yet."

"Obviously you're omnilingual, and I assume immortal?"

"What? The Muse of Mischief is immortal? No! Say it isn't so!" Bartala quipped, getting up to retrieve more snacks.

"So I assume those are all things your grandfather said about Clyreans?" M asked.

"Yes, they were looked upon favorably long ago. They were always helping others, it seemed to be their purpose - defending the weak, protecting the vulnerable. The heroes of the Universe."

"Did he say who had attacked Clyreans?" Brzko asked.

"He described them as tall and slimy, with tentacles on their faces, he said it was a species that wanted to take their powers. Sounds like the VReoria to me."

"Yes, it does." Brzko said. "We can chat about this again, once you've had more time to recover. We don't need to tire you out completely. But if you don't mind one more question?"

"Not at all."

"Did your grandfather ever tell you where Clyrea X9 was? And would you be able to find the location on a chart?"

"Oh I think so. It's a very special planet." Iysuno said.

"How so?" Lelelu asked.

"Grandfather called it a world engine. It has dual rings - they cross at a ninety-degree angle. He said the dual rings create a bizarre effect that outsiders can't seem to withstand, and that's if they can even get past them to land on the surface. But if it's true that they scattered throughout the Universe then maybe the VReoria figured out some way to get through. Oh Le, I wish you could have met your great-grandfather. You are very much like him, an explorer."

M and Brzko had to make an effort to stay calm. Could they actually be close to finding the planet where their species originated?

Brzko once again unrolled his tablet, this time he extended it and used it to display a chart of the Universe, he started with the area near them on the Planet of Portals.

Iysuno leaned over the chart, taking his time. "We're here." He said, pointing to the Planet of Portals. "So if my grandfather was correct Clyrea X9 would be out this way." He was dragging his finger along the tablet toward the left, it responded by extending the chart in that direction. "Oh, I see there have been advancements in technology." He continued. "So do you see this 'hazy' looking area here? Grandfather said the 'haze' is created where the rings intersect, it keeps Clyrea hidden."

"Interesting." Brzko said. "That's not too far from Trella."

Zri got up and went over to the chart to see the area they were discussing. After studying the chart for a moment, he asked Bartala a question. "How soon will the new ships be ready?"

NALAU BECOMES...

The training on Gaznzul hadn't just changed Empress Nalau physically. While it was true that her muscles were larger, she was much more limber, and her body was toned, the training had also enhanced her confidence. She is now a fully trained pilot, able to plot courses and handle most ships on her own. But Nalau isn't on her own - she handpicked a team of six from the beings that she helped rescue from the VReoria specimen ships.

Her first officer is Numia, the Keateran that first thought she'd like to return to working in shipping. After meeting Empress Nalau she wanted nothing more than to be at her side. As far as they knew, there were only four Keaterans in this universe, and she would not find her way back to her universe if she spent every day hauling roinad from one place to another.

The remainder of her team consisted of Kyruzia a Wrexnian with amazing technological abilities; Guug, a young Suus; G'uld, a Xinood; Snov, a Sarfet; and Strupa a Ploosnarian. They had all been captives of the VReoria for so long that they no longer had homes or families to return to. Each of them had attended the training on Gaznzul with Empress Nalau and Lelelu, and each of them had done exceedingly well. Zri could find nothing wrong with any of them.

After the intense training, Nalau was looking forward to being home on Ploosnar. Her ship was ready, honestly she didn't know if she was more excited about seeing her husband or her new ship. She stood on the bridge of Zri's ship - he was taking Nalau, her crew, and the other Keaterans to Ploosnar. She was deep in thought, gazing at the universe as they rushed through space. After a while she became uncomfortable, Nalau realized someone was looking at her. It was Zri.

"What?" She said turning to look at him.

"I'm wondering if Emperor Bartala will recognize you." He grinned.

"What do you mean, I haven't changed that much have I? It's only been a few weeks."

Zri laughed. "Have you really looked at yourself? Look at how you're standing. You're a soldier on assignment. And you've traded in your evening gown for a flight suit, and your palace jewels have been replaced by a pulse weapon on your hip."

Suddenly aware that she was standing military stiff, with her feet exactly shoulder width apart, and her hands clasped behind her back. She tried to relax. "Oh, you're right. I see what you mean. Maybe I should stow the weapon before we land."

"Good idea. Go easy on Bartala."

"And maybe even let my hair down."

This made Zri laugh. She handed the weapon to one of Zri's crew, and sat down to release her hair from its tight restraint. "I'm sure he'll be very proud of you Empress. You did even better than I thought you would."

"Thank you Zri. So do you think I'll be able to handle myself in tough situations?"

Zri looked down at his lap for a second, finding just the right words. "Empress, I'd gladly have you at my side on any mission." There was no better compliment he could give, and she knew it. Empress Nalau let the compliment surround her like the embrace of a dear friend, for that is what it was.

She felt the ship slow just slightly, a quick look at the nav station confirmed what she thought. "Oh we're there."

"Sir, we've been cleared for landing." Zri's officer announced.

"Thank you, we'll be staying in orbit. Empress," He turned toward her. "Take the shuttle down, when you're ready for your crew send it back on auto pilot. You've been gone a while, take as long as you need. We're fine up here."

"OK Zri, thank you." She headed for the cargo hold and the shuttle.

Technically Gaznzulian protocol prevented Zri from landing on the surface, anyway. Ships were not to land on the surface of alien planets unless there was another Gaznzulian ship in orbit, or of course extenuating circumstances.

Even though she was more excited than she'd been in a long time, Nalau handled the shuttle with calm precision. She landed next to the palace, knowing that her beloved Bartala would be there waiting for her. After shutting the engines down, she opened the door and stepped out. Wisssi came running toward her, screaming, "Maaaaaaaaaa!"

She grabbed him and twirled him around, making him scream. He had grown but he seemed lighter because she was so much stronger. She buried her face in her son's neck kissing him, taking him in. She put him down and turned to her patiently waiting husband, "Bartala my love. Oh I've missed you."

He didn't say anything, he just embraced her and held her for at least a minute. Finally he stepped back and looked her up and down. "Wow! I didn't think you could be more beautiful than you were but... My darling you have left me speechless. He looked past her toward the shuttle door. "Where's Zri."

She cocked her head slightly, a little confused. "In orbit."

Bartala covered his mouth with his hands, trying to hide a smile, "Oh, of course. My darling this is going to take some getting used to. Not only are you a pilot now, you've got a crew at your disposal. Where is your crew? I can't wait to meet them."

"They're on Zri's ship. I'll send for them soon. Now tell me what you and Wisssi have been up to." She said taking his arm and walking toward the palace. "C'mon Wisssi, I'm hungry, let's see what we have to eat shall we?"

Wisssi trotted up alongside her, "We shall, we shall, we shall." He chanted as they walked.

Seated comfortably in the green sitting room, Nalau looked around. The room looked different. "Has something changed?" She asked Bartala.

"Only you my love. The palace is the same."

"Interesting. I do see things a little differently I guess. Wait a minute, what's that over there?"

"Ahhhh, that is a gift from the Muse of Mischief. It's called a piano, it's a musical instrument. She gave it to Wisssi. One of the humans you rescued is something she calls a 'musical genius', he has been teaching Wisssi and other children here on Ploosnar to play."

Upon hearing his name Wisssi jumped up from where he sat on the floor playing with building blocks, "Wisssi pay Wisssi pay…" He laid his belly across the bench in front of the piano and wiggled until there was enough of him on it to climb up. Nalau covered her mouth, it was a priceless scene but she feared that if a giggle escaped her, she'd ruin the moment.

Wisssi placed his little hands on the keys, lowered his head and said something that sounded like 'focus'. He started to play an amazing melody. When he finished, he slid off the bench and bowed toward his mother as he said "Ta-da!!!!" He then returned to playing with his building blocks as if something extraordinary hadn't just happened.

"How did he learn to do that? In just a few weeks?"

Bartala's smile covered his entire face. "We have M to thank for that, she provided the instrument and the tutor. But it's our son that has the talent." He said beaming with pride.

Empress Nalau got up from her seat across from her husband and joined him on the sofa, "You are an amazing father Bartala. Thank you for all you do to raise our son." She snuggled up next to him, and they sat this way for a short time, just watching Wisssi build a tower with his building blocks.

"I suppose it's time for you to meet my crew. Is their residence ready?"

"Oh yes, I think you will be pleased with the way Ferocity's quarters were refurbished."

Nalau manipulated the Gaznzulian armband she wore, she was returning the shuttle to Zri's ship via autopilot.

"I'm sure that you have provided them with every possible luxury. Are you ready?"

"Yes my darling." He said standing up and smoothing the wrinkles from his jacket. "Wisssi, let's go. It is time for us to behave like diplomats, we have official business."

Wisssi immediately stood up, running his hands down the front of his little jacket, smoothing the wrinkles, then he spit on his hands and ran them over his hair. He stiffly walked over to where his parents stood.

"Eh, we're still working on the official palace walk."

"I see." Nalau said and giggled.

Wisssi fell in step with his father as they left the room, one step behind the Emperor, and to his right, as he always escorted his wife on his left. By the time they got to the landing pad, the shuttle had arrived. The aft door was open and the crew stood in a single line, standing at full attention. Numia stepped forward, "Empress, your crew reporting for duty." She stepped back in line with the others, again standing with her feet shoulder width apart, hands clasped behind her back.

"At ease, all of you. You are not on duty today. Today you will meet my family and receive your accommodations." Nalau said as she stepped forward. "I present to you my husband, Emperor Bartala and my son Ezopica Mischievous Wisssdartai."

"Bartala, this is my first officer Numia."

He stepped forward, grasped her hand and raised it high above their heads. "May you be honored with good fortune and long life my friend, welcome to Ploosnar." He then brought her hand down and to the center of his chest, holding it just for a moment, above his uppermost heart, providing her an official Ploosnarian greeting. "Numia, it is a pleasure to finally meet you. I've heard about you from Chuna and Blona. And of course Scomia. Kilome tells me she is hoping to follow in your footsteps and become a soldier."

"It is an honor to meet you Emperor. I… Your Majesty, you have my sincere gratitude for providing employment for Chuna and Blona, and a home and surrogate for Scomia." She bowed her bright yellow head toward him.

Because Bartala could feel the bond that was already developing between Numia and his beloved wife, he already felt a certain intimacy with Numia. He waved his hand in typical Bartala fashion, dismissing the compliment. "It's just what we do here on Ploosnar. We…"

He was interrupted by Wisssi, who had suddenly realized that the being they were speaking to was yellow. "Yellow, yellow, color yellow. She yellow." He announced as he reached out to touch Numia's leg exposed beneath her bright red skirt."

She squatted down, coming to his eye level. She extended her hand, "I am Numia, and yes I'm yellow. I also have pointy ears see?" She turned her head so he could get a good look at her ears. He reached out and touched the tip of her ear, she wiggled her ear.

Wisssi squealed with delight. He ran off to his nearby nanny, feeling it was important for her to know about the yellow being he had just met.

"He is wonderful Empress, probably a real handful but very entertaining."

"A handful indeed, but lucky for him, he has the Universe's best father caring for him."

They continued down the line until Guug, G'uld, Snov, and Kyruzia had been introduced. The last member to meet Bartala was Strupa, the Ploosnarian. Bartala embraced him. "Welcome home Strupa, welcome home."

"Thank you Emperor, thank you." Strupa said with tears in his bright blue eyes. "I never thought I would see home again, none of us did."

"How long has it been since you've been here on Ploosnar?"

"Three generations have passed, maybe more."

"Well we are glad to have you home, and I am very pleased that you have decided to be a member of the Empress's crew. Now come, all of you, we have renovated a wing of the palace for you." Taking Nalau's arm, he started walking toward the palace. She could feel him caressing her bicep, admiring it. "Mmmmmmm, I look forward to having you all to myself later." He said quietly as they walked.

~~~

Emperor Bartala stopped in front of the main entrance to the west wing of the palace. There is a huge double door, ornately carved from the bright blue wood of a native tree. He waited for everyone to gather in close. "Long ago this was the original palace, it's been renovated many times and used for many different things. I had them keep the great hall as it originally was, three stories tall." He nodded to the guards at the door, they opened the doors and stepped back, the small group entered the room. No one spoke, they just stood there absorbing the opulence. The main room, or great hall, has been refreshed since Ferocity lived here. There is a variety of furniture, all of it brilliant shades of blue, from the peaked ceiling there are blue tapestries hanging, billowing lightly. On each side of the room there is a large fireplace, Bartala had both of the fires lit for their arrival.

Bartala clapped and a stocky being immediately came from another room and stood next to him. "This is Zushiri, your head butler. He will take care of anything you need."

Zushiri stepped forward and bowed to them, they all just stared at him. Empress Nalau broke the awkward silence. "Zushiri, it is a pleasure to meet you, this is Numia, Guug, G'uld,

Snov, Strupa and Kyruzia. Please tell us a little about yourself." What she really meant was, tell us what you are. Zushiri wore a suit similar to the style worn by most of the palace staff, the visible parts of his body are covered in fur, even his face. He is a luxurious brown color, with a cat like nose and whiskers. His face is surrounded by a mane.

"Ah yes, pleasure. I am a Feliovis. Like many others I was taken by the VReoria and I cannot get back to my universe, at least not yet. Feliovis are social beings, like most advanced beings we live in family groups. The questions I hear most often are, am I completely covered in fur and do I have a tail. Ah and the answers are yes and no. I look forward to getting to know each of you." He stepped forward and took the time to greet each one, repeating their names to make sure he was saying them correctly. "If you will follow me I will show you around, there are private rooms for each of you, and a garden patio out back." He didn't wait for a response, he turned and headed out of the room knowing they would follow.

"Oh Bartala, you've outdone yourself this time!" Nalau exclaimed as they headed to the door.

"Do you really think so? So you're pleased then my darling?"

"Well I don't know." She teased. "I think so, but I haven't seen my new ship yet."

"Ha! Listen to you! Would you like to see your ship? I had a special hanger built for it, you may have noticed it when you landed the shuttle."

The couple slowly walked down the path leading from the west wing to the main palace entrance. Empress Nalau took a deep breath, enjoying the scent of the flowers along the path. "Actually darling, the ship can wait until tomorrow. I'd love to spend the evening alone with you and Wisssi, maybe some quiet time in your study. Do we have any espidrun?"

"Of course! We'll never run out. The Muse of Mischief keeps a large supply of it hidden in her rooms. I could always 'borrow' a bottle from her. Why don't you go and change into something more comfortable and meet me in the study? I'll find Wisssi and have the kitchen prepare a casual dinner for us." Bartala said as they entered the main palace.

"That sounds divine my love. I just need to return Zri's shuttle so he can leave." Empress Nalau veered away from the entrance, heading to the shuttle. She activated her earcom link.

"Zri, are you on com?"

"Yes Empress. What can I do for you?"

"We're all settled in here, I'm sending the shuttle back up. I'll see you tomorrow on Misko."

"OK Empress, enjoy your evening at home."

Empress Nalau manipulated her armband and watched as the shuttle ascended until it was out of sight. She had two more calls to make before she was ready to relax with her husband and son. Again she activated her earcom link.

"Numia, are you on com?"

"Yes Empress Nalau."

"How are your accommodations?"

"They exceed all of our expectations, thank you."

"Good, I'm glad to hear that. We'll be leaving for Misko first thing tomorrow. Please make sure everyone is ready. Until then, enjoy your first evening on Ploosnar."

"Will do Empress, thank you. See you tomorrow."

"Muse of Mischief, are you on com?"

"Yes Empress Nalau, I'm here. Is everything OK?" M answered

"Yes M, everything at home is fine. I just wanted to confirm that I'll see you tomorrow on Misko."

"Are you at the palace now?"

"Yes, in the side garden."

The Muse of Mischief appeared before her. "Empress." M walked toward her and embraced her. "It seems like you've been gone for so long. You look fantastic! I heard all of your training went well."

"It sure did. I realized I'm even stronger than I thought I was."

"I'm not surprised. You impressed all of us on the VReoria rescue mission. How's the crew? Are you comfortable with all of them?"

"Yes, so far. I'm looking forward to taking them on a mission though. They all excelled at the training and testing on Gaznzul but in action things could be different."

"We'll come up with something tomorrow, something you and your crew can do right away."

"Good. I haven't seen the ship yet, but I've reviewed the specifications. So I don't expect any delays tomorrow and…."

"Oh I should have known it was you that was detaining my wife." Emperor Bartala bellowed as he walked toward them. He grabbed his oldest friend in his usual bear hug. "How are M? I haven't seen you for a while."

"I'm doing well Bartala, doing well. How are you and that little rug rat of yours?"

"Oh he keeps me on my toes, we can't thank you enough for the piano. He's really learning to play. Come in, please, have a drink with us and let Wisssi play for you."

"Next time Bartala, tonight enjoy your wife. Tomorrow she'll be busy."

"OK, Give Agent Brzko my best."

"Certainly will, g'night." M left Ploosnar, returning to her dining room.

"How's the Empress, glad to be back at the palace?" Agent Brzko said as he sat their dinner plates on the table.

"She's great. I'm sure she'll enjoy her own bed and shower tonight but she's also eager to get to work. Oh and of course she's glad to see Bartala and Wisssi." M said mischievously.

"Of course. So what's the plan for tomorrow?"

"We need to work out a plan for getting to Clyrea X9. I think we should ask the Empress to take Iysuno and Faaf to Suus. It will give her a chance to test out her ship and her crew."

"Good idea. But you know Iysuno is going to object, he'll want to be on the mission with us, to see if his grandfather was right about Clyrea X9."

"I know, but it's just too dangerous. Besides, we can't let anything happen to him for Lelelu's sake."

"Agreed."

THE SUPERHEROINES HEAD TO TRAPHUS

The guest house on Misko, originally intended as a getaway for Emperor Bartala and Empress Nalau, has been dubbed "the house". The huge dining room, with its massive table makes a great meeting space for planning, and with multiple guest rooms there is plenty of personal space. It is here that the team gathers to plan.

The Muse of Mischief and Agent Brzko sit at the head of the massive table, while Lelelu, Zri, Waaw, Nalau, Numia, and Ferocity take their places along the sides of the table. They were all chatting, excited about their new union.

M stood up, grabbing their attention. "OK, listen up." She was met with immediate silence. "Let's get started, we need to talk about our first mission. We're going Clyrea X9." She sat back down and Brzko jumped in.

"Zri, who is your new first officer?"

"Actually it's still ShyUst. He also resigned from his official position on Gaznzul to work with us."

"That's great news." Brzko continued. "Nalau, how is your new crew working out, have you had enough time with them to trust them in a potentially dangerous situation?"

"Absolutely. We worked well together when we took Iysuno to Suus."

"Good. Nalau, how empathic is Snov?" M asked.

"Very. It seems that many of the beings held in stasis by the VReoria were able to develop the power of their minds. I think it helped them survive."

"Right, like my father being able to develop the ancient Trelod ability of telepathy." Lelelu interjected.

"Exactly." Nalau confirmed. "So when do we leave for Clyrea X9 M?"

Just as she was about to speak Lelelu interrupted. "There's a small situation that I think needs to be handled before you head out on that mission." Everyone just looked at her, so she continued. "We received a message from Vustia, the Ruling Council has requested assistance."

"What's wrong?" Brzko asked.

"There is a single portal in Traphus and it seems to have been hijacked. It leads to Luchybos and is generally used for transporting small goods. But it's been closed and the locals say they can hear someone in them, singing."

"Singing?" M, Brzko and Zri said in unison.

Lelelu smiled, her eyes sparkled, making her even more beautiful. "I know it sounds crazy. And if it's OK with you, I'd like to help handle this." She said looking at M.

"By all means, please do. If you can work it out quickly then we'll leave for Clyrea X9 the day after tomorrow."

"Nalau, would like to come with me?"

"Most definitely! Wouldn't we Numia?"

"Yes, when would you like to leave?"

"Now?" Lelelu said looking back and forth between Nalau and Numia.

"OK, let's go." Nalau said, standing up. As she activated her transporter she said "Hopefully we'll return very soon. Lelelu, there's no point in taking two ships, why don't you ride with us?"

"OK, I'll be right there." Lelelu turned to Zri and kissed his cheek. "I'll be back soon."

"Be careful Le." She activated her transporter and all three of them left for Nalau's ship.

After a quick preflight check, they were off, it would only take a few minutes to get to Traphus from Misko. Nalau let Numia handle the landing without comment.

Vustia was there waiting for them.

"Vustia, it's a pleasure to see you again, are you well?" Lelelu asked taking his extended hand.

"I am very well. How are you Lelelu? You look good. How is your father? Has he recovered?"

"Oh yes, mostly. He's visiting a friend on Suus right now. And you remember Empress Nalau I'm sure, this is Numia, Guug, Snov, Strupa and G'uld."

Nalau stepped up and extended her hand. "Of course." Vustia said. "It's a pleasure to see you, thank you all for coming to help."

"It's our pleasure, please show us where the portal is."

"Right this way." He led them to a solid metal doorway, standing alone in an open area between what looked like small warehouses.

M turned to Snov, "Can you feel anything? Anything from the other side of the door?"

Snov stepped forward and placed both his hands on the door. Something from the other side pounded against it and he jumped. He placed his hands back on the door, turned his head to the side and closed his eyes trying to focus.

"I feel frustration, despair, sadness."

"No anger or hostility?" Lelelu asked.

Snov turned his attention to the door again, focusing. After a moment he moved back. "No, I do not sense anything threatening."

Nalau turned and looked at the group, they were ready. She nodded to Guug, he grasped the handle and something pounded again.

"Open this door now or we're coming in!." Guug projected with as much force as he could. He turned the handle and with his

incredible strength, he was able to turn it enough for the door to unlatch. They all heard the click, and readied themselves for an attack. A massive force pressed into the door, slamming it all the way open. There was a loud hissing sound as a bright purple cloud surrounded Guug. Numia grabbed his shoulders attempting to pull him back. But it was too late, the purple cloud surrounded both of them. It wasn't causing them any harm but it was too thick to see through. Before they could decide which way to go to get out of the cloud they heard Nalau.

"Afrit, stop this NOW! I demand that you take a solid form immediately."

Afrit? Lelelu thought that sounded familiar, then she remembered why. Was Nalau right, was this Afrit the Great of Jinn?

"NOW Afrit. Or I'll have the Dragon breathe fire in your general direction. You'll be scorched no matter what form you're in." Nalau continued.

The purple cloud began to get thicker in front of Nalau, slowly it began to take shape. The shape of Afrit the Great. Afrit looked around, taking the time to note each individual. "Hey! There's no Dragon here! Empress you've changed!" He said looking her up and down.

"Afrit." Lelelu called, getting him to turn in her direction. "How did you find your way to the Planet of Portals?"

"This is this is the Planet of Portals?"

"Look Afrit, we're not in the mood for games. How did you get here?"

"I was banished. Well, sort of. I was actually given a choice. A choice between akenn kote or banishment from Jinn."

"Akenn kote?" Nalau asked.

"Right, akenn kote." He looked at her and realized she wasn't familiar with the term. "It's an ancient way to say nowhere."

"What did you do to deserve banishment?" Nalau asked.

"What makes you think I deserved it?"

"You were my houseguest for a while, I'm confident that you deserved it."

"Ohhh you really have changed! I bet you're a blast at parties now, Nalau."

She didn't take the bait and scold him for addressing her by her first name. Instead she stood still and gazed at him. Once again he looked around, assessing the group.

"So where's this Dragon you were threatening me with?"

When no one answered him, he finally gave up. "OK, OK. I was involved in a little scandal on Jinn. I had a little bit too much fun at a party and it turned out my drinking pal was the daughter of the ruling Jinn. He was furious, accusing me of corrupting her. Ha! Little does he know." He looked around, trying to find sympathy. He didn't find any so he continued. "So he gave me a choice, I could step through a portal leading to akenn kote or be banished from Jinn. I chose the portal, but it seems like the same thing because now I'm stuck on this hideous planet. No offense to my blue friends here." He said nodding toward Lelelu and Vustia. They all just stared at him.

"What is akenn kote like?" Lelelu asked.

"Lonely, that's what it's like." Again no response, so he continued. "It's like a single, huge room, there's lightning dancing at the top of the room. But no other discernible features."

"How long were you in there?"

"I don't know for sure, a few weeks maybe."

"You can survive that long without sustenance?"

"Ha! I was a houseguest on Ploosnar wasn't I?"

"Let's put him back." Nalau said, sort of kidding, but taking a step forward to emphasize her point.

"No, no, no. I'm sorry sister. I just hate being alone, I can't help myself. I don't know how to describe it in there. It's almost like time stands still, but not really. It's a terrible place. The door on the other side should be locked"

"Where is the other door?" She asked.

"One of them is on Jinn, and it's one way."

"There are more of them?" Vustia asked.

"If the stories are true, yes. Jinn children are told stories of akenn kote being used to travel between places undetected, or to hide. But it's risky. If you can't find an exit, or if it's locked, you may be trapped nowhere for eternity because time doesn't move the same in akenn kote. I don't know how long I was in there looking for a way out. Once I realized I was hearing industrial sounds, I stayed in this area because I figured there was a way out."

"So now what do we do with you? I don't think you can stay on the Planet of Portals." Numia said.

"Well technically I wasn't banished from Jinn..... But I don't think I want to go back there. Maybe I should spend a little time here. My ancestors spent time on this planet."

"No." Vustia, Lelelu, and Nalau said in unison.

"Umm OK then." Afrit put his hand on his chin and looked up at the sky tapping his foot. It made the pointed tip of his shoe jiggle. He snapped his fingers as he lowered his hand. "I've got it! Foskpruchu."

"Do you speak Foskpruchu?" Lelelu asked.

"How difficult can it be? Besides I love a riddle!"

"OK, Foskpruchu it is. Where's your bottle?"

"Back on Jinn."

Nalau rolled her eyes at him. "Fine. We'll take you to Foskpruchu but if you start anything on my ship I'll have Guug and G'uld put you down." She began walking toward her ship.

He ran after her, "Wait, this is your ship? And HEY what do you mean 'put me down'? I'm not some feral Koblenipi on Ploosnar!"

She kept walking at a quick pace, knowing that she'd gotten to him pleased her. But he couldn't see the grin she was wearing from behind her. The remainder of her team followed Afrit aboard the ship.

Lelelu and Vustia were still standing in front of the portal. "I'm sorry Vustia, we solved one mystery but have given you another. How the Jinn were able to send someone through a portal... I can't explain that."

"I've heard of other portals that lead into the Planet of Portals but I've never seen them. They are supposed to be in a deserted area, and locked down. But those were stories I heard as a child, I never believed them."

"But maybe it's true. Maybe there are portal that aren't one way. That would change the planet, wouldn't it?" She knew Nalau and her crew were waiting. "I've got to go Vustia, I guess we're going to Foskpruchu. You know how to reach us if you need anything else." She turned and as she jogged toward Nalau's ship, she realized that for the first time since being captured by the VReoria she felt completely recovered.

The Muse of Mischief

A QUICK CHECK ON THE EMPEROR

"The Muse of Mischief, Your Majesty." The palace guard announced as she reached the top of stairs and Emperor Bartala stepped out of the palace with a rug rat in tow.

"Autuania, Autuania, Autuania!" Wisssi called running to her. She whisked him up and twirled him around.

"Ezopica Mischievous Wisssdartai you are getting big! How are your piano lessons going?" She asked setting him down.

"Good." He trotted off saying something about playing the piano.

M embraced her old friend. "Bartala, how are you?"

"I'm fine M. Is everything OK?"

"Yes, Nalau is fine if that's what you mean."

"It is. She said had to take a trip to Foskpruchu and she would be home later today."

"Yes, did she tell you she found Afrit the Great on the Planet of Portals?"

"Yes, what was he doing there?"

"It's a long story. I'll let your wife fill you in on the details. I'm really just here to raid the kitchen with my old pal, it's been too long."

Bartala lit up. "Fantastic! I could use some fun. Let's go find Wisssi. He's probably playing the piano, waiting to show his Autuania his latest song."

Sure enough. The young pianist was playing something that sounded classical, Motzartesque, when they entered the green sitting room. He played for a few more minutes and then jumped off the bench, bowed dramatically and declared the end of his performance with an enthusiastic "Ta da!"

"Bravo, Bravo!" M said clapping.

He was delighted to have pleased his Autuania, but he was done performing. He went over to the corner of the room where a small table held a three-dimensional puzzle and settled in with a serious look of determination.

"He's been focused on that for a few days now. It's a Xinood puzzle, a gift from G'ist."

"How are G'ist and Rogs? And G'saar?" She said the name G'saar with a little question, as though she weren't sure she had correct name.

"They're all doing well. G'saar is even bigger! He is growing so quickly, they must employ a full-time tailor to keep up with him."

"Speaking of tailors, how is Scomia adjusting to life on Ploosnar? Is she getting along with Kilome?"

"Yes, they are very close. In fact Kilome registered the documentation needed to make Scomia his official heir. He said he wanted to make sure that she'll be cared for should anything happen to him. I told him that the palace would always provide for her but I think part of the reason he did it was to make sure that she knows she belongs here, with him."

"Oh that's great. So she adjusted to the Ploosnar schools OK?"

"She's a little behind the other students in language, but her mathematics knowledge exceeds that of her peers."

"Good. I'm glad she's not so far behind that she's uncomfortable. So how are you old man?" M said asked.

"Ha! I'm no older than you."

"Yeah, but you're a dad and I might be immortal."

Bartala laughed and finished his drink. "I'm doing well. I'm very thankful that I've got Wisssi now that Nalau has found a new calling. Or did Nalau find a new calling because I had Wisssi? Hmmm. Either way, the palace seems quite large when you're alone. But I'm hungry. Hey Wisssi, let's go raid the kitchen with your Autuania."

"Hey when he's old enough maybe he can take over for you and you can work with Nalau. She'd probably give a place in her crew. Well, after you went through some training."

Bartala opened his mouth to respond but couldn't think of a good come back. Instead he just laughed. They laughed like old times, when they were young and free of responsibilities as they headed to the kitchen. Wisssi wasn't sure what 'Raid the kitchen meant' but he wasn't going to miss a chance for adventure with his Autuania. He followed them down the hall.

M got to the kitchen first and peaked around the door. She put her finger up to her lips and looked at Wisssi "Shhhhhhh, the coast is clear." She whispered.

He just stared at her with his huge, bright blue eyes as she opened the door and motioned for him and Bartala to enter. She scooped him up and plopped him down on the counter across from the main refrigerator while Bartala started removing containers and setting them on the counter next to Wisssi.

M uncovered one of the containers, it was filled with lusimis. "Mmmmm" she said, as she dipped her finger into it and licked it. "Lusimis."

Wisssi had never seen this before! He plunged his fingers into the bowl "Lusimis." he declared and starting licking his fingers.

"Close buddy, it's lusimis."

He didn't bother to try the word again, why would he, he was busy licking his fingers.

Bartala handed him a vegetable that looked like a carrot, "Here Wisssi, use this instead of your fingers. M you're going to turn my son into a barbarian!" She could tell he wasn't serious, his grin covered his entire face.

"Mmmmmmm" Wisssi said as he dipped the vegetable into the lusimis, attempting to get more attention from M.

"Hey, remember that time we took a picnic up to the top of Mt. Brara and then found out we didn't have anything to eat with?"

Bartala laughed. "Oh yes. I remember that. We didn't even have serviettes with us. But we were far too hungry after hiking up there to forgo the food. We ate like animals."

"Aminals, aminals." Wisssi chanted as his father handed him a slice of fruit cake.

"So are you going to let him have fun as he grows up, the kind of fun you had, or will you shelter him?" M asked as she slid herself up on the counter, diving into a bowl with some kind of pasta.

"I want to shelter him, to protect him." Bartala said with a serious look. "But I know that I can't protect him from everything."

"And you wouldn't be who you are, if your father hadn't given you the freedom to explore yourself and the Universe." M said.

"I know. Sometimes I think that he gave me more freedom after you stumbled into the palace."

"Ha ha." M said sarcastically.

Wisssi immediately picked up on that one and started mimicking her, "Ha ha, ha ha…"

"No really, I think it's true M. He knew you had some.. *unusual?* abilities, and that you would protect me." M nodded in agreement, thinking that might just be true. Bartala continued. "That's why I wanted to explore the idea of Nguvu being bonded to Wisssi. If they're bonded by the time he's old enough to explore I would worry less."

"Hm, I see your point. Hey Wisssi, do you like Dragons?" M teased.

"Dragons, Dragons like Fercty." He answered.

"Yes, like Ferocity."

One of the nannies peaked in to check on Wisssi, her face momentarily displayed shock when she saw the Emperor and his son sitting on the kitchen counter sampling food directly from the storage containers. "Your Majesty." She said.

"Oh yes, yes. Come in. Wisssdartai are you ready for a nap or a bath or both?"

The look on his face was priceless as he realized his first kitchen raid was about to end. He shook his head no and started to pout.

"Ezopica Mischievous Wisssdartai, is that how an Emperor would behave? Suck it up and behave with dignity."

Instantly Wisssi's posture changed and he was ready to be whisked away. M took him off the counter and hugged him, "See you later little Bartala."

"Bye Autuania M."

The nanny took him away.

Just as M was about to ask Bartala about Nguvu one of the kitchen staff appeared. No doubt taking advantage of the Nanny's interruption. "Your Majesty. Shall I straighten up now?"

"C'mon M, we've overstayed our welcome in the kitchen." He said smiling. "Yes, please. We'll get out of your hair now." He said to the servant.

As they headed to the door he turned to M and in a quiet voice said, "Kitchen raids are much better in the middle of the night, don't you think? Let's go have a drink."

"OK, so what's up with that *suck it up* think? Are you purposely teaching Wisssi about Earth slang?"

"Sort of."

"What does that mean?" It took her a few seconds to figure it out. "OH! You've been letting him watch Babylon 5 haven't you?"

Bartala didn't answer, he just grinned. They were almost to his study, once inside he said, "Yes, I let him see a few episodes and it was hilarious. He thinks Londo is me, or I'm Londo. But then I became concerned that it might confuse him."

"Oh I bet it is confusing for him. Although he's developing so quickly." M said pouring the first round of espidrun.

They settled on the sofa, feet up on the table, slowly sipping the hot pink liquid with blue steam floating down the sides, it was still early. After a few minutes an idea occurred to M, she blurted it out. "So are you going to have another kid?"

"I'm not done raising this one yet!"

"Uh huh, but I bet you've already been thinking about it."

"So you read minds now?"

"Ha! I knew it!" M said, punching her old friend in the arm before reaching for the espidrun bottle.

"I've been thinking about it, once Wisssi is independent I may want to have another child. I want him to have what we have, we bonded like siblings while we were young. But that is a few years off, IF I even do it. When was the last time you heard about Nguvu? How is she doing?"

"Hold on." M reached for Ferocity. "*Ferocity.*"

"*Muse of Mischief, what can I do for you?*"

"*I'm with Bartala, and he's wondering how Nguvu is.*"

"*I spoke with Kwaai earlier today. He feels that she is ready to return to Misko under my supervision. If you and Lord Brzko don't need anything from me tomorrow morning I will return to Dragona to retrieve her.*"

"*OK, sounds good Ferocity, I'll see you later at home.*"

"*Understood.*"

Bartala was staring at M. "I really hate that telepathy thing."

"Hmm. I think you're just jealous."

"You're right." He said filling their glasses. "What did he say?"

"Nguvu will be returning to Misko tomorrow. Kwaai feels that she's ready to be mentored by Ferocity."

"Excellent!" He lifted his glass and clinked it against M's, "To Wisssi and Nguvu!"

"To Wisssi and Nguvu!" M said, finishing her shot in one gulp.

Bartala immediately reached for the bottle.

MEANWHILE, BACK ON MISKO

"I take it you went to Ploosnar?" Agent Brzko had just returned home to Misko. The Muse of Mischief was at the kitchen table eating lusimis, drinking espidrun and reviewing correspondence.

"What makes you say that?"

"Because it looks like you're a few espidruns ahead of me."

She grinned at him. "You're right. Here." She offered him her glass. He gladly took it and poured another, taking a seat at the table.

"Did you hear what they found in Traphus?"

"Yes, I was just talking to Zri about it."

"I wonder how many portals there are leading to, or from, akenn kote."

"Me too."

"I also wonder if they're all on Jinn."

"I have a feeling we'll never know."

"Will Nalau be back in time to leave for Clyrea X9 tomorrow?"

"Yes, they'll be back later today. Having the jump drive technology from Dragona is really helpful."

Brzko sat down at the table. "I agree. Did you hear Waaw's house is finished? I think she's settling in now." Brzko said, refilling her glass and keeping it for himself.

"Oh I'm sure. Did you see the size of her greenhouse?"

"I know, it's the biggest part of the house."

"Luckily for her, Ferocity lives right next door. She won't have to venture very far for philosophical conversations."

"Philosophical conversations? What have they been talking about?"

"They seemed to be having a great time when I was over there earlier. They were in the midst of a deep conversation - debating the origins of Ploosnarian opera. Waaw thinks it sounds like the melody of a bird found in the forests there, and Ferocity thinks it sounds like screams of a dying Koblenipi."

Brzko was laughing so hard that espidrun came out of his nose. He put the glass down. "I don't even know what a Koblenipi is, and I find that hilarious."

"It's basically a wild boar, found on Ploosnar."

"So then Ferocity is not a fan of opera?"

"At least not Ploosnarian opera."

"Did you see the thank you that Princess Cluthea sent?" M asked, getting up to get another glass.

"Briefly, is it here?"

M slid something that looked like a folded note across the table to him. Princess Cluthea had written a note to them on a leaf from a Neter tree.

"I'm glad to hear that she was able to reconnect with her parents. It sounds like Queen Eyjdra was serious when she threatened to leave the King if he didn't accept their daughter's marriage to a Blenia."

"Sometimes the females just have to put their foot down." M winked at him.

"Ha! Like you ever have to do that with me. This leaf is really amazing, it seems dry but it's still flexible - and I love the color. How do you feel about framing it?"

M didn't answer, she just shifted her eyes to the perfectly sized, empty frame leaning in the corner.

"Always a step ahead, I love that about you M."

"Yeah well, I'm female... not feeble."

"That you are. I was thinking about checking on Ferocity and Waaw, want to go?"

"Sure."

"Ferocity. Are you up for some company?" Brzko reached for his dragon telepathically.

"Yes please Lord Brzko. Waaw and I discovered something that you should probably see. We're in the library."

Brzko looked at M to see if she had picked up Ferocity's answer. She had - they both went to Ferocity's library.

Waaw was sitting on a stool, she was slumped really. Since they both had tails, the furniture that Ferocity had selected also provided comfortable accommodation to a Suus.

"What's wrong with Waaw?" M walked over to her, thinking there must be something seriously wrong with her. *"Waaw, can you hear me? Are you OK?"*

"Fine, fine, fine. Oh my." She projected back.

"What's wrong, are you ill?"

"Espidrun."

She turned toward Ferocity. *"She's a Suus, how could espidrun have an effect on her? She can't drink it."*

"The blue steam is basically a vapor." Ferocity projected.

"Oh shit, she's drunk!" M's hands flew up to cover her mouth.

Ferocity and Brzko both laughed.

"Waaw, are you OK, do you need anything, how do you feel?" M asked.

"I feel marvelous! I see why you drink espidrun now. But... But... four is too many for me. Next time I want to stop at two. Wait...." She grasped the edges of the stool she was sitting on with her lower arms and sat up straight. *"If Ciic finds out what I've done, there won't be a next time. I don't know what she will do, I've never heard of a Suus misbehaving to this degree, I just wanted to*

celebrate my new home with Ferocity. Oh no, I'm doomed. I will be banished." She slumped again.

Agent Brzko stepped forward to handle this, projecting calm as he spoke telepathically. "*Waaw, that's not how we do things around here. We're a tight group and we watch out for each other. Ciic won't hear about you from us, what you tell her is your business.*"

Waaw sat up straight again and looked at Brzko, blinking her eyes a few times. She stood, and extended all four of her arms, intent on embracing all of them. "*I love all of you. I finally feel like I belong here, I've found my home.*" They shared a momentary group hug. "*OK, Waaw sleep now.*" He turned and headed to the guest room without another word.

Whotov appear right away, "Do you require anything master Ferocity?"

"No, thank you Whotov. I'm going to leave for Dragona in the morning."

"Very good then, I will be here to help Waaw should she require any assistance." Whotov turned around and headed for his quarters.

"*We'll see you when you get back with Nguvu.*" Brzko projected as he and M left.

~~~

"*We're landing now.*" Ferocity projected to Agent Brzko and the Muse of Mischief. They headed out, so they would be there when they landed. Waaw was still recovering from her overindulgence.

The rear ramp descended from the back of Ferocity's ship. He walked down the ramp, Nguvu followed a step behind him. "Lord Brzko, Muse of Mischief, I'm sure you remember Nguvu." He said, motioning for her to step forward.

"Thank you for granting me the opportunity to live with Ferocity Muse of Mischief and Lord Brzko, I am in your debt." She said, bowing her head. She was very different from the terrified, feisty little Dragon they had recently pulled out of a stasis tube on a VReoria ship.

"Welcome to Misko Nguvu." Brzko said, extending his hand.

Whotov, with the impeccable timing of a seasoned butler, arrived, "Nguvu. Welcome. It's good to see you again. If you will follow me, I'll show you to your quarters so you can settle in."

She nodded toward M and Brzko, then Ferocity, before dutifully following Whotov into her new home.

"How was the trip Ferocity?" Brzko asked.

"Fine." There was something about his tone.

"But…." M inquired.

Ferocity looked past them, over the edge of the island to the Schwarth Sea, considering his words. "Dragona has a different feel now that Dragons have come out of hiding and taken a place in the Universe."

"And do you think that's a good thing?" Brzko asked.

"Yes. It's long overdue."

M and Brzko waited to see if he had more to offer, but he didn't. He needed time to adjust to the idea of Dragons no longer isolating themselves.

"If you don't need anything right now Lord Brzko I'd like to see how Waaw is. Maybe she's ready to move into her new home. And I'd like to take Nguvu flying later. I need to assess her abilities."

"Of course, we don't need anything."

~~~

"I think we should assume Iysuno's grandfather was right, and the Clyreans scattered after an attack by the VReoria. And if that's true, we need to be extra cautious as we approach that area of the Universe." The Muse of Mischief suggested to the group.

Once again they were gathered around the large table in the guest house on Misko. They were planning how to approach Clyrea X9.

"We should drop out of jump farther away than we normally would and approach slowly, while we scan the area." Zri said.

"Why don't we approach from all sides?" Agent Brzko suggested. "We've got five ships, let's space them out and come at the area from all sides. We're more likely to find any cloaked VReoria that way. And with jump drives we should be able to take retreat quickly in case of trouble."

"Good idea Brzko." M said. It seemed that everyone agreed. "If everyone is ready, we should go."

All five of the ships dropped out of jump at the same time, equal distances from the planet - a distance that put Clyrea X9 just at the edge of their scanner range.

The Muse of Mischief was on Zri's ship and Agent Brzko was on Ferocity's. She reached out to him with her mind, *"Do you see it Brzko?"*

"Yes M, it looks like a big dust cloud off in the distance."

M activated hear earcom link and video screen on the bridge of Zri's ship.. "Begin long range scanning."

"Confirmed." Ferocity replied.

"Affirmative." Lelelu replied.

"Affirmative." The Empress replied.

"Confirmed." Waaw projected.

"Check your scan data and begin approaching Clyrea X9." She said via earcom link, taking a seat in the commander's chair. She noticed Zri standing nearby and jumped up.

"Oh, sorry Zri. Please," She motioned to the seat.

He laughed. "No, I insist M. It might be my ship, but you're leading the mission." She sat back down and he took the secondary seat next to her. She adjusted the front video screen to show the view from the other ships.

"It still looks like a giant dust cloud from here." She said.

"Yes, it does. It almost looks like a storm. Look at how you can see the dust, or whatever it is moving there on the left."

"I wonder if that's where the rings intersect. ShyUst, can the scanners detect anything solid in the dust cloud yet?"

"No, Muse of Mischief, we are still not able to detect a mass." She and Zri continued to watch the cloud get larger as they slowly progressed toward it. Again she adjusted the front video screen to display the other ships for the benefit of Waaw. She needed a visual connection to non-telepaths to be heard.

"Is anyone detecting any activity in the area, anything unusual that would suggest we are not alone?"

Everyone responded with a negative so she changed back to watching the target dust cloud.

"*M?*"

"*Hey Brzko what's up, everything OK over there on Ferocity's ship*" She projected.

"*Yes, we're fine. When we get there I think one of the ships should land on the surface while the others stay in orbit.*"

"*And something tells me you'd like to be the one to land, right?*"

Zri looked at her with concern, he could tell she was communicating telepathically with someone. She gave him a brief smile to reassure him that everything was OK.

"*It makes sense for Ferocity and I to land. His ship is sentient and if we run into trouble it may react faster than the other ships in an effort to protect itself.*"

"*I understand. We'll be there in a few hours, I assume Ferocity concurs.*"

"*He does.*"

M turned to Zri. "So, Brzko thinks a ship should attempt to land once we're all in position. And of course he'd like it to be Ferocity's ship."

"That makes sense since Ferocity's ship is sentient." Zri agreed.

"Exactly what he said."

They all slowly watched the cloud that presumably surrounded Clyrea X9 come into view over the next hour. No activity was detected in the area, maybe they really had eliminated the VReoria from this Universe.

The cloud was gold and brown with streaks of bright red. It looked like an emission nebula, bright and glowing. Their scans were not able to detect any significant solid mass beneath the clouds.

The ships were evenly spaced in position around the cloud, continuing to scan what they presumed was the surface as well as what may be approaching from space. Brzko made a visit to Zri's ship.

"Are you sure you still want to take the ship down? None of our scans can penetrate the clouds, we can't tell what the surface is like." Zri said. "We can't even confirm that there is a surface."

"I don't think there's any other way for us to find out what's down there." Brzko answered.

"Brzko, I don't like it. I think we need to find another way to see what's down there." M said disapprovingly. "Zri, do we have any drones with us, anything that we could physically send to the surface?"

Zri considered her question. "Actually yes. I've got a hive drone in the cargo hold. Give us a few minutes to prep it. ShyUst," He called as he looked toward his first officer.

"On my way commander." ShyUst left the bridge with a quick jog.

"OK, so we'll send the drones down and at least try to get an image of the surface before anyone goes down then." M said, looking at Brzko.

"OK." He said reluctantly. "Let's see what the drones find."

Once the drones were prepped, all of the ships tied into the image feed. ShyUst released the drone from the cargo hold. Zri piloted the drone from the bridge of his ship, taking it directly down through the clouds. At first the image was just a blur, it was in the thickness of the cloud. Then it began to clear and there was indeed something below the cloud. Looking straight down the image the drone transmitted looked like a soft white clouds. The images disappeared.

"What happened?" M asked.

Zri looked at ShyUst, knowing that he was scanning for the drone. He looked up and shook his head. "It's no longer in orbit commander. It seems to have been repelled from the atmosphere, and it's been crushed. It's not worth retrieving."

"Iysuno mentioned that the unusual effect of the dual rings could make it difficult to get through the atmosphere." Brzko said. "I still think the sentient ship is the way to go."

"I still don't like it Brzko. At least make sure that Ferocity is ready to transport here if there's any trouble." M said.

"Will do." He swept her back in one of his infamous Hollywood style kisses. "I'll see you soon my love." He said releasing her, and then he was gone.

ShyUst adjusted the front video panel to display Ferocity's ship. They stood silently watching it approach the cloud.

"Are you ready Ferocity? Is your ship ready?" Brzko projected.

"Yes. We are both ready. The ship will take immediate action to keep itself safe should it need to."

"And your transporter is ready to transport you to Zri's ship."

"Confirmed, it's programmed, I would need only hit one button."

"OK, then let's make our first attempt."

The ship began to slowly descend. Their view was completely blocked by the clouds as they descended. Just as the clouds began to thin the ship began to shake. The surface of the planet came into view. There were dome like structures that seemed to be on individual cliffs, floating in clouds. Ferocity's ship began to emit a high-pitched whine, it could not take any more of the odd pressure and reversed course. It began to ascend. As it reached the top of the cloud the shake and whine ceased.

"What happened?" Brzko asked.

Ferocity remained silent for a moment. He was communicating telepathically with his ship.

"Pressure." He answered with his earcom link engaged for the benefit of everyone. "A crushing pressure, the ship could not withstand it. We would have been crushed."

"We'll find another way." M said, also via earcom link. Brzko transported himself to Zri's ship again while Ferocity guided his ship to a comfortable distance..

Brzko looked up at her. She could see his disappointment. "M, I know you're going to object but I'm going to use an aperture to get to the surface."

"I don't object Brzko. Iysuno's description makes it seem like only some beings can get through the effect of the dual rings. And I wonder if that means only a Clyrean. I know you'll be careful. If you can, send me images of what you're seeing."

"I will. I'm going to attempt to get to the dome we saw." Brzko began sending M his current vision via their telepathic link. She closed her eyes and saw herself.

Brzko opened an aperture and focused on the floating dome, instantly he was there. M could see what he saw - randomly spaced floating surfaces seemingly suspended in clouds. She could see rings above him.

"Those rings don't look real Brzko."

"The look like part of a machine. And..."

It suddenly became very bright. *"Brzko, what's wrong?"*

"There's some kind of energy building up, it's like lightning. I can hear it."

"Brzko, either get back here or wait for me." She opened her eyes and looked at Zri.

"He made it to the surface there's sound coming from the rings. I'm going down, I can't let him go alone."

Zri reached out and put his hand on her shoulder. "Be careful Muse of Mischief. We'll be here waiting for you."

"OK Zri, keep everyone safe." She left Zri's ship and arrived on the dome's platform, next to Brzko. The lightning jumped from Brzko to her and back. There was a loud grinding sound.

"What is that sound?" She asked Brzko.

"I think it's where the rings intersect. Look." He pointed to an opening in the dome, just at the edge of their sight. Just as she turned to see what he was pointing at, a short being with red hair stepped out and walked toward them. "Welcome, welcome. I am Hekwagter Gatekeeper. We weren't sure you'd be able to find us. Oh! Where are my manners. I know you have questions. Please come inside." He turned and walked toward the dome.

Neither M nor Brzko moved from where they were.

When he realized they weren't following him, he turned back. "Oh of course, of course. You are just as skeptical as the others."

"The others?" M asked.

"Yes Muse of Mischief, the other Clyreans."

"Where are the others?"

"Oh well, scattered throughout every universe."

"Is this where they used to live?"

"No, no. No one ever lived here. Well, Hekwagters do. But we're just Gatekeepers. This is Clyrea X9, it is technically not a planet. It is a World Engine."

"What is the purpose of a World Engine?" Brzko asked.

"Very good question Agent Brzko!" Hekwagter said, turning toward him. "A World Engine is a machine. It provides a permanent transfer point between universes - for beings that don't have the ability to travel between them on their own."

"So if Clyrea X9 isn't actually a planet, where are Clyreans from?" M asked.

This seemed to confuse the Hekwagter Gatekeeper, he looked off in the distance as though he was searching his own mind for the answer. He regained his focus. "I either do not know or am not authorized to answer that question."

Both M and Brzko wanted to pursue this line of questioning but knew that it would not get them the answers they were looking for. M tried to take them in another direction.

"Do you know where we can find any other Clyreans? We'd like to speak to them."

"Oh yes. Of course. There are two visiting here now. I think they have been waiting for you. Clyreans always seem to know when there are others around." Hekwagter Gatekeeper turned toward the doorway. He stopped in front of it and seemed to be speaking with someone. He turned and looked at them, and then stepped back.

Someone stepped out, it was a tall dark being. It looked like a black human. He said something else to Hekwagter Gatekeeper and then turned toward the M and Brzko. While looking at them he extended his right arm and reached into the doorway. His hand was taken by a smaller, fair skinned being. She stepped out and turned toward the Muse of Mischief and Agent Brzko with a smile. They began to approach.

"Greetings and salutations. I am Agent Qmkos and this is the Muse of Banter." He extended his right hand toward them, "The Muse of Mischief, it is an honor to meet you, Agent Brzko, a pleasure." The Muse of Banter also extended a greeting. She had light hair and skin; she was wearing heels with a long dress, slit all the way up one side - and a black wool beret. She looked very similar to the Muse of Mischief. Agent Qmkos also wore a black wool beret. And like Agent Brzko, he wore a long black jacket over black slacks and a button up shirt with a vest. He also had dark skin.

"Are you Clyrean?" M asked.

"Yes, Clyrean, just as you two are." Agent Qmkos said.

"I'm sorry, we don't mean to stare, we've just never met anyone similar to us." Brzko said.

"Mhmm, mhmmm, we understand." the Muse of Banter said. "You probably won't see another Clyrean anywhere but here."

Agent Qmkos looked from the Muse of Banter to M and Brzko, picking up where she left off. "You see Clyreans are too powerful, too complicated to be comfortable in close proximity to each other, but the world engine seems to absorb the friction."

"Do all Clyreans look like us? I mean our skin color..." Brzko asked, holding up his hand looking at the back of it.

"Yes, all of the males have dark skin and the females have light skin. It's how we're created." Agent Qmkos answered.

"Created?" M asked.

"Yes, we are specifically created for each other - we're created in pairs and then placed with pretend parents. We are naturally drawn to our partners once we're mature. Clyreans do not raise their own offspring. And most, but not all, usually make their way here at some point." Agent Qmkos said as he used his left hand to gesture toward all of the other domes that could be seen from where they were standing.

"What's the purpose of the domes?" M asked.

"They are noplaces. Protected areas that lead to other universes. This one here leads to a young universe where most of the planets have very little gravity. We call it No-grav. That one over there leads to a universe where the timeline is broken - we call it Fractured-time, and that one over there leads to a universe where every planet seems to be ruled by some evil force."

"Is this the only way to travel in multiverse?" Brzko asked.

"No, but it's the safest way and the World Engine is the only place that has multiple portals. There are fractures that lead to other specific universes but they can be unstable. Like the ones that the VReoria are using to stay hidden from this universe." The Muse of Banter said.

"You know about the VReoria?" M asked.

"Yes, they're always trying to capture one of us. Hey we heard about you destroying two of their specimen ships and rescuing all of the beings. Very impressive." She said looking M up and down.

"Do you know what universe the VReoria hide in?" Agent Brzko asked, looking at Agent Qmkos.

"No not for sure. They've been spotted in what we call the Furverse, but we've never seen them there."

"Furverse? Let me guess, the beings there are all covered in fur?" M asked.

"Yeah, mostly." The Muse of Banter said. "None of the universes have actual names. The inhabitants always think they're in THE UNIVERSE, but little do they know… Anyway, Qmkos and I use a naming system that work for us. Other Clyreans probably call them something else."

"So do all Clyreans move around through Multiverse?" Brzko asked.

"No, no, not at all. Some of them stay in one universe. But some do like to be on the move, like us. We rarely stay in any place for too long." The Muse of Banter said.

"Can other beings be taken through the portals, into a different universe?" M asked.

"Hmmmm, yes and no. Technically yes, you can each take one non-Clyrean with you, just like you would when you travel using an aperture. But each dome is home to a Hekwagter Gatekeeper, and they can be a little, mmmm persnickety." The Muse of Banter said, placing her hand on her hip to emphasize the point. "Maybe that's not the right word. You see, they're AI's - you know artificial intelligence - and sometimes they can be a little unpredictable. Never dangerous, more like illogically logical." She looked over at Agent Qmkos to see if he had anything to add. He didn't, so Brzko asked another question.

"So we could, technically, use the portals to return some of the beings we rescued from the VReoria to their home universe?"

"Yes, but because universes don't have names it would take a lot of exploring to find the right one. By the time you find the place you're looking for, they would have settled into a new life. Besides, you two have more important things to do." Agent Qmkos said, looking from Brzko to M.

"We do?" M asked.

"Uhhhh yeah." The Muse of Banter said with serious attitude, as if M should have already known that. "It wasn't a coincidence that you met the father of your namesake."

"Emperor Bartala?" M asked. But before she could finish her thought her earcom link came to life.

It was faint and broken, but they could hear Zri, "….Muse…. Boost… Can you… Status…"

Ignoring their new friends for a minute, M looked at Brzko to see if he had also heard the transmission. He had. She attempted to respond to Zri. "Zri, we are OK. Please hold your position until further notice."

"....Af...tive."

She looked back toward Agent Qmkos and the Muse of Banter.

"And that's our cue to leave. You have much to do, we ALL have much to do. We're going to check out a place we call Water-verse." They turned and headed back in the direction they came from although the door was now closed. They walked arm in arm, much as the Muse of Mischief and Agent Brzko often did. They disappeared. But before M and Brzko could even contemplate their next action, the Muse of Banter appeared before them again.

"OK, one more thing." She said quietly, leaning toward them. "That little Dragon is part of your future too, protect her." And with that she was gone.

M and Brzko looked at each other. M opened her mouth to speak but couldn't find the words. Instead she pictured the bridge of Zri's ship, shared it with Brzko, and they left Clyrea X9 with a few answers, but more questions than they had when they'd arrived.

~~~

The time that the Muse of Mischief and Agent Brzko had been out of contact with their team had been very stressful for Zri. He'd spent almost the entire time pacing back and forth, across the bridge of his ship. When they returned to the bridge, he did something he rarely does, and never in front of his crew, he displayed emotion.

He rushed over to M and grabbed her. "Muse of Mischief, you're back!" He released her, stiffened slightly, gaining control of his emotions, and turned to Brzko. "Agent Brzko, I'm relieved to see you." He said, extending his hand and grasping Brzko's elbow.

They stood looking at each other, M finally broke the silence. "I think we should gather everyone together so that Brzko and I only have to go over this once. Zri, can you have them all transport here?"

"Of course, of course." He looked at ShyUst who was already on it.

Ferocity was the first to arrive. *"Lord Brzko!"* He said telepathically, as he embraced his bond.

It took less than two minutes for them all to arrive, they headed down to the lower level of the ship. The room that had been set for the group's comfort on the trip to Trella has been returned to its normal, slightly sterile state. The sofas have been replaced with a large meeting table. The Muse of Mischief, Agent Brzko, Ferocity, Nalau, Numia, Lelelu, Zri, ShyUst, and Waaw were all seated at the table.

M started to explain what they'd learned, or most of it anyway. "We learned a few things, but ended up with more questions. But here's what we do know - Brzko and I are Clyrean, but this place is not where we're from, it's not even a planet."

This piqued everyone's interest.

Brzko jumped in, giving M a chance to take a sip of water. "The World Engine is a series of portals that lead other universes. There doesn't seem to be any kind of map or guide to the other universes so it would be difficult to use the place to track the VReoria."

"Is this place how they travel in multiverse?" The Empress asked.

"No." M answered. "Only Clyreans can access Clyrea X9, well other beings can but they would need to be with a Clyrean. We were told that the VReoria exploit fractures between universes in order to travel between them.

"Told?" Ferocity asked.

"Yes." Brzko started to answer.

M sent him a telepathic thought, *"Don't mention Wisssi or Nguvu yet."*

"Told." He continued without missing a second. "We met two other Clyreans, Agent Qmkos and the Muse of Banter." He let that sink in for a second, but before he could continue, Numia raised her voice.

"Excuse me, may I speak?"

"Of course Numia, you don't need to ask for permission first, you're one of us." M said.

"Thank you Muse of Mischief. Is there any chance of using these 'portals' for me to return to my home? She asked.

"We're not sure yet. It seems like it, but it wouldn't be easy since universes don't have official names and there doesn't seem to be any sort of guidance system." M said.

"Oh I understand." Numia said, leaning back in her chair.

"We would have to investigate each universe to see if it's 'the one.' If we could find a way to get information from other Clyreans, and figure out a way to quickly identify the universe we're looking for, that would speed the process."

"Other Clyreans? Did you meet anyone other than the two you already mentioned?" Zri asked.

"No." Brzko answered. "We're not even sure how, or if we could contact other Clyreans. They told us that there is a certain 'friction' when we are near each other, and that Clyrea X9 somehow stifles the friction. I suspect that was the cause of the lightning when we first arrived on the surface."

"So do you think what Baba said his grandfather told him about Clyreans scattering around the Universe is true?" Lelelu asked.

"Yes and no. Clyreans are scattered, but it could be intentional, not due to any actual event. And it's not just throughout this Universe, it's all universes."

~~~

The conversation continued much the same, the only thing they didn't share with the group was the mention of Wisssi and Nguvu. They decided to head back to Misko - they weren't ready to start traveling in other universes so there was nothing more to do here right now.

The Muse of Mischief and Agent Brzko elected not to return via ship with the remainder of the group. Instead they returned via aperture.

"*I think we should go to Lincoln City.*" M projected to Brzko, before they left Zri's ship.

"*Agreed.*"

It was early morning in Lincoln City, the fog still clung to the trees. Even though there was a chill in the air, they took their coffee out on the deck.

"So what do we do now?" M asked, pulling a chaise lounge cushion out of the storage bin and handing to Brzko before she retrieved a second for herself.

Brzko took a deep breath and let it out. "Uh I don't know for sure. We need to keep watch over Wisssi and Nguvu, but we don't know what we're watching for." He rubbed his face, they were both tired. "M, they suggested that you didn't meet Bartala by chance. It was arranged. I'm really sort of creeped out to think that one, we were 'created', and two, things have happened due to someone else's influence."

"It is annoying isn't it. But then again, we were hidden on Earth, so we sort of already knew that someone, or something, else was influencing our lives."

"That's true, that's true." Brzko acknowledged. "It seems like we need to do something to increase the safety of Wisssi and Nguvu. But I don't think we can do that without divulging - to at least a select few - what we were told about them. Maybe we should share the information with everyone."

"Maybe we should. What do you think it means? I mean what do you think Agent Qmkos and the Muse of Banter were suggesting?"

"Well if it's true that you meeting Bartala was arranged, maybe the reason for that was to protect Wisssi from something in the future."

"Or maybe just to guide him through something."

"True. And Bartala has already expressed a desire for Nguvu to be bonded to Wisssi, so maybe that's where she fits in."

"That's probably where it starts, but there's got to be more to it than that."

"I agree. But whatever it is may not happen until they are both adults. And how do we even know if what we've been told is reliable? How do we know that they've provided us accurate information, or that they can be trusted? What if they are attempting to influence us in a way that benefits them?"

"Great. So after finding Clyrea X9, and meeting other Clyreans, we have more questions than we did before." M said getting up to get more coffee.

When she returned with refilled mugs Brzko continued. "I don't think we have more questions M, I think we have different, or more specific questions."

"Good point Brzko. So what do we do about it?"

"Ensure the safety of Wisssi and Nguvu, just in case Agent Qmkos and the Muse of Banter are right, and then return to Clyrea X9 and see if we meet anyone else."

"Do you want to use the portals to explore other universes?"

"Maybe. Are you up for some adventure M?"

M paused for a second, looking at what remained of her coffee. She looked up, met Brzko's gaze and said, "Oh hell yes, I'm always up for an adventure."

Brzko laughed. He loves her sense of adventure and enthusiasm. "OK. Do you want to tell everyone about Wisssi and Nguvu together?"

"Bartala first, then everyone else."

"That's what I figured. I think you two have a few things to talk about."

"Indeed, and there's no time like the present."

Brzko got up and stretched. The sun was fully up by now, providing enough warmth that the fog was almost gone. "I'll catch up with you back on Misko, my love." He bent and kissed her before heading inside.

The Muse of Mischief used her earcom link to contact Emperor Bartala.

"Bartala, are you busy?"

Bartala was in fact busy - in a meeting with a transportation liaison. He could tell that his oldest friend had sent her message privately, to just him. That meant something was wrong, or something important was going on. Instead of answering her while the liaison was in the room, he touched the earcom link and activated the microphone. "It sounds like you have it all under control." He said to the liaison. "I trust that you will continue to handle things with your usual expertise. If you would be so kind as to excuse me, I've just received a message I must respond to." He stood to make it clear that he expected his guest to leave.

"Of course Emperor. I thank you for your time today. Your confidence is appreciated." The transportation liaison said as he headed toward the door.

Once the door was closed, Bartala answered the Muse of Mischief. "M, are you OK?"

"Yes. I need to have a private conversation with you. Where are you?"

"I'm in my public study."

He hadn't even finished speaking when she appeared before him.

"Where have you been? You look like you're dressed for the frozen tundra."

She was wearing jeans and a sweatshirt that said *Female not Feeble*, standard Earth garb. "Almost, late fall on Earth."

"It's a good look for you." He teased, moving from behind his desk to take a seat on the sofa. "So what's wrong M?"

She sat down on the other sofa, facing him. "Nothing's really 'wrong' but there are a few things I think you need to know. You know that we recently went to Clyrea X9 right?"

"Yes, Nalau told me about the trip. She said you confirmed that you are Clyrean, and met other Clyreans."

"Right. Where is the Empress today?"

"She's on a mission with Waaw, something about delivering medical supplies and food to refugees in the Zenbliuq Galaxy. I expect her to return late tonight."

"Good, and Wisssi?"

Bartala consulted the clock above the door. "At this time of day he'll be in a language class with other children. Why?"

M ignored his question. "There is a guard with him anytime he leaves the palace correct?"

"Two, and now you're causing me concern. What's going on M?"

"On Clyrea X9 we met Agent Qmkos and the Muse of Banter, and they told us some interesting things. First, they claim that we didn't meet by chance. You and I." She said.

"Hmmm, we've considered that before. When we went to Trella, we talked about that possibility."

"Yes. But they suggested that it wasn't necessarily about you and I, instead it has to do with Wisssi."

"Exactly how does us meeting have to do with Wisssi?"

"They didn't provide details, they only suggested that Brzko and I make sure to keep him safe."

Bartala inhaled sharply, held it for a second, and slowly released the breath, calming himself. "Do I need to send for him? Have him return to the palace?"

"I don't think there's any immediate threat. But there's more."

Bartala looked as though he wasn't sure he could take any more. He stood up and went to a side table, poured two glasses of nekmid, and returned, handing one to her without saying anything.

"It's about Nguvu. The Muse of Banter suggested that she has something to do with this as well. But we don't know what 'this' is."

"Is Wisssi in danger M?" Bartala asked with almost no inflection. Which M knew meant he was having to keep himself calm.

"I don't think so Bartala. But... I can't be sure. I don't even know if the Clyreans we met can be trusted. Did they suggest that we watch over Wisssi and Nguvu out of kindness, or do they have something to gain?"

Bartala finished his nekmid and motioned for M to drinkup, to finish hers. She did and handed him her glass. Nekmid was not nearly as strong as the espidrun they had been drinking lately, it had a nice mellow calming effect. He handed a refilled glass to her and took his seat again.

"Gaznzulians. Zri can help."

"I agree. But first we need to speak with the Empress. I don't want..."

"I'll tell her." Bartala said, interrupting M.

"OK. If you think that's best."

"I do."

"Look Bartala, I know that you have your own palace guards, and I know they're well trained, but..."

"You want Zri to assign a Gaznzulian guard to Wisssi."

"Right, so are you developing telepathy now too?" M teased.

"No, no...." He laughed.

"So Bartala, we never really explored the details of the idea that us meeting was arranged. Do you think your father or anyone on Ploosnar could have been involved?"

The question startled him. "Oh! I... Hmm, I never considered it before, but I suppose it's possible. You know my father was the Emperor of Ploosnar for a very long time, I suppose it's possible that he obtained information about our futures. After so many years of leading the roinad empire, his social network was vast. And we did find crystals identical to the ones that grow in caves here on Ploosnar on Trella."

"Are you sure he was Ploosnarian?" M interrupted.

Bartala opened his mouth, intent on saying that he was, but he then he paused. "My father, I um never considered that he wasn't. But I guess it's possible. If…"

There was a knock at the door, a butler stepped in. "Your Majesty, please forgive the intrusion, Commander Zri is here, he said he was summoned."

Bartala looked at M as he said, "Yes, yes, send him in."

The butler opened the door wide and Zri came in. His posture demonstrated that he was on high alert. "Your Majesty, Bartala I came as soon as I could, is everything alright?"

Instead of answering him, Bartala looked at M. "Really? You called him in my name? Why didn't you just call for Zri yourself?"

"It's more fun this way, more mysterious, don't you think?" M said, standing up.

"More mysterious no, more mischievous, yes!" Bartala scolded.

"Hey Zri, thanks for coming on such short notice. Please have a seat."

"Hello Muse of Mischief." He said, taking a seat as asked. There was a hint of question in his tone.

"Zri. We want to hear your ideas for providing additional security for Wisssi."

"Has Wisssi been threatened? What are we protecting him from?"

"We aren't sure yet." M said as she got up to retrieve the nekmid bottle and another glass for Zri. It would take a while to bring him up to speed.

The Muse of Mischief

PREPARE FOR DEPARTURE

The next morning the group once again gathered around the huge table in the dining room of the house on Misko. The Muse of Mischief had already told Zri about their concerns for Wisssi and Nguvu, and Empress Nalau had of course heard the details from Emperor Bartala. Agent Brzko had brought Ferocity up to speed the night before. They began the morning by explaining the situation to the others. Once they were up to speed, Zri explained the steps they'd taken to ensure Wisssi's safety.

"He will have a Gaznzulian guard with him at all times. They'll be clothed in the uniform of the Ploosnarian palace guards, in order to attract less attention. Wisssi has also been fitted with a personal alarm. It's similar to your armbands but his does not provide any transport, instead, it simply sounds an alarm. I'm not sure that he really understands what an emergency is yet, but Emperor Bartala assures me that they will work on this."

Lelelu and M both looked toward the Empress to see if she had anything to share about her son's safety. At first it didn't seem that she did, but after taking a moment she addressed the group.

"I'm confident that Bartala will be able to teach Wisssi how and when to use the alarm. I find it sad that these conversations need to happen with my son at such a young age. But as the future Emperor, it was inevitable that he would need to be made aware of his personal safety at some point." She said.

The group stayed silent for a few seconds, giving the Empress a chance to continue. She did not have anything else to say, so Brzko spoke up.

"Ferocity, what did you decide about speaking to the Great Assembly on Dragona?"

"I spoke with Kwaai. I did not want to bring our concerns to the Great Assembly yet. Kwaai has agreed that I am to be recognized as the official guardian for Nguvu. Although her upbringing is different than other Dragons, she is to be groomed for a bond. She is to be bonded to Ezopica Mischievous Wisssdartai of Ploosnar if she would like to be." He paused and looked across the table at Empress Nalau. This was the first time the bonding had been confirmed.

The Empress was speechless for a moment. "Thank you Ferocity. Please extend Ploosnar's gratitude to Kwaai."

"I will Empress, I presume you will inform the Emperor?"

"With pleasure."

The conversation momentarily lagged, Lelelu took the opportunity to move the conversation along. "OK, so if Wisssi and Nguvu are reasonably protected, what's the next step. What are you and Agent Brzko planning to do next?"

M looked down the table toward her faithful assistant. "You know me well Lelelu. Brzko and I are thinking of exploring the portals on Clyrea X9. We'd like to meet other Clyreans, to…. Uh 'validate' the information we received. And supposedly we can only be near them on Clyrea X9, so that's where we'll start."

"I know that you don't need a ship to get there, but I'd like to orbit the planet while you're gone. I was just barely able to communicate with you while you were on the surface. I've boosted my com signals, so I might be able to get through the interference now. And I'd like to keep watch for the VReoria."

M looked at Brzko to see if he wanted to respond. He did. "Even though I don't think the VReoria can get to the planet's surface, that's a good idea Zri. And appreciated. We don't want to be surprised by the VReoria. But you have to promise to jump out of there if you detect VReoria, we can't have them capture you."

Zri nodded, accepting the terms.

"Lord Brzko, you said that you could each take one being with you…" Ferocity said.

"I think I know where you're headed with that Ferocity, and you know I always prefer to have you with me, I don't think it would be wise on our first mission." Everyone stayed quiet, hoping for more of an explanation. Brzko obliged them. "Each of the portals is guarded by a Hekwagter Gatekeeper, an AI being that can be difficult. We need to get comfortable with them first. And we're not sure how other Clyreans would react. We just found the planet, we wouldn't want to offend anyone so soon."

"I understand." Ferocity said.

M looked around the table, she could tell that Numia had something to say. But she was not yet comfortable enough to address the group without being called upon. "Numia? Is there something you'd like to ask?" M said.

"Thank you Muse of Mischief. Yes. Will you be looking for something specific as you explore the portals?" She said, blinking her large almond shaped eyes and tilting her head just slightly.

"If you mean, will we be looking for the universe that you're from, yes. That is one of our goals. Your home planet is called Keatera?"

"Yes, that is correct."

"What is unique about it - for example Ploosnar is vividly blue and full of roinad."

"Half of the planet is uninhabitable - the atmosphere at the northernmost pole is in constant turmoil. 'Storms' I think you would call them."

"OK, that might help us to find it."

Again the conversation lagged. Waaw took the opportunity to seek direction. *"I understand that Zri will be in orbit around*

Clyrea X9 while you are exploring. What would you like the rest of us to accomplish?" She projected.

"We may not be gone long, but in case we are - there are still evacuees on Gaznzul that need to be taken home, or relocated to new homes. Please continue to aid them. And Lelelu, I assume there is no shortage of requests for help?" M asked.

"Never. Afrit has even asked for our help, again. It seems he needs a ride home to Jinn."

M really wanted to say something about Afrit, but managed not to. "Prioritize the requests and do what you can. I think you should stay here on Misko - that will leave three ships to work with. Work together to decide if you should handle things alone or as a group."

Everyone at the table nodded in confirmation. The plan was understood.

"Anything else?" Agent Brzko asked.

"Two things." Lelelu said. "The Myaads have requested a meeting. I think they are looking for some advice on how to re-initiate the Rogsaar explorations. And Iysuno has been invited to take up permanent residence with Faaf on Suus. They will actually split their time between her home on Suus and his home here on the Planet of Portals, but you know what an honor it is for him to be accepted on Suus. I've been invited to visit Faaf's home. I'd like to go before you leave."

"Of course! That's an honor you can't pass up." M said. "When were you planning on going?"

"As soon as we're done here today. Zri, will you accompany me?"

"Yes. ShyUst can prepare my ship for the Clyrea X9 trip while I'm gone."

LELELU VISITS SUUS

"Why am I nervous?" Lelelu was pacing back and forth on the bridge of her new ship. Zri was seated in the command chair, just watching her.

"Lelelu." He waited for her to stop and look at him. He stood up and went to her, embracing her. "You're just excited. You thought you lost your father so long ago, and now you have him back."

"You're right. But it's also being invited to Suus. They don't invite many outsiders to the planet, I just don't want to make a bad impression. I…"

"Lelelu, you're not an outsider. You've worked personally with Ciic, you are the assistant to the Muse of Mischief, one of her dearest friends, and now your father has partnered with one of the Suus rescued from the VReoria. Relax, I assure you, they aren't going to see you as an outsider." He could feel her begin to relax, she sat down waiting for clearance to land.

"Excuse me, Lelelu." Her communications officer approached. "You've been cleared to land, the shuttle is ready."

Too nervous to speak, she stood and nodded before heading to the shuttle. Zri followed. She was too nervous to pilot the shuttle, she seated herself in the co-pilot's chair and let Zri fly them down to the planet. As they neared the landing coordinates they'd been given, she could see an entire group of Suus gathered, waiting for her. They were flying the customary red banners used for ceremonies. Now she was really nervous. After setting the shuttle down, Zri stood and took her hand.

"Come Lelelu."

She obeyed.

He led her to the side door, opened it, and allowed the ramp to descend. There was in fact a group of Suus waiting to greet her, and one of them was Ciic.

They made their way to the bottom of the ramp where Ciic and Muum greeted them. *"Lelelu, Zri, on behalf of Suus, I welcome you both. And offer our sincere gratitude for rescuing some of us from the VReoria."* She stepped forward and embraced Lelelu first, then Zri. Muum presented her with a huge bouquet of Leel flowers, the vines were woven together to create a handle with a complete sphere of flowers hanging from it. The smell was intoxicating.

"I know that you have much lost time to make up for with your father. We won't keep you.".

"Ciic, thank you for allowing us to visit Suus. It is an honor to be here." Lelelu said.

Ciic looked back toward her. Projecting only to Lelelu, she took her arm with her upper arm and encircled her waist with her lower arm. *"I consider you to be family Lelelu. Should need anything, you have only to ask."*

Before Lelelu could respond Iysuno came rushing forward with Faaf beside him. Ciic and Muum stepped back.

"Le!" He exclaimed, scooping her up and holding her. When he finally let her go, he stepped back and looked at her beaming with joy. He turned to Zri. "Commander Zri, thank you for coming." He took a slight step back and with his arm around her, he presented Faaf. "And you both remember Faaf, now my wife." He looked at Lelelu to see her reaction to the news that he had remarried. The only emotion her face displayed was joy. Her mother had lived a long, full life - why shouldn't her father have a partner now that he was back?

"Thank you both for coming to Suus. We are honored to receive you." Faaf projected.

Lelelu handed her bouquet to Zri and went to her, and embraced her. "Thank you Faaf, I'm so pleased that you and Baba are together."

As the pleasantries died down, Ciic came forward again. She reached for Lelelu's hand, *"I hope that you will join us at the palace for a reception this evening Lelelu."*

"Thank you Ciic, we will be there."

The small crowd dispersed, and they headed to Faaf's home. The walk was enjoyable, Suus is a very clean, heavily floral planet. It's also a very safe place. Lelelu and Zri could feel eyes upon them as they walked, but there was not hostility in the stares, only curiosity. They arrived at a small residence, tucked away on a path with many others that looked similar. Each had a stone wall and a wooden gate. When they arrived Faaf opened the gate, Lelelu and Zri stepped into the courtyard. It was overwhelming - like stepping into a different world.

"This is amazing Faaf!" Lelelu exclaimed.

"Thank you Lelelu. I am honored to have a home such as this. It is very similar to the home I had before, before I was captured." She paused, momentarily overtaken by memories of the decades she spent in a stasis tube on the VReoria specimen ship. *"Luckily Iysuno is also passionate about gardening, we enjoy cultivating here in the courtyard."*

The courtyard is filled with a variety of flowers, most of which Lelelu had never seen. There was every color and shape imaginable. Along the fence line to the left she noticed a vine with long bean pods.

"Are those atus beans, like we grew in the garden when I was a child?"

"Ah yes!" Iysuno said, heading over to the vine. He was very proud of them. "This is one of our experimental plants, and it's been a great success."

"Experimental?" Zri asked.

"Uh-huh, you know that Suus sustain themselves on vapors, but I need actual food. We've been experimenting with plants that create food for me, and flowers that can be vaporized for Faaf. Sort of allowing us to 'eat together' even though we have such different needs."

"The vapor created from the flowers of the atus bean are surprisingly flavorful. It is unlike anything here on Suus, sort of hot." Faaf projected.

"Hot like spicy?" Lelelu asked.

"Yes, I think spicy would be the correct description. Suus do not have anything like this. We've shared it with friends, and it has been well received. Others are now growing the vine here on Suus."

"Oh I see. You two are becoming trendsetters here on Suus." Lelelu teased.

Faaf looked at Iysuno and her eyes sparkled. It was as close to a smile as a being with no mouth could get. Lelelu assumed they had shared a private moment via telepathy.

"Let's go in, we can continue our visit inside. I want to show you the plans for the greenhouse and garden we're adding on to the house on the Planet of Portals. Are you hungry?" Iysuno asked.

"No Baba, we're fine." Lelelu said as they all followed him into the house. She was happy to see that her father seemed to have recovered from being held in a stasis tube for decades - recovered physically at least. Lelelu knew that having a partner who had suffered the same incarceration would be a benefit to his emotional recovery, she felt a weight lift as she realized that Baba would be fine.

They sat in the living room, sipping tea and reviewing the plans for the greenhouse addition that was to be built onto the house that Lelelu had grown up in.

"This tea tastes like jasmine, the tea that M gets on Earth."

"Yes, it is the same. After the Muse of Mischief shared the tea with Ciic, she began to cultivate both the tea and the jasmine

flowers here on Suus. Vapor from the jasmine flowers are enjoyed by many here."

"Well, we should prepare for the reception. It's not every day that we're invited to a reception at the palace!" Iysuno said, gather up the tea cups.

The Muse of Mischief

ALL AROUND THE MULTIVERSE - THE CLYREAN CHASED THE VREORIA

The Muse of Mischief stood in the center of their living room. "Well?" She said, with her feet planted a shoulders width apart and her hands on her hips.

Agent Brzko was circling her, looking her up and down. "Hmmmmm. Well M, I've just got to say... I love it!" He teased.

They had both had new garments created for the trip. Their new derbies had hidden compartments, the inside of their long coats were lined with invisible pockets, and surprisingly, M had decided to wear solid black leggings, no stripes.

"I know, I know." She said. "It just doesn't seem like me without the stripes right?"

Brzko laughed and hugged her. "Nah, I don't need striped stockings to know who you are. Zri is already in orbit around Clyrea X9, are you ready to go?"

"Oh I'm more than ready! We haven't really gone exploring since we took the Jeeps out in the forest on Earth to find Rogsaar. Let's go!"

Arm in arm they left the Planet of Portals, and arrived on the World Engine known as Clyrea X9. They were on the same stone cliff floating in the clouds, where they had met Agent Qmkos and the Muse of Banter.

M reached up and activated her earcom link. "Zri, can you hear me?"

"Yes, M, I can hear you. Your signal is faint but it's clear." He answered.

"As is yours. Standby, we don't know how long we'll be here."

"Affirmative, good luck and travel safely."

"Thanks Zri." She said. Then she turned to Brzko. "So where do you want to go first?"

"Well, if we're where we think we are, this noplace leads to the young universe with very little gravity. Numia didn't mention low gravity in her description of Keatera. Let's try...." he turned and looked at the seemingly endless domes on stone cliffs, floating in the clouds, "that one!" He pointed to one that was a ways away, a little behind them.

"OK, let's go."

On the cliff of this new dome, they began to circle it slowly, looking for the entrance. "This reminds me of ancient Ireland and walking around the cairn at the Mountain of the Hags." Brzko said.

"Oh don't say that! I don't want to run into Mahb today!"

They continued on, walking slowly. A doorway opened, sliding upward, and a short, redheaded Hekwagter Gatekeeper stepped out of the dome.

"Welcome to noplace! Won't you please come in?" The little being said as he gestured toward the doorway.

"Where does this portal lead?" M asked as they slowly approached the door.

"The place you need to be. Or maybe it's the place you want to be. Or maybe it's the place you should be. I guess you will find that out once you're there." The Hekwagter Gatekeeper said.

"*I can see what the Muse of Banter meant about illogically logical!*" M projected to Brzko.

They stepped through the doorway, the Hekwagter Gatekeeper followed and the door closed. Leaving them in complete darkness. They both tensed. M let go of Brzko's arm and stepped aside just slightly, preparing to defend herself. The ceiling lit up with a map of a universe.

"Take your time, look around." The Hekwagter Gatekeeper said.

They both just looked at him. The colored lights from the ceiling were reflecting on his skin, they gave him a sickly multi-color glow. But they did nothing to lessen the shocking red of his hair.

"Ah, yes. I see. You are new to Clyrea X9 no?" He didn't wait for an answer. "Point at any galaxy and more detail will be revealed."

"Can you provide any information about this universe?" M asked.

He looked them up and down. He was AI but he was certainly displaying emotion - her question annoyed him, he didn't hide his impatience.

"Tick tock tick tock, I am a Hekwagter Gatekeeper. I am not an information provider."

"*Wow.*" She decided to use telepathy with Brzko.

"*Interesting attitude. OK, why don't you try?*"

"So Hekwagter Gatekeeper, how long ago did other Clyreans pass through here?" Brzko asked.

"Tick tock tick tock, time is a relative term."

"Hmmm. OK then, what did the last Clyreans to pass through here call this universe?"

"Gears." The Hekwagter Gatekeeper answered.

"Show me the planet they went to please."

The Hekwagter Gatekeeper looked Brzko up and down. He pointed to the map above their heads. It shifted and brought a small solar system into view. He pointed to one of the large planets in the system and brought it in close. Clearly he wasn't going to volunteer any information. They would have to learn the right questions to ask.

"Is this planet a frequent destination?" M asked.

"Tick tock tick tock, frequent is a relative term."

"Have the last Clyreans to go to this planet been there more than once?" Hekwagter Gatekeeper opened his mouth to respond, but M wasn't done yet. "And if they have, how many times have they traveled there from this portal."

"Yes. Four."

"Have Clyreans used this portal to travel to any other planets in this solar system?" Brzko asked.

"Yes."

"Show us."

The Hekwagter Gatekeeper manipulated the map to bring the other large planet into view.

"Is there a significant difference... "Brzko realized *significant* would no doubt be a relative term to the Hekwagter Gatekeeper. "Which planet is more often a destination and what percentage of the time is it the destination."

The Hekwagter Gatekeeper gave Brzko a hideous grin, confirming that he had noticed they were catching on. "This one," He manipulated the map back to the first planet. "eighty-nine point four."

"That's all for now." Brzko said, hoping the Hekwagter Gatekeeper would give them some space. It worked, he retreated to the wall waiting to be called upon again.

"Let's see if we can get closer." Brzko said pointing at the planet. The map zoomed in on the surface close enough to see land and bodies of water. He took it even closer and slowly rotated the planet. They could see signs of advanced civilizations in some areas, other areas seemed mostly uninhabited. "This looks like an interesting place, it seems like an advanced culture - you can see some kind of hovercraft or low flying ships." Brzko pointed to one of the smaller communities.

"It looks interesting, like it might be worth a visit at some point." She looked over her shoulder to see how close the Hekwagter Gatekeeper was. He was still standing next to the wall, waiting to be needed again. M decided to switch to telepathy in order to keep the conversation private.

"Do you want to see more of this universe or move on to a new portal?"

"Let's move on." He turned and headed toward the doorway.

The Hekwagter Gatekeeper moved toward them. "Tick tock tick tock, leaving so soon?"

"Yes Hekwagter Gatekeeper. But we appreciate your hospitality while we were here." Brzko said.

The Hekwagter Gatekeeper cocked his head to one side, like a puppy that was trying to understand its new master. "Good bye then." Was all his AI mind could think of to say.

The door opened as they approached, they stepped out of the dome and the door closed behind them.

"Where to now?" M projected.

Brzko looked up, they were directly beneath one of the rings. *"Let's try to stay in line with the ring."*

"Sounds good, so that one next?" M said looking at a nearby dome. Brzko turned in the direction she was looking.

"Sure, why not. Ready?" He took M's arm and they went. Again, they slowly walked around the dome until the door opened.

This time they weren't greeted by a Hekwagter Gatekeeper, it was an Agent. He greeted them as he walked out of the door, donning a long heavy duster and a cowboy hat. "Well howdy! Y'all must be the Muse of Mischief and Agent Brzko. Darlin' c'mon over here and say howdy!"

~~~

Ferocity, Lelelu, and Waaw had gathered for a status update on the Myaads from Empress Nalau. She and her crew had just returned.

"Lelelu, you were correct about them wanting to have the Rogsaars begin exploring again. But they're going to take a different approach this time."

"How so?" Lelelu asked.

"Now that their communications equipment has been upgraded, they're going to research before they go - in other words... they'll be avoiding infantile places like Earth."

"That's probably a very good idea. Poor Rogs was there alone for so long." Lelelu said. "How are the young Myaads, is there any sign of aberidus?"

"Healthy, there are no signs of the disease in the young ones or the hives. They've decided to continue repopulating with a new method. They are incubating Bivoors, Dumeers, and Rogsaars all in one hive, and using the other hives to stagger their development."

"*Interesting.*" Waaw projected. "*Is there still only one Queen per hive?*"

"No, there are several now. They're experimenting with rotating shifts. I think the shifts are a few weeks at a time. It seems like they've made great progress."

"Do they need anything from us?" Lelelu asked.

"Yes, they've asked for help updating the Rogsaar ships that were recovered. I took the liberty of having a team of engineers from Ploosnar dispatched to Myaad. At this time I don't think there's anything else they need from us."

"Excellent." Lelelu said. "Ferocity, how was your trip to Dragona with Nguvu? You went for a type of ceremony with other young Dragons?"

Ferocity paused, looking down at the table while he gathered his thoughts. After a moment he looked back up and spoke. "Yes. When Dragons complete basic education the decision of what they will devote their lives to must be made. As you know, some of us are bonded, and some stay on Dragona to serve. The ceremony was for Dragons that aspire to be bonded. They will now leave Dragona, and live in seclusion as I did on Trella. But because Nguvu spent so many years in seclusion on the VReoria ship, she will not live in seclusion. This seemed to make her feel superior to the other Dragons."

"Was there a problem?" Nalau asked.

"She was challenging her peers inappropriately, more specifically her male peers."

"Oh, she was trying to establish that she's just as fierce as the males?" Lelelu asked.

"Yes. How did you know?" Ferocity asked a little surprised.

Lelelu looked across the table at Nalau and they both smiled. "It's a common trait in the females of species where the males are dominant."

Ferocity didn't know what to say so he just nodded his head.

Waaw helped them move on. *"Will she be ready for bonding soon?"*

"I am unsure, Kwaai and I have discussed this many times. Because she was not raised as other Dragons, it is difficult to tell just how mature she is. In some ways her maturity far exceeds her age. But I am concerned about her temper."

"Do you think she would be a danger to her bond?" Nalau asked.

"No. Absolutely not. But if anyone were to threaten her bond..." He paused, considering his words carefully. "...I suspect that she would use all available force to defeat them, rather than just enough force to handle the situation."

"It sounds like she would benefit from training on Gaznzul." Lelelu said.

This threw Ferocity of course for a moment. "A Dragon being taught self-defense from Gaznzulians? She can breathe fire and ice, and fly. I do not see what else they could teach her."

"No, no, not self-defense. I think what Lelelu is referring to is self-discipline. They can help her learn self-discipline."

"I see your point. It may be good for her, and unless anyone objects, I'd like her to accompany us on a few missions. I know it may seem early, but it might help to... humble her."

"Since she was not raised by Dragons, she is already on a different path than you, and the others like you have taken. She is one of a kind, tradition and rules may not apply to her."

"As always Waaw, you speak the truth with wisdom."

"OK, moving on." Nalau said. "Lelelu, do you have new challenges for us?" She asked.

"Of course. Have you heard of Jastea MJ?"

"*In the Xeiwynia galaxy?*" Waaw projected.

"That's right."

"*The sun in one of the smaller solar systems is dying.*"

"That's right. And it's having some very profound effects on Jastea MJ."

"Jastea MJ is still inhabited?" Ferocity asked.

"Yes, a small population remained after the main evacuations. They assumed that they had a few thousand years before the sun actually died. I guess it was a group of what they call 'science seekers' that thought they would gain valuable information by monitoring the death of the red giant."

"How many beings are we talking about?" Nalau asked.

"Around three hundred. We probably can't fit all of them on our ships, but that's not the worst part." She unrolled her tablet and brought up an image of the solar system. "Their sun has expanded into a red giant much faster than they anticipated. It's about to consume Jastea MJ."

When she saw the image Nalau took a deep breath and let it out loudly. Ferocity moaned. And there was a general feeling of dread emanating from Waaw as they looked at the image of Jastea MJ. It looked like the atmosphere was being pulled toward the red giant.

Lelelu looked up at her peers. "No one will risk getting near the red giant to rescue them. They're all going to die." She paused and let that sink in. "And... yes it's their own fault. I mean they challenged what M calls Mother Nature and they lost, they made a mistake. So will we leave them to die because they made a bad decision?"

"No." They all said, or projected in unison.

"Good. We need a plan. How can we transport three hundred Jasteas?"

"Is there time for a Gaznzulian transport to get there?" Nalau asked.

"Probably not, they don't use jump drives." Lelelu answered.

"What is the final destination for the evacuees?" Waaw projected.

"The other inhabitants were relocated to Gcugrawa, not far from this solar system. I don't know where they want to go, but I'm not sure it matters. The most important thing is that we get them off of a planet that's about to be consumed by a red giant. And there's another problem. I'm not sure if it's solar flares or radiation, but communication with the surface seems to be intermittent at best." Lelelu explained.

"Dragons." Ferocity said. Everyone looked at him waiting for him to continue, to explain what he meant. "Dragons would be able to jump and get there almost instantly. Three hundred beings will fit in the cargo hold of a large transport ship.

"Dragona would be willing to help?" Nalau asked.

"Yes. The Great Assembly has agreed that it's time for Dragona to end their seclusion. If no one objects I will contact them."

"I don't object but," Nalau said "I'm concerned with the panic it may cause for Dragons to show up on the surface of Jastea MJ. Most beings in the Universe aren't sure Dragons are real."

"Hmm I see your point." Ferocity said. "Perhaps you, I and Waaw should appear first." After seeing the look on Nalau's face he revised his idea. "Or you could approach them first and explain to them that they have nothing to fear."

"That could work." She smiled at him. "When do we leave?"

"I'll contact the Great Assembly on Dragona and have them meet us there. Lelelu will you be able to reach the Jasteas to tell them we're on the way?"

She checked the current time. "Soon. They're almost out of today's communications blackout."

"I think we should depart as soon as possible. We could rendezvous with the Dragons here." Ferocity zoomed in on a map of the solar system, drawing a circle with his finger around an area that was just beyond the reach of the red giant.

Nalau stood up. "My crew and I can be ready in less than an hour. We'll meet you there." As she manipulated her arm band to transport back to her ship Waaw also stood.

"*Agreed.*"

They both disappeared, heading to their ships to get ready for departure.

"Lelelu, do you need anything before I go?" Ferocity asked.

"No, thank you Ferocity. I'll contact the Jasteas and tell them to expect you. Well, to expect evacuation." She smiled at him.

He smiled and nodded, heading to the door.

~~~

The Muse of Mischief and Agent Brzko stood looking at the Agent wearing a cowboy hat. A Muse came out of the dome and joined them. She also wore a cowboy hat, and a short patchwork denim skirt with bright green cowboy boots that matched her plaid shirt. Her ensemble was hideous, worse than his.

"Howdy y'all. I'm The Muse of Slight and this here is Agent Strno. We're mighty pleased to meet ya." She stuck her hand out, toward M. Reluctantly M took her hand.

"It's a pleasure to meet you. I'm The Muse of Mischief and this is Agent Brzko."

"Oh we know who you are darlin'! We ALLLL know who you are." She said drawing out the word all as she rolled her head back for emphasis.

M was at a loss for words. Brzko came to her rescue.

"You've heard of us?"

"Lawd yes we've heard of you two. Who hasn't?" Agent Strno said, comically drawing out the word Lord. "I mean shucks, we all heard about how you kicked ass on them VReoria. You two are old school all the way!"

"Old school?" Brzko asked, M was still too grossed out to talk.

"Yeah, you know, like our ancestors, before Clyreans got all selfish and stuff." The Muse of Slight chimed in.

M was so busy thinking about how unintelligent this being seemed that it took a second for her process what she'd said. She scratched the side of her neck, activating her earcom link before bringing her hand back down.

When he didn't hear her say anything, Zri attempted to initiate contact. "M, I'm receiving you. If you need help just…"

"Mmmm" She cleared her throat interrupting the voice in her head. "Selfish? Clyreans are selfish now?"

Agent Strno and The Muse of Slight looked at each other like 'oh, here we go.'

"Why yes darlin'" he said in a most demeaning tone. "Ain't you ever wondered why the two of yas are the only ones working on fighting the VReoria? It ain't like we don't know 'bout them. It's just that, they can't catch us, so why should we care? Shiiit, we're having too much fun exploring, to spend any time risking our lives to protect lesser beings."

"Is that an agent I hear?" Zri asked.

"Uh-huh." M said, as though she were speaking to Agent Strno and The Muse of Slight, but really speaking to Zri, "So the other Clyreans we've met here were just talkin' shit when they told us what they knew of the VReoria?" M asked, mimicking their Southern drawl.

"Well I suppose there must be other… Um *overachievers* like you two." The Muse of Slight said, using her fingers to make quotation marks in the air when she said the word overachievers.

"Overachievers?" Was all M could say.

"Course darlin', who ever said it was our duty to save every insignificant life form out there?" Agent Strno said.

M was at a loss for words. She couldn't decide if she wanted to continue the conversation or kick these two country ass idiots in the shins and then box their ears so hard that they'd never stop ringing. Agent Brzko rescued her, while Zri stayed silent, listening.

"Wait, wait, wait, so you two are saying that you know other Clyreans?"

The looked at each other and shrugged. The Muse of Slight answered for them. "Well *know*" again with the air quotes, "might be a little strong. We've seen a few. Even a few of them devoted to the *losers* of their universes, like you two." She looked over at her partner, Agent Strno when she said losers, with air quotes.

M wanted to kick her more than ever now.

"So you see these other Clyreans here, on Clyrea X9?" M asked.

"Sometimes." Agent Strno said, as though he were speaking to a child.

"So then, you're telling us that this isn't the only place where Clyreans can mingle without consequence?" Brzko asked.

"*I'm done Brzko.*" M projected to him.

"Lawdy no, someone's been feeding you a line of horse dookie. Oh probably some stingy Agent and Muse, wanting to keep you outta all these here domes." He turned toward the Muse of Slight with an overemphasized frown when he said stingy.

"Thank you so much for your time. Good luck in your travels." M said without waiting around for a response. She pictured the bridge of Zri's ship at the same time she projected it to Brzko, and disappeared.

"Well!" The Muse of Slight said. "She's not really all that friendly… and did you see that outfit? They ain't got nothin' on us sugar." She turned toward Agent Strno, and reached for him.

Brzko decided not to interrupt them, it might be better to just leave Agent Strno and the Muse of Slight before they had a chance to share their impending PDA.

DRAGONS TO THE RESCUE

Empress Nalau, Waaw and Ferocity were all near Jastea MJ, but they had no intention of getting close until they actually began the evacuations. They were on the bridge of Nalau's ship, discussing their options.

"*Our scans show that there is barely any atmosphere remaining. We don't have time to shuttle a few evacuees at a time. I'm going to land.*" Waaw projected. "*Lelelu, please have them send landing coordinates.*"

"Wait, are you sure you want to do that? If something goes wrong you may not be able to get your ship out of there in time." Nalau said.

"*I don't see another way.*" Waaw added.

"How soon will the Dragons get here Ferocity?" Nalau asked.

"They are arriving now." Ferocity said, receiving information telepathically. "And they brought a newly designed transport ship. It's large enough to hold over 500, we won't need to land our ships."

"Good, let's go. Numia I think you should stay up here and coordinate. Ferocity, can we all transport to the Dragon ship? As the only humanoid in the landing party, I think I should be the one to greet the Jasteas. They've been told to expect Dragons, but…" Nalau said.

"Of course. I agree." He reached for Nalau's armband and programmed in the transport ship's coordinates. He didn't have time to program Waaw's transporter, it was subcutaneous, so instead he reached for her and activated his own transport.

He reached for Nguvu who was waiting on his ship, *"Nguvu, transport yourself to the cargo hold of the Dragon transport ship that just arrived."*

"Understood."

The group arrived in the cargo hold of the Dragon transport ship. It was a huge empty space with a console toward the back, they headed that way. As they were walking, Nguvu arrived.

"Reporting as ordered Ferocity." She projected.

He didn't respond, only looked at her. In her excitement she had forgotten that speaking was the expectation when in the company of non-telepaths.

"Reporting as ordered Ferocity." She said falling in step with him as they headed toward the back of the cargo hold.

There was a line of stools, most of them were already occupied with Dragons ready to handle the evacuees, but there were enough seats left for Ferocity, Nalau, Waaw and Nguvu to have a safe place to sit while the ship descended.

It was like being on a ride at an amusement park, the ship descended as quickly as possible. The second they felt it touch down, everyone in the cargo hold jumped up and went to the door, ready for it to drop. They lined up - Dragons and Waaw splitting up so that they were lined up to either side of the door. Empress Nalau was front and center; her hair pulled back tight, wearing a brilliant green bodysuit and a pulse gun strapped to each thigh. Ferocity had just a second to think that Emperor Bartala had probably never seen her looking like this.

The upper half of the door lifted, and a ramp descended from the lower half of the opening. The heat was stifling and the dirty air was thin. The hot wind was almost unbearable. She ran down the ramp looking for the beings they came to rescue. Suddenly the area around her began to darken and she was confused, ready to retreat from a threat. But then she realized the darkness was a mass of beings, running toward the ship. As she got closer they became visible, there was one out in front. She hadn't thought to ask what a Jastea looked like. They were intelligent humanoids, that was all she knew.

A bright red tri-ped standing over two meters tall, presented itself to her. "Thank you for coming, I am Lornv these are the science seekers." Lornv said, gesturing with one large arm toward the masses directly behind where they stood. Nalau noticed that on the other side the being had two small arms. She didn't have time to reflect on how odd the Jasteas were, she had to get moving.

"You're welcome. We need to move quickly, we have much less time than we thought. You've been told that you're being rescued by Dragons right? We don't want to create panic."

"Yes. But we assumed the transmission was damaged by the radiation, Dragons are not real."

"They are, and they're the ones here to save you so get everyone moving. Now!" Nalau stepped to the edge of the ramp and gestured for Lornv to take up position on the other side. They started routing the Jasteas up the ramp. Just inside the door, the Dragons and Waaw began guiding them toward the back of the cargo hold so that they didn't block the entry. Most were so relieved to be off of the planet that they didn't notice the Dragons at first. There were a few shrieks and many gasps as the evacuees took note of their rescuers.

It seemed like it took an eternity to load them all. Finally the last one was aboard. Lornv went and joined the others. Ferocity walked down the ramp toward Nalau. "Is that all of them?" He asked.

"I think so." She said.

But it wasn't all of them. They heard shrieking and turned toward the sound. There were three more beings approaching, but two of them collapsed. "We don't have time for this!" Nalau exclaimed, running out into the dirty air.

"Empress NO!" Ferocity yelled and grabbed for her but missed. He followed her with Nguvu right at his heels. The planet began to shake violently just as they reached the last three Jasteas.

"GO! GO! Get on the ship, NOW!" Nalau literally shoved the standing Jastea. "We'll take care of them." She said, following the Jasteas gaze toward it's fallen mates.

Surprisingly her directions were followed. Nguvu went to the smaller of the collapsed individuals and scooped them up in her arms. Without saying a word she spread her wings and flew back to the ship with her precious cargo.

As Ferocity bent to pick up the fallen Jastea, the planet shook again. He knew the ship couldn't stay any longer. "Nalau get back to the ship. I'll take this one via transport."

She hesitated.

"GO!" He both yelled and projected telepathically to her. The single word hit her brain like a lightning bolt and she sprinted for the ship.

The ramp was already closing. They were departing without Ferocity. Nguvu ran for the door and lifted off, flying toward the small opening. Shrieking as she went, "Ferocity!"

Waaw saw what was happening and jumped as she passed over him, he managed to grab her foot and throw her off balance. They both fell to the floor as the door closed and the ship began to ascend.

"*Nguvu, we must follow our orders.*" He projected to her.

"*But he's going to die out there.*"

"*Perhaps, but I'm sure he has a plan, and if you had flown out that door you would have distracted him from whatever it is that he's trying to do and we'd end up losing two friends today.*"

"*I understand.*" She projected as she got to her feet.

"*Now, let's go see if anyone needs assistance.*" Waaw projected.

Just as Ferocity lifted the Jastea, the planet shook again, and as the atmosphere was stripped away, fireballs began to rain down on him. He dropped the Jastea, already dead, and reached for his own transporter to save himself. But the fireballs were too much, they knocked him to the ground as they burned him. He'd been without air for too long, he wasn't going to make it. With his last thought, he reached for his bond. In desperation, he reached for Lord Brzko, not expecting to be rescued, but to say goodbye.

~~~

"Oh my GOD!" The Muse of Mischief exclaimed as soon as she and Agent Brzko were on Zri's ship.

"Are you OK?" Zri asked with concern.

"Yes, I'm fine. I just want to take a shower!" She turned to Brzko, "I really wanted to kick her ass. And Agent Strno… I'm sorry, apparently he missed the memo that says no one wearing a cowboy hat can be condescending! ARRR!" She roared in frustration. "I'll never wear a hat again!"

Zri stayed silent, knowing that the two of them would bring him up to speed once M had calmed down.

"M, I'm not sure I want to explore the other universes. Something doesn't seem right about Clyrea X9." Brzko said.

"I agree. Can you believe the two cowboy clowns we met?" M said. "They were nothing like The Muse of Banter and Agent Qmkos, these two seemed skanky and…. Brzko what's wrong."

Brzko looked like he was about to faint, he grabbed the railing near him and steadied himself. He closed his eyes and threw an image to M. "I'm going." He said before disappearing.

Ferocity was in trouble, he had given M an image - the view from Ferocity's own eyes. He seemed to be surrounded by molten fire. His skin was burning, but worse, the atmosphere was almost gone. He couldn't get enough air.

"Zri! Call Lelelu, find out where they are and if anyone else needs help!" M didn't wait for a response, she opened an aperture and went to the image Brzko had sent her.

She was hit with instant heat, it was so hot she couldn't open her eyes. She forced them open and they instantly flooded with tears. She looked for Brzko, he was just ahead of her.

"M, help me. He's not breathing!" Brzko projected. Even without spoken word she could detect his panic.

M ran toward them, knelt on the other side of Ferocity, taking his arm, and threw Brzko an image of the lawn in front of Ferocity's home on Misko, they went. It was a relief to be away from the heat of the red giant, but they had to work fast to assess Ferocity's condition.

"I don't think he's breathing M, what do we do?"

"Hold on!" She opened an aperture and arrived inside Ferocity's house, in the kitchen. It was a good guess, Whotov was there. "I need Nguvu here NOW!" She left, returned to Brzko.

"Any change?" Brzko shook his head.

Whotov came running out of the house, wringing his hands. They heard Ferocity's ship break through the atmosphere and begin to descend above them. Whotov had been successful at reaching Nguvu. Before the ship even touched down, she jumped from the open doorway. Extending her wings, gliding down to where they were.

"Get back, get back!" She took a deep breath and blew a layer of ice over Ferocity. She knelt next to him and put her snout up to his ear and purred, making the same sound that Ferocity had used to resuscitate her when they removed her from the stasis tube on the VReoria ship.

It seemed to go on forever, the ice layer had melted from everywhere but the claws on his toes. Nguvu was having a difficult time deciding if she would stop purring long enough to cover his with ice again, she kept purring.

First the toes on his right foot twitched, then his foot moved. He opened his snout and drew in a huge breath and slowly let it out. Ferocity was wracked with a coughing fit. He turned his head to the side and spit red bile. He was taking very shallow breaths in order to avoid coughing again. Too weak to stand up, he first turned toward Nguvu and said "Even" and then he reached toward Brzko.

Brzko settled on the ground next to him. Explanations would have to wait.

"C'mon." M said to Nguvu, leading her away. "Let's let them have some time alone. You handled yourself well Nguvu, I'm impressed."

At this she absolutely beamed, a compliment from The Muse of Mischief was not something to be taken lightly. "May I ask a question Muse of Mischief?"

"Nguvu you never need permission to ask a question, you should question everything, and after today, please call me M."

As her smile widened, even more of her teeth were showing. Dragons were one of the many species that were not attractive while expressing joy.

"What do you think Ferocity meant when he said even? I, my, well my purring was consistent and steady so..." She noticed that M was smiling so she waited for the forthcoming explanation.

"I suspect he meant that he had saved you, and you have now saved him. Repaying the debt so to speak. It means you are two are even. You have become his equal."

"Oh."

"Nguvu, do you have the same telepathic link to other Dragons that Ferocity has?"

"Yes."

"Good, contact Kwaai and tell him what's happened. I'd like a Dragon with medical training to come to Misko and check on Ferocity."

"Understood." She nodded and turned away from M to find a quiet place to complete her task.

"Lelelu, are you on?" M asked as she activated her earcom link.

"Yes M, I'm on. Where are you?"

"Misko. You?"

"I'm here M, something terrible has happened. It's Ferocity, he…"

"He's here Lelelu, he's on Misko."

"How did you find him? He was on Jastea MJ, Nalau said he was with the last few evacuees when the planet started breaking apart and falling in on itself. All at once the atmosphere disappeared."

"He managed to get an image to Brzko. We got him back here, and Nguvu helped to revive him but we need a Dragon with medical experience to…"

"Hold on." Lelelu interrupted.

Within a minute there was a flash above M as a ship entered the atmosphere. A ship that looked a lot like Ferocity's landed in an open area near M. A Dragon walked off of the ship and came running toward her, it was Hasira.

"Where is he?"

M looked over her shoulder toward Brzko and Ferocity in the lawn. Hasira went to them without saying another word. M followed him. As they neared Ferocity they heard another ship landing. A small, fast cruzer landed near them. Dr. Q'osp ran toward them as soon as the door opened.

"I was in the area, how can I help Muse of Mischief?"

DEBRIEF

"I've asked Lelelu, Empress Nalau, and Waaw to join us. I want to hear what happened from them." The Muse of Mischief said.

Agent Brzko was sitting in his favorite spot, on the deck overlooking the Schwarth sea. "Hmmm." He hadn't really been listening, but he tried to recall what she'd just said. "Oh OK M. Good."

"Hey, are you OK?"

"No. Yes. Well, this has been…" Close to breaking down, he didn't finish.

"But everyone is OK, Ferocity is expected to make a full recovery. And this is what we do, this is what our team does."

"I know, I know. It's just that I can't help but wonder what would have happened if we'd been in a different universe, off exploring somewhere. I don't think we could have made it in time. I doubt if our telepathic links would work form another universe."

"I see your point. So are you saying you don't want to explore other universes?"

He turned and looked at her, trying to gauge her reaction before he answered. She saw that he was concerned that not wanting to explore would upset her, she decided to make it easy on him.

"Because I hope that's what you're saying. If we'd been somewhere else when Lelelu was kidnapped we would have lost her, if we'd been somewhere else today, we would have lost Ferocity." She gave him a second to process what she was saying. "Besides," she continued, "if I ever run into The Muse of Slight again, I'm going to have to teach her how to dress. And it won't be pretty!"

Surprisingly he laughed. "Oh M, you are too damn funny." One of the many things she loved about him was his ability to laugh, always.

"Oh I'm not kidding." She said, feeling herself getting fired up again.

"I know you're not, I know." He said grabbing her arm and pulling her down into his lap.

"But what about meeting other Clyreans?"

"First, I doubt the validity of any information we've been told so far. We heard that we can be near other Clyreans and we heard that we cannot. So who is telling the truth, and what does the other one have to gain by misleading us? And I'd like to try and figure out if meeting Bartala was arranged, because…"

"And who arranged for Ferocity to be bonded with me. Remember? He said that someone made a request for me to have a Dragon. I'd like to know who that was."

"That's right. Have you asked him about it?"

"No, I actually forgot about it until now. Hopefully the bond with Dragona is good enough now that they'd be willing to help us figure it out."

There was a commotion at the top of the stairs, it was Lelelu, Empress Nalau, and Waaw. Nalau had her hair down, and Lelelu and she both wore casual, loose fitting attire. Waaw had a bottle of espidrun in each of her lower hands, and bottle of nekmid in each of her upper hands.

"*I think we need to let off some steam.*" She projected to all of them.

Nalau and Lelelu both roared with laughter. M pretended to be unimpressed. "Oh Waaw really?"

She looked confused and considered explaining that she was referring to the blue steam released when espidrun is exposed to air. She was sure that this was a joke that they would all find humorous.

"Oh damn Waaw, you're fitting in better and better all the time!" Brzko said, pushing M off of his lap and getting up to embrace the big four armed being.

"Good one Waaw!" M said, clapping her on the shoulder. "Uh, let me help you with one of those." She said as she liberated one of the espidrun bottles.

Her relief that M had only been teasing her was felt by them all.

With the espidrun poured they all lifted their glasses, "To a successful rescue!" M toasted.

"A successful rescue!" They chimed and projected, four of them tossing back the shot, Waaw inhaled the steam and then sat her glass down. M looked at her.

"I've learned to be a little more cautious with the espidrun. I do not need a repeat of the first time."

This made them all laugh. Lelelu and Nalau had heard the story of the time that Waaw had discovered the steam of espidrun had an effect on Suus.

Brzko felt Ferocity reach for him. *"Hey, what's wrong Ferocity? Are you OK"*?

"Yes Lord Brzko. I am OK, I'm tired of being inside. I would like to take a walk or get out of here for a while."

"Why don't you join us on the lower deck, but bring the hover chair, I don't think you should walk that far. And bring Nguvu."

Brzko stood up and poured another round for everyone but Waaw, and then went to the bottom of the stairs.

"What's wrong?" M asked.

"Nothing, Ferocity and Nguvu are going to join us."

"Oh! He must be feeling better!" Empress Nalau exclaimed, joining Brzko at the base of the stairs. She hadn't seen him since he was on the surface of Jastea MJ.

~~~

Ferocity couldn't stand the hover chair any longer. He complied with Agent Brzko's request and used it until he was at the bottom of the stairs. With Nguvu's assistance he stood. Empress Nalau could hardly wait for him to stand before she embraced him. They stayed like that for several minutes - his large, now scarred wings wrapped around her. The last time she had seen him he was on a planet being consumed by a red giant, a planet with no breathable atmosphere - she was devastated to think that she'd lost one of her dearest friends.

Once Lelelu had also had a chance to confirm that Ferocity was indeed alive, he took a seat on the stool next to Brzko. "Pour a Dragon a drink, will you Lord Brzko?"

Brzko, well everyone, turned and looked at him. "Really?" Brzko asked. "Are you well enough to drink?"

"It will soothe my throat and help me relax. Nekmid if you like." Ferocity said slowly.

Waaw was up and offering him a glass with each of her lower hands - espidrun in one, nekmid in the other. "*Your choice...*" She projected.

"Oh! I see you have a partner in crime now." The Muse of Mischief teased.

"*I know of no one else that can debate the nuances of every opera in this galaxy, I am honored to provide him comfort.*" Waaw projected.

Ferocity took the espidrun from Waaw's left hand, and then quickly grabbed the nekmid in her right. He held a drink in each of his scarred hands looking back and forth between them, making everyone laugh.

"*Are you really OK Ferocity?*" Brzko projected privately.

"Yes, Lord Brzko. I assure you, I look worse than I feel." He responded without looking away from the glasses he held

"I don't know which to take first." Ferocity teased.

"So are you on medication Ferocity? You seem a little… uninhibited tonight." Lelelu asked.

"No, no medication Lelelu. Taking your last breath, on a planet with no atmosphere, can cause one to gain a new perspective. Nguvu!"

She had been quietly standing on the outskirts of the group, almost unnoticed. "Yes Ferocity." She said as she came forward, toward him.

"Find a stool and join us. Tonight you join us, as an equal."

She followed the direction of her mentor, rescuer, and closest companion, and pulled up a stool near Ferocity. He handed her the nekmid and raised his other hand in toast.

Waaw quickly refilled the other glasses with espidrun, everyone lifted their glasses and waited for Ferocity to find the words.

"Nguvu, you are like no other. You are strong, independent, and wise beyond your age. The mission to Jastea MJ was dangerous and difficult, but you performed the mission with the inner strength and discipline of a mature Dragon and put the needs of the evacuees before your own. While I'm happy to continue as your mentor, you've demonstrated that you are ready to determine your own path through life. To Nguvu!" He lifted his glass a little higher and then tossed it back.

The others mimicked his sentiment. "To Nguvu!"

Nguvu was smart enough to sip her first nekmid.

Empress Nalau caught The Muse of Mischief's eye. She didn't have to say anything, M knew exactly what she was thinking. She got up and walked to the edge of the deck for a little privacy.

She activated her earcom link. "Hey, old man. Are you in bed yet?" She was of course calling her oldest friend, Emperor Bartala.

"No M, I'm up, waiting for my wife. But as usual you are keeping her busy." Bartala fired back playfully. "What are you two doing tonight, planning another rescue mission?"

She ignored his question. "Can you sneak out? We need you here with us."

"Yes! Meet me in your rooms, I'll be there in two minutes."

Without saying a word to anyone, The Muse of Mischief disappeared from the deck. She returned almost instantly with Bartala.

"Bartala! Welcome." Brzko called to him.

"Thank you Agent Brzko." He said as he walked over to Ferocity. "Ferocity. I..." He didn't know what to say.

Ferocity stood slowly and embraced him with his wings. After a moment he released the Emperor of Ploosnar and took his seat again. "I'm OK Bartala, thank you for coming."

Bartala was having a difficult time pulling his attention away from Ferocity but Waaw was there to help. *Here, you have some catching up to do Emperor!*" She projected to everyone as she shoved a steaming glass of freshly poured espidrun toward the Emperor.

Emperor Bartala immediately tossed it back and held the glass out toward Waaw, while he turned to look at his wife. "Darling, as always you are a vision of beauty."

As soon as his glass was filled he went and sat with her.

"Emperor?" Ferocity said.

The Emperor didn't answer, he just looked across the deck toward the Dragon with a raised brow.

"May I share an image with you?"

Bartala didn't really know what to say, or what that really meant, so he just nodded. Suddenly it was as if he was standing on the deck of the Dragon ship. The ramp was down, open to a fiery red planet. In the distance he could see the red giant, pulling the planet's atmosphere toward it - everything glowed a hostile shade of red. At the base of the ramp stood his wife, the Empress of Ploosnar. She donned a brilliant green bodysuit. Every part of her body was firm and tense, ready for action. With a pulse weapon strapped to each thigh, she stood confidently with her feet at a shoulder's width, ready for action. She turned and looked toward him, she was of course looking toward Ferocity - this was his memory. Bartala had never seen the love of his life look more beautiful - not even in her most elegant gown decorated with jewels. As quickly as it came, the vision ceased. Bartala looked up, across the deck toward Ferocity.

"Thank you." He said as he tried to discreetly dab the edge of his wet eye.

Ferocity just nodded to him.

Empress Nalau leaned toward her husband and whispered in his ear. "What is it darling, are you alright?"

He kissed her forehead. "Yes my love."

The Empress sat back in her own chair, "So Nguvu, have you given any thought to bonding?" she asked.

Bartala's hand was casually resting on her thigh, but when she asked Nguvu about bonding he squeezed in excitement.

"Empress Nalau I..." Nguvu started. But she was interrupted.

"Hey! You started the party without me!" Zri said as he came down the stairs.

Lelelu was up, and in her lover's arms in a flash. Zri embraced her, and the moment he let her go he went to Ferocity.

"Close call huh Ferocity." He said patting his shoulder.

Ferocity didn't answer, he stood and embraced Zri. At first Zri was completely rigid, unaccustomed to being touched by anyone but Lelelu. But there's something about being wrapped in a Dragon's wings that relaxes even the most rigid.

Ferocity released him without a word and sat down. Waaw was right there handing Zri his first espidrun of the evening. Zri took it with him, and sat down with Lelelu. Waaw made the rounds and refilling glasses. She saved Nguvu for last. *"Nguvu, would you like another?"* She asked as she extended the arm holding the nekmid bottle.

"Only if you are having another Waaw." She said extending her glass toward her.

They all laughed. "Nguvu you fit in perfectly." M teased. "So, before Zri arrived, you were about to say something about bonding…"

Nguvu took a breath, about to respond but was interrupted again.

"Please forgive the interruption." Whotov as he descended the stairs. "But I'm quite sure you are in need of refreshments, especially you Ferocity. You need to keep your strength up." Once again, the Ploosnarian butler that served Ferocity the Dragon, came to everyone's rescue. He was balancing an unbelievably large tray, filled with a variety of fruits, vegetables, and lusimis. He set it on the table and turned to leave, he noticed the Emperor and simply nodded to him. Knowing that the Emperor of Ploosnar is not supposed to leave the planet without a full escort of palace guards, he was uncomfortable with openly greeting him but at the same time accustomed to seeing him here.

"Thank you Whotov. You always know just what we need." Agent Brzko said as Whotov ascended the stairs.

"Pleasure!" he called over his shoulder as he climbed the stairs.

"Remember Whotov, we'd be happy to have you back at the palace anytime you tire of this Dragon." Bartala called after him.

Whotov just waved his hand and kept heading up the stairs. He was glad that they couldn't see his face, he couldn't hide how happy it made him to hear these things from the Emperor of Ploosnar, whom he had served for decades. But he wouldn't leave his post with Ferocity for anything. He often bragged about his position to family and friends, sharing tidbits of his most interesting days.

Glasses were filled again, snacks were grabbed from the tray, and the group settled again. As usual, they were quite a sight - two Clyreans, two Dragons, a Suus, a Trelod, a Gaznzulian, and the Emperor and Empress of Ploosnar. But there never has been, nor will there ever be, a tighter group.

M was afraid that saying anything would interrupt anything Nguvu may have to say. So instead of speaking she leaned forward and look past Brzko and Ferocity toward Nguvu, catching her eyes.

"Yes Muse of Mischief." Everyone went silent when Nguvu spoke. "I have spent time considering the possibility of bonding. I've spent time on Dragona with unbonded Dragons that devote their lives to politics, or other duties of servitude. But I've also spent time with Ferocity, a bonded Dragon. And recently, I realized that I am in a unique position. Ferocity's bond to Agent Brzko was arranged, as are most bonds. But because I was in stasis on the VReoria ship for so long a bonding was not pre-arranged for me. I have the luxury of having a say in who I bond to, and I would like to be bonded."

He couldn't help himself, Emperor Bartala blurted out, "Would you consider being bonded to our son Wisssi?"

The only sound was the waves of the Schwarth sea crashing below. Everyone was looking at Nguvu. She was looking at the ground in front of her.

Ferocity attempted to come to her rescue. "Perhaps..." Nguvu looked at him and he stopped speaking.

"Emperor Bartala, Empress Nalau, I would be honored to be bonded to Ezopica Mischievous Wisssdartai when he is ready." She said.

"Ready? I do not understand." Bartala said.

"A bond cannot be undone, it is for eternity. He has to be old enough to know what it means to be bonded to a Dragon before I can be bonded to him. And it needs to be *his* choice." She said.

Bartala just looked at her, then finally said, "You, Nguvu, are more insightful than I imagined. Would you consider spending time getting to know him, before he's old enough to make a decision about bonding?"

"Of course." She answered. "I think we will have a great time getting to know each other."

The Muse of Mischief

~ Part Two ~

The Muse of Mischief

THE EMPEROR QUITS

"He is the youngest, the youngest ever." Emperor Bartala said.

"Why are you doing this? Why are you deviating from the centuries old traditions of Ploosnar?" The Muse of Mischief asked.

They were sitting on the patio of her and Agent Brzko's home on Earth. Listening to the waves of the Pacific Ocean below them, she was trying to determine if her oldest friend was all right. Her first thought was that he may have been infected with mind altering bacteria.

"Wisssi will be the youngest Emperor that Ploosnar has ever had. Has any other ever surrendered the title to his offspring while still in his prime?" She asked.

"No M. It's never been done."

"Then why Bartala, why are you doing this? With a lifespan of more than 200 years you're really only in your prime."

"Exactly." He answered. "I've been thinking about his since you mentioned it."

"Me? You're going to put this on me?"

"You don't remember." He said. "You came to see me before you left for Clyrea X9 the first time. It was the time we taught Wisssi how to 'raid the fridge', as you say. You suggested that he could take over for me and I could work with Nalau."

"That sounds like something I'd say."

"So you see, this is your doing."

She just looked at him, waiting for more. She wouldn't let him off that easy. He'd be trapped here on Earth with her until she was satisfied with his answer.

He took a deep breath and slowly released it. "I envy you M. I've always envied your freedom. I don't think I ever really held it against you, but I longed for it. When we were young we had great fun planet hopping and causing a little trouble. But then my father passed and I became the Emperor of Ploosnar. The position certainly has benefits, but for more than a decade now, I've watched you, and my wife, and my best friends make a difference in the Universe. And Wisssi has had plenty of time to explore and enjoy the freedom of his youth. He and Nguvu have been all over the Universe."

"But..." She attempted to interrupt.

He held his hand up to silence her and continued. "I know what you're going to say. I've made a difference on Ploosnar, and even to some degree throughout the Universe - like when I helped the Rogsaars get back to Myaad. I see the deep personal satisfaction that comes from the work all of you do, and I want that for myself. I also want a chance to share that with my wife. Wisssi will excel as the Emperor of Ploosnar. In fact, I suspect he may be a better Emperor than I ever was. He has new, innovative ideas about the roinad empire. He's already expanded the market by working with the Dragons. At his age, he won't let tradition stop him, he'll forge ahead in new directions and I think Ploosnar will be better for it." He paused and took a sip from the fine china teacup beside him. "What do you call this stuff again?"

"Espresso."

"I like this stuff, I REALLY like this stuff. I feel invigorated!" He said.

M just laughed at him.

"So if Wisssi becomes the Emperor of Ploosnar you'll be homeless. What's your plan?"

He looked at her and smiled.

"Oh I see." She said sarcastically. "You want to live in the spare house on Misko."

"Well you DID have it built for me and Empress Nalau - under different circumstances, but nonetheless."

"Bartala you know I'd love to have you that close, even though it probably won't be good for us." They both laughed. "You realize that you'll be taking orders from your wife right?"

"Yes. And I fail to see how that would be any different than it is now."

"She has a full crew, they've been working well together for many years. Numia and her make a great team - they can anticipate each other's needs when they're working. How will you fit in?"

"It is a shame that Numia will never be able to return to her home, but she seems to enjoy her new life. I don't intend to intrude on to my wife's ship. I'm having my own built - I'm still the Emperor of Ploosnar, and can use the resources as I see fit." They both laughed.

"Oh, this is where you two are?" Agent Brzko said as he came out of the house.

Bartala turned to see who was behind him, he jumped up and greeted Brzko. "Agent Brzko, it's nice to see you."

"You don't usually hang out here with Bartala M, what's up? Everything OK?" He asked, pulling up a chair.

"Yep, it's all good. I wanted to find out the real reason Bartala is stepping down as Emperor of Ploosnar, and I figured if he refused to tell me the truth I'd threaten to leave him here." She grinned at Bartala.

"Oh you are an evil one M."

"Yep. Hey Brzko, Bartala wants to come live on Misko. Are you OK with that?"

"Really? How can you be the Emperor of Ploosnar and live on the Planet of Portals?" He asked, taking a sip if M's espresso.

"I'm relinquishing the throne to Wisssi."

"Seriously?"

"Yes, I want to do something else with my life, and he will be a better Emperor than I ever was."

"I'm surprised you don't keep a residence at the palace. I would have guessed you'd want to keep the... luxury. I guess that means M will have to give up the purple rooms too."

"He doesn't know does he?" Bartala asked, looking at M.

"Probably not, he's been out with Zri in the Vaproutov Galaxy."

"What don't I know? What did I miss?"

"Ezopica Mischievous Wisssdartai is not just to be bonded with Nguvu - they are to be bonded." He could tell that it hadn't clicked for Brzko yet. "Bonded, as in marriage."

"Holy shit! Are you serious? I had no idea they were involved that way."

"No one did, they kept it very discreet." M said.

"Has a Dragon ever married outside their species before?"

"No. This will be the first. So you can see that my place is no longer at the palace on Ploosnar."

"I do see that now!" Brzko said. "Has there ever been an Empress that wasn't Ploosnarian?"

"Yes, but never one as... well, never one that could breathe fire." He said grinning.

"Wow. So are you going to play house husband to Empress Nalau on Misko?"

M laughed so hard that she lost the sip of espresso she'd just taken.

"Hardly Brzko!" Bartala said, doing his best to look insulted. "Actually my new ship will be ready in a few days, and my crew and I have already attended flight and defense training on Gaznzul. We're ready to join you."

"Wait, you said you lost weight because you'd become vain about your appearance. You were actually training with the Gaznzulians." M asked shocked. "I can't believe you were able to hide that from me. Does Nalau know?"

"Of course."

"Wait, you said crew." Brzko said. "You've already selected a crew? Who?"

"Several that you rescued from the VReoria specimen ship have been living on Gaznzul, but not really settled in."

"Oh, so they've all been there for a while." M said, thinking out loud.

"Yes, with the exception of my first officer." M and Brzko just looked at him, waiting. "Do you remember Scomia?"

"Of course, the young Keateran that Kilome adopted. She's going to be your first officer?"

"Yes. You know we stayed close while she was finishing school on Ploosnar. She's never really settled into a profession, she's restless and eager to explore more of the Universe."

"What about Chuna and Blona? Are they still running roinad freighters?"

"Mmmm hmmm."

"So when and where is the ceremony for Wisssi and Nguvu?"

"Next week - there will be three ceremonies. First a mostly traditional bonding on Dragona, then a wedding, then the ceremony of ascension on Ploosnar."

"Mostly traditional?" Brzko asked.

"The Great Assembly of Dragona has agreed to open the ceremony to immediate family/"

"Oh! Are you serious?" M asked.

"Yes. It's true."

"I wonder why Ferocity never said anything." Brzko considered out loud.

"Because he doesn't know. I only found out minutes before I was kidnapped and brought to this beautiful place on the most infantile of planets." He said pretend frowning at M. "Now I've had a lovely time M, but will you please take me home. There's little time to prepare and I need to see Schatorren. As the father of the groom I must be impeccably dressed."

THE BONDING

The Muse of Mischief was surprised by the smell of Dragona. The strong scent of the red salty ocean water wafted up toward her. She was at the end of the walkway that connected the landing platform to the castle of the Great Assembly. She stood on one side with Agent Brzko and Ferocity, Emperor Bartala and Empress Nalau were on the opposite side.

Nguvu's ship descended through the atmosphere almost silently, landing just as Ferocity's ship had all those years ago when he was bonded to Agent Brzko. M looked over at her old friend Bartala just as the ship set down. He caught her glance and a grin spanned the entire width of his face. The ramp descended from the rear of the ship - everyone tensed. Nguvu came out first, she paused at the bottom of the ramp waiting for Ezopica Mischievous Wisssdartai, her bond, and soon to be her husband.

Wisssi had grown into a fascinating young man. He was fonder of business than his father, but he was also more mischievous, living up to the reputation of his namesake. Although Wisssi was taking today's ceremonies seriously, he couldn't help but dress with his usual flair. The suit he'd had made for this occasion was a brilliant scarlet color, trimmed in black. His hair was styled as his father had worn his many years ago - sticking straight up and forming a crown around the top of his head. He looked even more like Londo the science fiction character from Earth than his father ever did.

Nguvu began to walk past them with Wisssi following. When they exited the castle here today, it would be she who followed Wisssi, and when they complete their marriage ceremony later today, they will forever walk side by side.

The young dragon is also a bit rebellious - because she did not receive a normal upbringing on Dragona, she often struggles with the stringent customs. As she passes Ferocity she steps out of place to reach for his hand. He has recovered from his experience on Jastea MJ, but his hands are forever scared from the fire balls. Nguvu never tires of hearing the story of how his Bond saved him. She continues past them without the traditional battle cry of the soon to be bonded Dragon.

As they progressed, the Dragons that had been standing still along the edges of the bridge begin to take flight. M was surprised by the amount of wind they create. She wants to ask Agent Brzko if it was like this when he arrived on Dragona to bond with Ferocity, but she doesn't want to distract him.

The five of them follow behind Wisssi. Empress Nalau wearing a long black elegant gown with a long trail behind her. The fabric makes a whooshing sound as she progresses across the bridge.

At the door Nguvu raises her hands, makes fists and bangs one fist on each door twice. The huge doors open inward. It's difficult to see inside the castle from outside, it's dim. Nguvu takes Wisssi's hand and steps over the threshold. The Muse of Mischief, Agent Brzko, Ferocity, Emperor Bartala, and Empress Nalau follow them in. They position themselves in a loose semicircle behind Nguvu and Wisssi.

"*Lord Brzko...*" Ferocity projected, allowing M to hear his thoughts.

"*I know Ferocity, there must be three times as many Dragons in here today.*"

Today the walls were lined with rows of Dragons, they are grouped by the color of the cord that holds their medallions. The Dragons begin ticking, communicating in one of their ancient languages. Again Kwaai stands on a platform at the head of the room with the scepter topped with a glowing red orb. He raises the scepter and silence falls.

"As we have for millennia, Dragons bond to those that are worthy, those that are a positive force. Before us stands Nguvu, she comes to us today to be bonded. Nguvu! Present the Bond." He raises the scepter and brings it to the floor, making a deep clanking sound.

"My fellow Dragons," Nguvu said looking around the room, "Today I stand before you with Ezopica Mischievous Wisssdartai of Ploosnar. He lives in service to his people, ever diligent in their empowerment and their protection. He is worthy of a Dragon." She took a half step to the side and turned to look at Wisssi. He stepped forward with his head bowed.

"Ezopica Mischievous Wisssdartai, Nguvu finds you worthy of bonding, you know that only death can break this bond, if you are willing to accept it then step forward and kneel before the Great Assembly, kneel before Dragona!" Kwaai said, again banging the scepter to the ground.

Just as Agent Brzko had done all those years ago, before Wisssi was born, Wisssi steps forward and takes a knee. "My Lord, it is my honor to accept Nguvu as my bonded Dragon." He says as he bows his head.

She kneels beside him and whispers to him, "This is going to hurt, but it won't last long." He knew what to expect.

Kwaai extends the scepter toward them, the bolt of red light jumps from it and encloses Nguvu and Wisssi. In his mind, he's seeing Nguvu's life up to now - being a captive on a VReoria specimen ship and then placed in a stasis tube for what seemed to be an eternity. How had she not gone mad he wondered, just reliving it in this way was driving him to the edge. He couldn't take much more, then the images changed, he was seeing her life after being freed. It finally ended, when the light disappeared his body lurched forward as though he had been leaning on a support that was removed. Nguvu quickly reached out to steady him.

"Stand!" Kwaai commanded. "You are now Ezopica Mischievous Wisssdartai and his bonded Dragon Nguvu."

The Dragons began ticking again. All at once they stopped. But instead of blending in and seeming to disappear, this time they came forward to mingle with the group of outsiders.

"*Things have changed since we were bonded here.*" Brzko projected to Ferocity.

"*For the better Lord Brzko, for the Better.*"

The soon to be wed couple was surrounded by the Great Assembly, being congratulated. Many of them will attend Wisssi's ceremony on Ploosnar, but they can't wait that long to congratulate them. M makes her way over to the parents of the groom while Ferocity and Brzko are engaged with other Dragons. She has to wait for them to be free, the Dragons have many questions for them - they are all excited that a Dragon will become an official dignitary on Ploosnar later today.

Finally she was able to break in. "How are you two? A bit overwhelmed?"

"Oh no M, we do this all the time." Bartala teased.

"I am." Nalau said. "I admit it, this was an unbelievable experience. Being around all of these Dragons, it's...." She threw up her hands with a beautiful smile upon her face.

"Agreed. It's..." M said. "And we're not done."

They were nowhere near done for the day.

THE WEDDING

"Are you nervous?" Agent Brzko asked the Muse of Mischief as he circled her, making sure there wasn't a single thread out of place.

"Me? No I do this stuff all the time. But hey, let's take a few shots before the ceremony begins. Just to relax." She smiled at him. In truth she is nervous. It's one thing to rescue a being from pending doom, or track someone that's become lost, but being part of a wedding - that was trying her nerves.

M is wearing a brilliant blue suit - Wisssi had Schatorren make it for her. The back collar stands taller than her head, creating a frame. The suit is identical to Wisssi's except that it is tailored to fit her body.

The wedding ceremony is smallish, and taking place on Misko. Wisssi and Nguvu both insist that this part of the day must be intimate. There are around thirty guests waiting for them on the beach. The ceremony will be led by Whotov.

There's a knock at the door, but before either of them can move to answer... "M, M, are you ready?" It's Wisssi.

"Yes Wisssi, I'm ready. Are you and Nguvu ready?"

"Yes, she's outside. Let's go."

M turned and looked at Brzko, it is his cue to leave. He should already be on the beach before they arrive. He kisses her cheek, pats Wisssi on the shoulder and heads to the beach.

"You look fantastic Wisssi." M says.

"Thank you M." He reaches for her, pulls her in and holds her close. "I'm honored to have been named after you. I'm lucky to have an Autuania like you - thank you for everything you've done for me."

"Oh Wisssi, you were also named after your father." She said, downplaying her importance in his life.

He laughed. "Yes, and he has been a great father. But not nearly as much fun as you Autuania M. You showed me things in the Universe that he's never seen. And without you, I never would have met Nguvu."

"Oh, yeah, I guess I did that didn't I."

"Shall we?"

He took her arm and gestured toward the door. They step outside and see Ferocity and Nguvu just ahead of them on the path to the beach. They follow in silence.

The guests are seated in a semicircle, looking out at the ocean. In front of them stands Whotov. Now too old to butler for Ferocity, but still residing with him as a companion. His pale grey hair makes his brilliant blue eyes even brighter. M and Wisssi pause at the edge of the beach and let Ferocity and Nguvu make their entrance. Silence falls as the crowd sees her - today she wears a string of leel flowers around her neck. Courtesy of Ciic of course. She stands before Whotov with Ferocity at her side. Wisssi walks toward them, M following close behind. He sneaks a glance at his parents, tears are streaming down his father's face. He breaks from the expected progression and greets his father, hugging him, sharing words that only he can hear. They continue on until Wisssi is next to Nguvu. He reaches for her hand and they face Whotov together.

"Loved ones we are here today to witness the joining of Ezopica Mischievous Wisssdartai and Nguvu the Dragon. Who will stand with them today?" Whotov begins.

"I will!" M and Ferocity answer in unison.

Whotov nods to Wisssi, indicating it's time for his vows.

"My dear Nguvu, I will forever walk beside you, I give myself to you. Will you walk beside me, grow old with me?"

Nguvu meets his gaze. "Wisssi, I will forever walk beside you, I give myself to you, and I will be honored to grow old with you."

"Friends!" Whotov called. "I present to you Ezopica Mischievous Wisssdartai and Nguvu the Dragon - husband and wife."

Wisssi embraces Nguvu, kissing the tip of her snout -she surrounds him with her wings, embracing him. When she releases him they turn and look at the small crowd as an official couple for the first time. Everyone stands and begins coming forward to offer their congratulations. M steps back from the crowd and finds Brzko. He's standing alone at the edge of the crowd. His long coat billows in the ocean breeze with the sun catching the small red paisleys on his vest.

"Damn you look good." M says, hugging him.

"Thanks M."

"Aren't you glad I turned you on to Schatorren?"

He laughs. "Yes, but… "

"Hey you two! Isn't this just amazing?" They turn to see Lelelu, Zri, and Waaw approaching.

"Le." M greets her with a hug. "You look lovely today. The color of that dress makes your blue skin even more beautiful than ever."

"Thank you," she says twirling so that they can see her from all sides. "Zri helped me pick it out." She turns and looks at Zri with an adoring look.

"Hmm." Zri says, uncomfortable with the idea of discussing fashion.

"Friends! Are you ready to go? There's one more ceremony to attend to today!" Bartala calls as he, Nalau, and Ferocity approach; saving Zri from having to discuss the finer points of fashion.

"Emperor, Empress, how…" Brzko says before Bartala interrupts him.

"Ahhhh Brzko, that will be one of the last times you can call us that. In a few hours Wisssi will become the Emperor of Ploosnar, and Nguvu the Empress."

Ferocity makes ticking sounds, uttering something in an ancient Dragon language. Everyone looks at him. He realizes they heard him.

"I was just expressing my… surprise, or disbelief, that a Dragon will become the Empress of Ploosnar. It was not that long ago that Dragons chose to live in secret."

"Does it displease you Ferocity?" The Empress asked, unable to *read* him.

"No Empress, it does not displease me. I am honored, as are all Dragons. I remember when we rescued Nguvu from the stasis tube." he looks off in the distance, recalling the unpleasant memory of the VReoria specimen ship.

They all stopped to recall the horrible conditions they had rescued so many beings from - and they all knew that there were more VReoria specimen ships, with more beings in need of rescue.

The Empress decided to move them along. "And look at her now Ferocity. Later today I will relinquish the title of Empress of Ploosnar to her. If you had not mentored her it would not have been possible. Do you remember how she used to breath fire with no warning, anytime she was upset?"

"Yes I remember." Ferocity said. "It took some work to get that temper under control."

"I can relate to that." Brzko interjected.

They all looked at him and then realized he was speaking about The Muse of Mischief, so they looked at her.

"And your point is?" She said oozing with sarcasm. "A temper is just an untapped tool. SOME of us learn how to use it to our advantage." She shrugged, making them all laugh.

"We should all go if we're going to be on Ploosnar before the Emperor to be arrives." Lelelu said, keeping them organized and on task as always.

BARTALA'S LAST DAY AS EMPEROR

The Muse of Mischief and Agent Brzko have been traveling the Universe and working with a vast number of species, in a vast number of places for decades now - but they have never seen an event like this one - the ascension of a new Emperor on Ploosnar.

This ascension ceremony was unlike any of the previous ceremonies on Ploosnar. When Bartala became Emperor, his father had died unexpectedly while traveling, there was a small ceremony held inside the palace, with only Ploosnarians in attendance. But today was much different.

In order to accommodate the huge crowd, consisting of Ploosnarians, Dragons, Suus, Gaznzulians, and many other species, a huge outdoor arena has been created. It's a theatre really, there is a small stage in the center. From there, the land gently slopes up and out in all directions - it's as if the stage is in the center of a large bowl. The gentle slopes are covered in finely manicured grass, the blue grass that is used in landscapes all over Ploosnar. The top of each slope has been decorated with huge emerald green flags. They billow in the gentle breeze. Between each flag stands three Dragons. The slopes are filled with observers.

From their position near the stage, M and Brzko look around, observing the crowd. "How many?" She asks.

He continues to survey the slopes turning to look over his shoulder. "There's got to be thousands."

"Ten thousand." Zri interjects from next to them.

Lelelu, at his side turns and looks up the slopes, taking it all in. "Are the Dragon's planning something Ferocity?"

He grins, exposing his jagged teeth, and nods in affirmation.

"*Interesting.*" Waaw projects.

The crowd suddenly goes silent as Emperor Bartala, wearing his crown, takes the stage. He turns back to the steps and offers his hand to Empress Nalau as she joins him on the stage, also wearing her crown. Looking more beautiful than ever, they stand arms linked, waving to the crowd in all directions. Everyone in attendance applauds, whistles, shouts - whatever their custom dictates - and the sound is deafening. Bartala and Nalau let them continue on for a moment, just standing in their brilliant blue attire. The sun is catching the crystals on the crowns, throwing brilliant blue flares of light around the crowd.

Bartala steps away from his wife and that cues everyone to be silent. Instead of speaking, he and Nalau step apart and welcome Wisssi and Nguvu to the stage. The crowd goes wild again, this time they don't want to stop. Wisssi and Nguvu take a tour around the stage, waving in every direction. Finally it begins to quiet.

Wisssi steps away from Nguvu and stands before his father, Nguvu stands before Empress Nalau.

"Ezopica Mischievous Wisssdartai, I am honored to have a son and heir such as you. Ploosnar will flourish with you as Emperor." Bartala began. "I Kufeter Whakeclyte Wissswara Bartapulnye hereby pass the title of Emperor of Ploosnar to you, with all of its responsibility, authority, and amenities. If you accept this bestowment willingly, kneel and accept the crown of the Emperor of Ploosnar."

Wisssi kneels in front of his father, Nguvu kneels in front of his mother. In the final act as Emperor of Ploosnar, Emperor

Bartala removes the crown from his own head with both hands and places it on Wisssi's head. Empress Nalau removes her crown and places it on Nguvu's head. As Emperor Wisssi and Empress Nguvu stand to face the crowd as officials of Ploosnar for the first time, Bartala and Nalau discreetly leave the stage.

Each of the Dragons at the top of the slope roar loudly as they tilt their heads back and breathe a long stream of fire straight up. The glow that it creates is amazing. The crowd goes wild again. Wisssi and Nguvu stand arm and arm on the stage.

"M." She turns and sees Bartala at her shoulder. "M we're ready to get out of here, can you and Brzko take us to Misko now." He looks toward the stage.

"You don't want to watch this?"

"No, this and the after celebration will go on for hours, and it's their day." He said.

"OK, let's go." She takes his arm and goes to Misko. Brzko takes Nalau's arm and follows.

"Wow." M said. "I really like the way you Ploosnarians keep your ceremonies short and sweet."

"For real." Brzko said. "There are places where it would have taken days of ceremony to name a new Emperor."

"Who has time to waste?" Bartala said. "Wisssi has an empire to run and we have beings that need our help. But first, we have espidrun to drink. Shall we meet you on the terrace after we change?"

"Of course! We'll see you there." M said. As she and Brzko turned toward their house, they could hear both Lelelu and Ferocity's ships landing.

The Muse of Mischief

WHAT'S IN A NAME

"Wait, look Brzko, what are they doing?" The Muse of Mischief asked. She and Agent Brzko were the last to arrive, the rest of their group had been on the terrace long enough to have enjoyed a few espidruns. They had some catching up to do.

"It almost looks like they are trying to balance full shots of espidrun on their noses." He answered.

"Well that hardly seems like a fair contest, Ferocity and Waaw have snouts!"

"Oh! Did you see that? Zri just spilt his. He's really changed hasn't he, relaxed a bit."

"Yeah, somewhat. He still takes the work seriously, maybe he's just learning to accept himself."

"Good point. Are you ready to go down and join them M?"

She nodded, took his hand, and started walking down the stairs. About halfway down she announced their arrival. "You better not have finished off that bottle before we got here!" She teased.

"M! Brzko! You're here." Lelelu called, excited.

"Ah, it's just like you to keep us waiting M." Bartala teased.

"What makes you think it was me, maybe I was waiting for Brzko."

Everyone just laughed at M's attempt at pretending to be insulted.

"Who's pouring?" Brzko asked, taking a seat between Ferocity and Waaw. Lelelu took care of his requesting, refilling everyone else's glass except Waaw's.

"Have I offended you in some way Lelelu?" She projected.

"No Waaw but you still have some in your glass."

"Ah yes, but it is only the steam I find appealing." She projected.

Ferocity leaned forward, reaching in front of Brzko, he grabbed the glass, quickly drank the remaining espidrun and said, "There, problem solved." as he returned the glass to Waaw, smiling and showing all of his teeth.

Lelelu just shook her head and pretended to be annoyed while she filled Waaw's glass and a few others.

Brzko realized that Ferocity and Waaw were much closer than it appeared.

M stood and raised her glass, "A toast!" Everyone lifted their glasses, "To my oldest friend Kufeter Whakeclyte Wissswara Bartapulnye, we are thankful to you for joining us, all the better for having you, welcome to the group!"

"Welcome!" Everyone yelled or projected.

"Thank y…"

"Whakeclyte? Your first name is actually Whakeclyte?" Zri teased.

"Mmmm, this from a being that has a single name, but masks his true form when in the company of others." Bartala teased back.

"Touchdown Bartala, touchdown." Zri said.

M choked, she laughed so hard that espidrun flew out of her nose.

"Do you mean touché Zri?" Brzko asked laughing.

"Yes! That's it touché! What is a touchdown?"

"Uh, something that would take time and visual aids to explain." Brzko answered.

"It's a term from a contact sport played on the barbaric place where M and Brzko were raised, Earth." Bartala said.

"Really? Contact sports? That place is worse than I thought." Zri said.

Bartala nodded in agreement. "So what do we call ourselves?"

"What are you talking about darling?" Nalau asked.

"M said welcome to the group. What is this group called?"

No one made a sound. "Uhhhh we don't really have a group name Bartala, it's not a clubhouse ya know." M said.

"We need a name. How will people refer to us - you know that group that consists of two Clyreans, two Ploosnarians, a Trelod, a Dragon, a Gaznzulian, and a Suus?" He asked sarcastically as he refilled glasses.

"The Regulators!" Zri said, excited.

"Zri, have you been watching Earth television?" M asked.

"Uh, yes. There is something called westerns. Have you heard of them?"

M and Brzko both laughed. "Yes Zri, we've heard of westerns. Be careful, too much Earth television will rot your brain." Brzko said. Zri leaned back in his chair to consider this as though it would actually make his brain begin to rot.

"Coalition." Nalau said quietly.

"What was that my love?" Bartala asked.

"We are a coalition, are we not?"

"Yes, we definitely are a coalition." M said. "But that sort of suggests a temporary bonding."

"Guild." Brzko said.

"That is a perfect word to describe us." Bartala said. Everyone agreed.

"But we can't be just the Guild" He said.

"Why is a name so important to you Bartala?" M asked.

Before he could answer Waaw projected, "*It provides a sense of belonging, acceptance.*"

"Exactly." Bartala added.

Lelelu who thus far had been quiet spoke up, "Everything we do is within the Cosmos."

"The Cosmos Guild? It doesn't sound quite right." M said.

"Advocates." Ferocity said. Everyone looked at him.

It hit the Muse of Mischief then, she stood and raised her glass. "To the Advocates of the Cosmos!"

And so it began. With glasses raised, standing in a circle, are two immortal Clyreans, a blue Trelod, a fire breathing Dragon, two royal Ploosnarians, a reflective Gaznzulian, and a four-armed Suus.

They are:

THE ADVOCATES OF THE COSMOS.

The Muse of Mischief

Afterward

Well here we are again. The end of the second volume in The Muse of Mischief series. Many of the questions from Volume One were answered, but we still have much to do.

By now, you know The Muse of Mischief well. We don't know where she'll go from here, but we do know she won't be going alone.

The ADVOCATES OF THE COSMOS will soon release their first adventure. Sign up to be notified of its release at:

amazon.com/author/catrinabriscoe

Thank you for joining M and Brzko on their journey to find out where they're from. The Universe's favorite **superheroine**, The Muse of Mischief, will return soon with Agent Brzko, Ferocity, Bartala, Nalau, Zri, Lelelu and Waaw!

See you soon,

Catrina

GLOSSARY

Aberidus - a respiratory disease resulting from the inhalation of spores that reside in soil.

Afrit the Great of Jinn - a mischievous creature with the ability to vaporize himself. He is extremely arrogant.

Bartala - the Muse of Mischief's oldest friend and the Emperor of Ploosnar. They met by chance when they were young. As Emperor, his main responsibility is running the roinad empire of Ploosnar. He is a quick-witted jokester that can actually keep up with the Muse of Mischief's high jinks. Physically Ploosnarians look very much like humans but they all have bright blue eyes and three hearts. Bartala is kind and giving, often using the assets of Ploosnar to aid the Muse of Mischief and Agent Brzko in their endeavors. Sometimes, he even gets to tag along.

Bispork - a species of four-legged rideable beings with the ability to speak. They resemble small dinosaurs with humps; they run very fast and enjoy transporting riders. Because they can speak they are treated like beloved pets.

Bivoor - one of the three beings from Myaad, they are asexual. Bivoors are responsible for the administration work in their society. They look like all Myaads with pale skin, messy white hair and black eyes. They tend to be shorter and more petite than Dumeers and Rogsaars.

Black Sea Planet - a dangerous planet covered entirely in water. The native inhabitants are aquatic, but many nefarious beings now inhabit the planet on floating structures, making it dangerous.

Blenia - a land dwelling species, native to Utkrora. Their purpose is to care for the Spubfurnia. They have brown mottled skin, pointy ears, and their eyes are on tentacles. Long ago they lived underwater with the Spubfurnia, but they evolved to breathe air.

Burdohnirc - aquatic creatures from Drolla O0. They are comprised of numerous small creatures that rummage and feed on their own, but they are connected and actually a single being. They are colorful with long flowing fins.

Cazoova - a planet of entertainment. Cazoovians are hoofed animals that race, similar to the horse races on Earth. The planet is ruled by a governing council that attempts to ensure the Cazoovians are not exploited.

Chyke 2C95 - a planet that is covered in active volcanoes. Because of the lava and the Haplogawas, the surface of the planet is uninhabitable. The occupants live in underground lava caves.

Ciic - the current leader of the planet Suus.

Clyrea X9 - possibly a planet where beings like the Muse of Mischief and Agent Brzko may have originated. The exact location of the planet is not known.

Cosliuq Galaxy - the galaxy where Utkrora is.

Drolla O0 - a planet where foods such as niptdyn is grown. They also produce products like espidrun. Markets and trading centers for everything they produce are located on Smd, one the planet's moons.

Dumeers - one of the three beings from Myaad, they are asexual. Dumeers are responsible for tangible operations (i.e. housing, food production, etc.) in their society. They look like all Myaads with pale skin, messy white hair and black eyes. They tend to be stocky and more muscular than Bivoors and Rogsaars.

Earth - an infantile planet where the Muse of Mischief and Agent Brzko were hidden as children. Although some Earthlings suspect that they are not alone in the Universe, Earthlings in general incorrectly think that they are the center of the Universe. The planet is not considered safe. There are numerous cultural problems such as famine, disease, violence, and oppression.

Espidrun - a liquor made from fermented niptdyn on Drolla O0. It is hot pink in color and lets off blue steam when it's poured. Espidrun is marketed in beautiful bottles made of heated titanium.

Ezopica Mischievous Wisssdartai - the son of Emperor Bartala and Empress Nalau. Named, in part, after the Muse of Mischief.

Feliovis - a species from an unknown universe. They are covered in fur, and have whiskers, but no tail.

Ferocity - a Dragon bonded to Agent Brzko. He is a flying bi-ped with golden eyes and telepathic abilities. All Dragons have the ability to breathe fire, but he can also breathe cold. His ship is sentient and has the ability to travel at jump speeds. Ferocity is a courageous member of the team.

Foskpruchu - a planet in the Glion Galaxy where they speak in confusing parables and riddles.

G'ist - a Xinood. Like all Xinoods his skin and hair are as black as obsidian, his eyes are bright green. Except when angry, then they turn bright red. G'ist is in a relationship with the Rogsaar that was stranded on Xinood 5.

G'saar - the son of G'ist and Rogsaar. He was created by combining DNA from both parents, carried by a surrogate.

Gaznzul - a small planet with a population of agamic beings. Gaznzulians are intelligent and loyal, they have the utmost integrity. Their mastery of technological gadgets has helped them to become the most highly sought-after security service providers in the Universe. They are reflective. To Ploosnarians they look Ploosnarian, to Sarfets they look Sarfet, etc. Very few beings ever see a Gaznzulian without their reflection.

Gcugrawa - the planet that Jasteas were relocated to when Jastea MJ was consumed by a red giant.

Glion Galaxy - a peaceful galaxy with many planets. One way to reach it is via the portals on the Planet of Portals.

Guug - a Suus rescued from a VReoria specimen, now serving on Nalau's crew.

G'uld - a Xinood rescued from a VReoria specimen ship, now serving on Nalau's crew

Haplogawa - a very large bi-pedal lizard that inhabits the surface of Chyke C295. They have large mouths, sharp teeth, and eat anything they can get a hold of.

Hasira - a Dragona and the youngest member of the Great Assembly on Dragona.

Haurangi - a Dragon the second oldest member of the Great Assembly on Dragona.

Igao - a whale like creature from the Planet of Portals.

Iysuno - Lelelu's father. Thought to have died while she was a child.

Jastea MJ - a planet being consumed by a red giant. Jasteas are tri-peds that stand over two meters tall. They have one long arm, and on the other side, two short arms. The sides vary by individual.

Keatera - a planet in a different universe. The upper hemisphere of the planet is uninhabitable due to storms. Keaterans are yellow with pointed ears, almond shaped eyes, and long tails. Their hands are made up of a thumb and two wide fingers.

Kiik -the lead researcher on the planet Suus.

Kilome - a designer working at Schatorren Designs on Ploosnar. He his half Ploosnarian and half Sarfet. He is the Muse of Mischief's favorite fashion designer.

Kufeter Whakeclyte Wisswara Bartapulnye - Emperor Bartala's full name.

Kwaai - a Dragon and the oldest member of the Great Assembly on Dragona.

Kyruzia - a Wrexnian rescued from a VReoria specimen ship. He now serves on Empress Nalau's crew.

League of Mongers - a group of interplanetary exploiters, criminals.

Lecur - a small community east of the palace on Ploosnar. Previously roinad was processed here but recently it was used as a gathering place for the abandoned Rogsaars.

Leel - white flowers with nebulas at the center of each. From Suus, they grow on vines and have a pleasant smell.

Lelelu - a Trelod, native to the Planet of Portals. Trelods have bright blue skin and no hair. They have fantastic memories, some even claim to be able to recount every moment of their lives. This exceptional memory makes her the perfect personal assistant to the Muse of Mischief and Agent Brzko. Lelelu is an amazing detective because she is objective, patient, and persistent.

Lusimis - a paste made from legumes. It's a delicacy on Ploosnar.

Mahb - the leader of Otherworld in ancient Ireland. She resides in Sidhe with other Irish Faeries but has the ability to travel between Earth and Otherworld. The extent of her power is unknown.

Misko - an island on the Planet of Portals, purchased by the Muse of Mischief and Agent Brzko.

Muum - Ciic's husband.

Myaad - a planet with no surface water. There are three types of beings on Myaad, Bivoors, Dumeers, and Rogsaars. They are parthenogenetic breeders that use hives to incubate their young. Each type of being is physically identical to the others in their group. However, they are individuals due to independent thought and life experiences. Recently the disease aberidus decimated their population. All Myaads have pale skin, white hair and black eyes. Bivoors function as administrators; Dumeers function as operation specialists, and Rogsaars function as explorers.

Naan - the ruling family on the planet Suus.

Nalau - Ploosnarian and Emperor Bartala's wife. She is truly a beautiful creature inside and out, always convivial and selfless.

Nekmid - a liquor that is colorless. It takes like spicy teriyaki sauce and is very potent. It is available throughout the Universe.

Niptdyn - a delicious fungus grown on Drolla O0, available in the markets on Smd. It is fermented to make the liquor espidrun.

Nguvu - a Dragon that was rescued from a VReoria specimen ship.

Numia - a Keateran rescued from a VReoria specimen ship, she now serves as Nalau's first officer.

Nyeeq'r Vupromia Flivus - a Blenia who is the concierge to the King and Queen of Utkrora. A thirty-second generation Vupromia to the nobles.

Okenn Kote - nowhere.

Planet of Portals - a planet with small communities, each containing different types of portals. Some lead to random places; some lead to specific places. All portals are one way. The portals are often used by desperate beings or criminals. There are a few restricted portals that lead to different times. Trelods are the native species on the planet.

Ploosnar - a planet with three suns and the only planet where roinad is mined. Ploosnarians are humanoids that have three hearts and bright blue eyes. All citizens benefit from the roinad empire, they want for nothing. Because of the roinad all plant life on the planet is blue. There is virtually no crime here; Ploosnarians are honorable and hard working. Emperor Bartala is responsible for running the roinad empire.

Pragma - a cross between grass and fruit that looks like a long, slimy blade of grass. It is considered a delicacy on Ploosnar with both a sweet and savory flavor.

Prujelst - a small bird on the Planet of Portals. Where one is said to have *prujelst bumps* when cold or creeped out.

Rogsaar - one of the three beings from Myaad, they are asexual. Rogsaars are the explorers of Myaad; responsible for establishing trade partnerships for supplies and knowledge. When there was an outbreak of aberidus on Myaad they were all stranded on other planets in the Universe and left to survive on their own. They look like all Myaads with pale skin, messy white hair and black eyes. They are larger than Bivoors and strong, but not as muscular Dumeers.

Roinad - a regenerating element mined exclusively on Ploosnar. It's bright blue and used in everything from atmospheric filters to fabrics. The mining methods used are considered sustainable. All Ploosnarians receive a portion of the profits from roinad.

Sarfets - native to Drolla O0, they are empathic humanoids with angled noses and flared nostrils. Because Drolla O0 produces and markets many products, most Sarfets work as producers or traders.

Schatorren - a Ploosnarian fashion designer and tailor. He is the founder of Schatorren Designs, the favorite designer of Empress Nalau.

Scorchbrooke, Oregon - established around 1857, it is now a ghost town between Pendleton and Hardman, Oregon. Rogsaar was stranded here when there was an outbreak of aberidus on Myaad.

Shwarth Sea - one of the oceans on the Planet of Portals; bordered to the north by Unilond, Luchybos to the west, Qoshnides to the East and open land to the south. It covers a quarter of the planet's surface.

ShyUst - a Gaznzulian, he is second in command to Zri.

Smd - a moon of Drolla O0, is home to many trading posts and retail markets.

Snov - a Sarfett rescued from a VReoria specimen ship, now serving on Nalau's crew.

Spubfurnia - a telepathic water dwelling species native to Utkrora, with gills they look like giant axolotls. They do not live in structures - they live in thick underwater plants.

Strupa - a Ploosnarian rescued from a VReoria specimen ship, now serving on Nalau's crew.

Suus - a planet of advanced beings. The Suus are tall with green skin, four arms, and tails. They do not have mouths. They communicate through telepathy and feed on vapors. They have devoted themselves to cataloging everything they can into a massive database. They also frequently assist in benevolent efforts throughout the Universe.

Sw'dell - a sea dwelling creature that looks like a hermit crab. Their shells look as though they are made of glass.

Thlethlut - the oldest knows Blenia on Utkrora.

Traphus - a city on the Planet of Portals

Trelods - are native to the Planet of Portals. They have bright blue skin, no hair and frequently integrate into other cultures. They have phenomenal memories, some claim to be able to remember every moment of their lives.

Unilond - a city on the Planet of Portals. All of the portals here lead to places in the Glion Galaxy. This is where Agent Brzko first interviewed Lelelu.

Universal Coalition - an organization taxed with setting some basic standards for its members. Membership is voluntary.

Utrkrora - a planet where the water dwelling Spubfurnia live, and the Blenia that care for them.

Vassbr - a waterfront city on the Planet of Portals. All of the portals here lead to random places.

Viiv - a family on Suus that feels they are entitled to rule. They attempted to assassinate Ciic before she could ascend to the throne.

VReoria - there are two types of VReoria, the enslavers attempt to dominate other worlds, any species they cannot enslave they attempt to exterminate. The collectors travel around multiple universes, collecting a few of each species and holding them in stasis.

Vustia - a Trelod, serving as the liaison to the ruling council of the Planet of Portals.

Waaw - a Suus commander. She commands most of their fleet before resigning her position to work with the Muse of Mischief.

Whotov - a Ploosnarian, now retired from serving at the palace on Ploosnar, he is the butler to Ferocity the Dragon.

Wrexna - a planet with great technology and bad food.

Xinood 5 - a planet with humanoids. There is also a Xinood 1, 2, 3, and 4. But only 4 and 5 are inhabited. Xinoods are as black as obsidian with bright green eyes. Their eyes turn blazing red with they are angered. They are a highly intellectual species that values education and relies on trading for income.

Zenbliuq Galaxy - a distant galaxy. Lelelu's ship ends up here when she's kidnapped.

Zri - a Gaznzulian. He has worked with the Muse of Mischief for a very long time. He is tireless, loyal, and selfless.

Zushiri - a Feliovis rescued from a VReoria specimen ship. He now serves as butler to Nalau's crew.

www.ingramcontent.com/pod-product-compliance
Lightning Source LLC
Chambersburg PA
CBHW061549170626
46811CB00001B/145